Adopting With The Doctor

Adopting With The Doctor

A Marietta Medical Romance

Patricia W. Fischer

TULE
PUBLISHING

Dedication

To all the mothers who choose to place their baby up for adoption, you are loved and amazing.

To all those sweet souls who deserve a safe, loving home, this is for you.

"We look at adoption as a very sacred exchange. It was not done lightly on either side."

—Jamie Lee Curtis, award-winning advocate, mom of two, and general badass

Chapter One

STARING DOWN THE barrel of a gun hadn't been the ideal start to a snowy Monday morning, but it wouldn't be the first time midwife Susan Davidson faced a firearm. "Calm down."

With a white-knuckle grip on the handle, the gunman wildly darted his eyes from Susan to the front doors. "You calm down! Bernie's got a serious situation here!"

A young woman braced against the main candy display, crushing multiple bags of M&Ms and other treats under her butt. Through clenched teeth, she Lamaze-hissed while cradling a protruding, watermelon-sized belly.

"I can see that." Despite having almost no sleep in the past few days, Susan's nurse brain kicked in with a large side of caution. Keeping a close watch on the nervous gunman, she moved out of the immediate line of fire. "Bernie? I'm Susan. Talk to me."

"Can't. It. Hurts." No more than twenty, the young woman wore no heavy coat, but instead several layers of unbuttoned oxford shirts over her petite frame. Her well-worn jersey knit skirt hugged flush against her hips as her phone sat between her cleavage. Her bleached, shaggy bob contrasted against the dark layer of black eyeliner along her upper lids.

Wiping her sweaty brow with the back of her hand, Bernie smeared eyeliner across her cheek as she relaxed when the contraction subsided. "There's gonna be another one, Carl. I just know it."

Yep, and another one after that. And another one after that.

The grogginess Susan fought for the past hour suddenly evaporated as the steady taps of thick snow hit the front windows. The blanket of white covering the parking lot reminded her of a scene from a standard holiday movie, but she'd be hard-pressed to find a film with an opening that included a raggedy gunman, a pregnant mother, and a caffeine-deprived midwife.

"Not now. Not. Now!" Carl tapped the barrel of the gun against his leg. "You just had to do this. Deliver on purpose."

Susan bit back *babies come out when they damned well please* from reaching oxygen. Educating a weapon-toting moron didn't seem like the smartest idea at the moment.

Carl held his arms wide. "You gonna help or what?"

As Susan shed her thick coat, her annoyance spoke louder than common sense. "Put the gun away."

"What?"

From the side pocket of her bag, she gently pulled out her stethoscope and held it up. "If you're waving that gun around, it's not safe."

Bernie's eyes filled with hope as her Lamaze breathing resumed.

His bushy forehead creased. "You a doctor?"

"A nurse. A midwife." Placing the stethoscope on top of her bag, she subtly scanned the store for security cameras.

Carl threw his hands up in frustration. "A midwife? What good are you, then?"

"A midwife delivers babies, dumbass!" Bernie snapped as the winds howled, violently rattling the front doors.

The noise reminded Susan of a hurricane she sat through back in Florida. It suddenly dawned on her how dangerous the weather had been. Seemed her vigilant but stubborn determination to see her siblings kept her safe, even during the dark hours of the night in an unknown, snow-covered world.

It was that or Susan was damned lucky to have made it from Albuquerque, New Mexico, to Montana without incident.

"We got three hours to make it to Milk River, so hurry up and push that thing out, woman!" Carl quickly shifted his weight before snatching a box of a popular donuts brand, shoving it into his coat pocket. "Lady, you gonna help or what?"

"Put the gun away or deliver this baby on your own." Undeterred by his nervous behavior, Susan's gaze swept the store for supplies.

His eyes momentarily widened, as if he didn't expect her pushback. "It can't be hard. They do it all the time on TV."

"But you're stupid. And gross." Fear danced in Bernie's eyes.

With a noncommittal shrug, Susan subtly winked at the girl. "Be sure to wear gloves since you're dealing with blood, amniotic fluid, and the placenta."

Despite her exhausted state, Bernie snapped a photo and tucked her phone back between her boobs. "You're a badass."

Carl cringed as though he smelled something foul, like his underarms. "What's a placenta? I'm not stupid!"

"It's the big, bloody ball of goo that feeds the baby while in utero. You gotta deliver that, too. *All* of it." If Susan had a nickel for every ignorant person who insisted birthing babies couldn't be *that hard*, she'd have a lot of damned nickels. Adding the graphic details always put things into realistic focus. "You'll for sure get shit on."

"Stop it!" He tucked his handgun in the front of his ratty jeans before messing with the handle. "Get the safety on."

If he reduces the gene pool, making it "safer," he's on his own. Unfortunately, the weapon remained silent.

With the immediate danger temporarily neutralized, Susan moved her bag and coat to the endcap of day-old pastries, and pulled out her phone and keys, tucking them in her hoodie pocket. "Bernie?"

With quick breathing, the girl endured another contraction. "They didn't say … it … would hurt … this much."

"Kind of hard to quantify childbirth." Susan's mental checklist ticker-taped in her brain while the weight of her keys reminded her what she needed most sat in her car.

Outside. In the freezing-assed weather.

April in Montana blows.

"Stop freaking out!" Carl blurted before stabbing his grubby fingers through his unwashed hair.

"I'm not freaking out! You're freaking out!" Mascara-tinted tears streaked down the girl's pale cheeks.

"We got on the road. She had to pee. Again. Then she pisses all over my front seat and freaks out about it."

Bernie clenched her fists. "I didn't freak out because of pee! You robbed this store!"

The bitter taste of bile coated the back of Susan's throat. *A robbery and a baby on the way? I hate Mondays.*

Like a petulant toddler, Carl stomped his well-worn boot before opening his thick coat to reveal his inside pockets stuffed with cash. "Told you last night we needed cash. You said hit this place."

"You idiot! Not hit it as in rob! Hit to use the bathroom!"

"You always need to use the bathroom."

"So would you if you had a watermelon dancing on your bladder twenty-four seven."

Already, Susan located paper towels, garbage bags, and a limited supply of hand sanitizer. *I need my medical bag.*

"Dammit, Bernie! Why do you always gotta mess things up?"

"If you'd taken me to the hospital last night, I wouldn't be in this mess. I missed a prospective adoptive parent interview because you couldn't be bothered to put on pants."

She's giving her baby up for adoption? Only yesterday, Susan received verification of her infertility, which destroyed her dreams of a family with an amazing guy.

Yet, on the quiet drive here, her always rational brain yanked her out of heartbreak and gave her a practical solution.

Adoption.

Then she walked into an insane situation with a woman who planned to give her baby up? Susan believed in kismet, but damn, this was bananas.

As for an amazing guy? That would be determined once she got to Marietta and met him. Officially. "You're giving your baby up for—"

Nodding, Bernie placed her hand on her belly as it re-shaped itself. "Settle down, kid."

"Holy shit! Did you see that?" Carl jumped backward, as did a teenage store clerk, who suddenly appeared from behind a well-worn Avenger life-sized cutout.

"It's like aliens!" The strength of the kid's prescription lenses emphasized his shocked expression, making him look extraterrestrial. "Nothing's gonna pop out of her, right?"

Susan noticed his name tag. "It will eventually, Ben."

Even with her negative caffeine levels and her well-earned exhaustion from her long drive and side trips, Susan's midwife focus remained sharp. "Guys. Please. If you can't handle this, go sit in the corner."

"I can handle this just fine!" Carl pocketed two mini bags of chips, a can of bean dip, and a handful of breath mints.

"I can't." Ben's shoulders drooped and he shuffled back toward the drink machines.

As the overhead sound system played Diana Ross's classic dance tune "I'm Coming Out," Susan bit back laughing at Ms. Ross's song timing. "How you doing, Bernie?"

The young woman winced before a long exhale. "This

really hurts. Is something wrong?"

I hope not. Reaching into her purse, Susan pulled out her favorite pink hair tie and placed it on her wrist like she always did when shit was about to go down. "How long have you had belly pain?"

"Yesterday. Evening. It's just gotten worse."

Carl tapped his watch. "We gotta get across the Canadian border before sunrise."

Susan's eye twitched. *Well, that doesn't sound concerning at all.* "Is that far?"

"It's over three hundred miles. Even if we drive one hundred miles per hour, we won't make it." Sweat pooled at Bernie's hairline.

Tilting his scruffy chin up, he snarled, "With me driving, we'll make it. And I'll do it without attracting cops."

"It's basic … math. But you're too … too stupid—"

"Stop calling me stupid!" His hand rose, but before he gained momentum, Susan instinctively stepped between him and the mom-to-be.

With a slow shake of her head, Susan anticipated his next move, mentally reviewing self-defense tricks her younger sister, Lucy, taught her long ago. "Don't."

The moans of the arctic winds momentarily filled the store as Carl's hand slowly lowered on the handle of his gun.

Sadly, staring down a woman's abuser had been a necessary part of her job working labor and delivery. For over a decade, she refined her fierceness, but it didn't mean she wasn't terrified. "Back off and let me do what you won't."

The purposeful words appeared to unnerve him. His

forehead unknotted as his hands rose in mock surrender and he backed away. "She's all yours, but you and I? We ain't done."

"Can't wait." Turning to her patient, Susan swallowed the bile dancing in her throat. *Be scared later.* "How you doing, Bernie?"

"No one's ever stood up for me like that." Bernie's bottom lip quivered.

That tugged on Susan's heartstrings. She knew all too well what it was like to have no one but yourself to rely on. "I'm sorry to hear that, but I'm here now."

"I bet you're a fierce mother." The girl's unexpected compliment hit Susan hard enough sideways that her tongue tripped.

"I'm not ... I mean, I can't have ... I mean ... no. Not yet."

With a head tilt, the girl's big brown eyes stared directly into Susan's soul. "Meeting all those prospective parents ... I've seen that kind of sadness before."

"What sadness?" A spotlight aimed at Susan's face would have been less jarring. *What is going on?*

"But you want to be a mom someday, right?"

More than I'll admit to anyone. "Absolutely. Someday."

For a few beats, a sad smile spread across Bernie's face. "Don't worry, Susan. No matter what biology says, you'll be an amazing mom sooner than you think."

How in God's name did she figure that out? Susan had known about her messed-up insides for only twenty-four hours. This girl took one look at her and knew?

Is there some sort of psychic fertility voodoo in the Montana air? Shaking off Bernie's commentary, Susan shoved her brain back into midwife mode. "Is this your first baby?"

"Yes. Contractions started after last night's dinner. I shouldn't have eaten hot dogs. Are you single?"

As intense and quick as they are, she's probably well into transition. That meant a baby could be born on this cold, dirty floor before sunrise if Susan didn't take charge ASAP.

Ignoring the question, Susan located a few overhead cameras and two screens behind the counter labeled FRONT and BACK. Even if monitored, the heavy snowfall would take one hundred years to dig out of, delaying EMS and police arrivals. Before arriving, Susan couldn't recall spotting any other cars on the roads for at least three hours. That brought her level of hope for backup to zero. *Seems my level of hope for everything right now is zero.*

She tamped down her anger for allowing a poor-me distraction. *Focus!* "You peed in the car? How long ago was that?"

"About an hour." Panting, Bernie placed her legs slightly wider than shoulder-width apart and rested on her thighs. "I think those hot dogs are giving me fits."

"Not any of our hot dogs." With his hands up, Ben recoiled from Bernie's death glare. "Feel better, Bernie."

"Need to go to the hospital." She took two steps before grabbing the edge of the counter. "It's happening again. Carl."

She held her hand out for him to take, but her abuser scoffed. "I ain't touching you."

What a gem. After a decade of helping miracles into the world, even without the bliss of magic morning brew, Susan's skills leveled up easier than breathing.

Juggling trauma and chaos weren't new. Twenty years ago, a drunk driver hit her and her family head-on, killing her father and permanently injuring their mother. Ever since, Susan bore the heavy weight of keeping her three siblings, their mother, and herself afloat, alive and accomplished.

So, navigating a snowy morning with a first-time pregnant mom, a grubby gunman, and socially awkward onlooker would be a quick walk in the park. "Bernie, the hot dogs aren't doing this. Your water probably broke in the car."

"What the hell do you know?" Carl sniffed a refrigerated sandwich before throwing it on the floor.

"She's a midwife, you stupid piece of shit! She knows more than you do!" Bernie balled her fists. "This. Fucking. Hurts!"

"What she said." Susan coached the young woman through the next round of pain as the hard stench of sweat, bad breath, and the thick smell of whatever lay in that colorful bin with NACHOS on the side hit Susan square in the face.

Working in labor and delivery, Susan experienced worse, so it wasn't the odors that caught Susan off guard. Contrary to her petite frame, Bernie's grip proved to be so painful that Susan wondered if her own fingers would ever function again. "Keep breathing, Bernie. You've got this. When is your due date? Holy shit, you're strong."

Bernie powered through until her petite shoulders fell. "Yesterday."

"We gotta go. We gotta go now!" Carl's thick coat dragged over the top of a discounted cans display, sending the top tiers rolling around the store.

"I just put those up." With his hands still up, Ben pouted as the fluorescent lights momentarily flickered before a low hum filled the store.

Immediately, Carl fired two shots into the ceiling before destroying the rest of the can display with a hard kick. "How much time before the cops get here?"

"What the hell are you doing? Put that away right now!" Susan's throat clenched when them not making it out of there alive became as real as the pain of Bernie's grip.

"Leave Ben alone!" Bernie rested her hands on her belly.

Ben shakily thumbed over his shoulder. "The coffee machines. When they all start at the same time, the lights flicker."

As a wave of freshly brewed happiness hit the air, Susan deeply inhaled. *I'd kill for an IV of caffeine.*

While flecks of the ceiling peppered his hair, Carl lowered his gun and kicked away an item that bumped against his boot. It rebounded off the wall and rolled to a stop under the homemade RESTROOMS THIS WAY sign near the back hallway.

Bernie moved her phone out from between her boobs and placed it on the counter. "I'm so tired. Am I almost done?"

Gently, Susan moved a lock of hair out of Bernie's tired

face as Taylor Swift's "I Knew You Were Trouble" played overhead. "How long?"

"Probably nine months," Carl snorted a bit too hard at his own joke while pocketing several more items.

Straightening to her five-foot-nothing height, Bernie launched an apple from the front counter bin at him. "Shut up!"

Laughing, Carl swatted it away.

"Hey! You've gotta pay for that." Frustration momentarily replaced Ben's fear. "And I'm gonna have to clean that up."

This is like herding squirrels. "Bernie. Find something to focus on." As Susan's fingers itched to dial 9-1-1, Bernie's wolf whistle seemed misplaced. "What are you doing?"

"Focusing on *that* guy."

"What guy?" Susan scanned the store for other customers she might have missed.

"Where? Where is he?" Carl's indifferent demeanor changed to panic as he randomly pointed his gun.

With trembling fingers, Bernie motioned. "Calendar. Sexy. Man."

It took less than a second for his face to register, but Susan refused to be derailed, no matter how quickly he always made her heart beat and her panties combust. "It's the Marietta first responders' calendar. I need gloves, Ben."

"Aisle five," he answered.

"Shit, Bernie. You got me upset over a calendar?" Carl tapped his temple with the muzzle of the gun before shoving it into the front of his pants. "Use your brain, woman."

Ben rolled his eyes. "My boss won't let me take it down. It's like ten years old."

"Less than two actually." And Susan would know since that same calendar sat in a bin in her car, permanently opened to the same month his boss appeared to favor.

"That guy is *hot*! This. Hurts!" Bernie sobbed while protectively cradling her belly.

"Dr. Reynolds comes in all the time. Nice guy."

Yes, he is. Last year, her younger sister, Lucy, FaceTimed, introduced Susan to the incredible ER staff on duty, but Thomas Reynolds stayed in Susan's thoughts the longest. A few days later, when she called the unit in search of Lucy, she talked to him again. Unbeknown to her physician siblings, that conversation led to another one and daily texting, and many late-night discussions.

The man unnerved her in the most delicious ways, and she had yet to actually meet him, but she would when she got to Marietta.

Today. Probably.

"Susan. You're blushing." Bernie took a slow breath as the smirk on her face indicated she welcomed the distraction.

"What? No."

"Uh-huh. Sure, Jan. That's why you didn't answer me when I asked if you were single."

Geez, this girl's observation skills. "I'm not gonna lie. Having an additional medical professional's help right now would be nice. Not these two idiots." She gave the girl a reassuring smile as her exhaustion momentarily let her guard down. "In reality, I am single since I've never even actually met him."

"But you've met him."

"We've talked, texted." *Why are you saying all this?*

"Sexted?" Bernie gritted her teeth. "It's starting again."

"No, we've kept things strictly platonic. Uncomplicated." Not making things awkward before actually meeting proved to be the responsible choice. More than once, Susan imagined the man screaming her name after she worked some sexy magic on him. "Not the point."

With a stressed smile, Bernie replied, "Susan, you've got it *bad* for him. You're gonna be an amazing couple. Family."

Here's to hoping. Meeting the man would be the first hurdle before bringing up the idea of family. Maybe take him on a date or two first.

She motioned for Bernie to continue. "Contractions?"

"Kicked in hard after dinner last night. I couldn't sleep because of it."

Susan's fingers tapped the keys and phone in her pocket. The itch to throw Bernie in her SUV and drive to the closest ER grew with each passing second. Ideally, driving to Marietta Regional would be her first choice since one of her siblings would probably be on duty.

Or Dr. Reynolds might be.

"You gotta pay for that." Ben's annoyance strengthened as the hot snack machine rotated a lonely eggroll.

Bernie rocked her hips from side to side, reviewing her symptoms as Carl rummaged through merchandise like a hungry bear.

When Ben yelled for Carl to stop, the gunman ripped

open bags of chips, peppered the floor, and stomped them into dust. "That's gonna be your head if you don't shut the fuck up."

"Any problems? Blood pressure? Diabetes? Keep rocking your hips. It'll help." Every time Ben complained, Carl's behavior escalated and Susan's worries multiplied.

After pocketing more items, Carl shoved an entire popular cream-filled sponge cake in his mouth and giving them the double middle finger salute.

Please let us get out of here alive. "All your prenatal check-ups good, Bernie?"

"No complications. Before you got here, I squatted and this big bloody booger fell out. Then it got worser." Bernie pounded her fist on the counter. "Like right now."

Throwing his hands in the air in frustration, Carl yelled as bits of cake flew out of his mouth, "Those hot dogs—"

"Hot dogs don't make your water break and dislodge your mucus plug." The thick blankets of snow had Susan wishing for the hot humidity of Florida. *Why did I move here again? Oh right. My siblings. My broken heart. And that calendar guy.*

Carl growled as if thinking hurt his brain. "What the hell is a mucus plug?"

"I'll take care of it. I need my medical supplies out of my car." But Susan didn't take two steps before—

"Put the gun away, Carl! Put it away right now!" Bernie's eyes went wide with terror. She threw more apples at him, along with multiple expletives.

As the fruit grazed Carl's face, Susan froze as Ben slowly

disappeared behind aisle three.

Carl stomped his dirty boot like a toddler. "*You* don't tell *me* what to do, woman. I'll point my gun at anyone I want to."

His gun remained tucked in the front of his pants. *What is she doing?*

Unfazed, Bernie's ferocity continued. "I'll say whatever I want to keep you from pointing that stupid gun at me. At any of us *three*. You keep that gun tucked away before you shoot someone. Again."

"Again?" Susan's heart dropped to her feet. *Shit.*

Instantly, that cold, sinister abuser returned as he closed the gap between them. "Woman, I told you to keep your yap shut about that or I'd shut it for you."

Throwing her hands up in surrender, Susan demanded, "Stop! There's an *innocent baby* on the way. A *child* who has nothing to do with any of this. Judges like healthy babies."

Carl shifted his weight, his shaggy forehead furrowed as if he juggled all his life decisions. "It's not my stupid kid."

So that's why he didn't react to her giving it up for adoption. "Does that matter? It's an *innocent baby*. Let me deliver her child and you can shoot me afterward? Deal?"

Anxiety thickened the air between them as Carl rolled his head from side to side before backing away. "Fine. But hurry it up. Gonna be light soon. And keep your mouth shut, you hear me, Bernie? Keep. It. Shut."

Relief flooded her veins, but Susan's pause was short-lived when Bernie screamed, "Susan! Here comes another one!"

As soon as the contraction ended, Susan refused to wait any longer to get her medical bag. "Bernie. Hang tight. I'll be back in thirty seconds."

"You're such a badass, Susan. I knew he'd back off. Because he's a stupid chickenshit. That's why he needs to get to Canada. He shot his best friend yesterday."

The moment Susan placed her hands on the frigid handle of the door, the cock of the gun froze her in her tracks.

"Deal's off."

Why does she keep provoking him? "Carl. Calm down."

His eyes narrowed, void of compassion. "I'm not a chickenshit!"

"You're not, but I need my medical bag. Some towels. Please, let me help her. Before it gets light."

"She'll tell everyone as soon as they get here."

"Then go! Leave before any police show up."

He hesitated, his hands trembling. "I could. But—"

"Take your useless ass out of here," Bernie snapped.

He slid off the safety. "I've had enough of your shit."

Throwing her hands up, Susan braced for the worst. "Wait!"

Suddenly, a flash of red and white rocketed across the room and slammed into the side of Carl's head, sending him straight to the floor.

As soon as the gunman's body went limp, it all processed in slow motion, making Susan wonder, *What have I gotten myself into?*

Chapter Two

TAKING OUT A gunman with a dented can of a popular side dish hadn't been the way Dr. Thomas Reynolds planned to start this snowy Monday morning but wouldn't be the first time he faced a fool with a firearm.

Whoever screamed about the weapon gave Reynolds a solid warning as soon as he walked in the back door. Otherwise this situation might be very different right now.

And whoever the negotiator was, she was brilliant. And familiar. Repeating the words *innocent* and *baby* probably kept them all alive.

"Is everyone okay?" Without waiting for a response, Reynolds picked up the gun, removed the bullet in the chamber before pocketed the bullet and gun. He then tossed the magazine in a basket of protein bars. Lying still, the grubby man appeared to be unconscious.

Is that part of the ceiling in his hair? Reynolds conducted a quick assessment. "Strong pulse. Airway patent. He's alive."

"That's unfortunate," a woman scoffed.

"Dude, you took him out with a can of pork and beans!" Ben's blue eyes were wide with amazement. "It had a perfect curve on it and everything."

"Guess those baseball skills still help. Everyone okay?" Finally, Reynolds took note of the three other people. Ben the clerk he met numerous times, a young woman holding her phone up, and … her. His heart lodged in his throat.

There weren't enough adjectives in the English dictionary to describe her beauty. Dark hair cascaded about her perfect, makeup-free face as questions floated through the intensity of her green eyes.

The impact of her presence slammed into his brain harder than that discount can he had just thrown. "Susan?"

"What?" As she put her arm out to shield the girl standing next to her, the corner of his mouth twitched at her protective nature. A quality her siblings mentioned more than once.

Reynolds cautiously removed his cap. "Susan. It's me. Reynolds."

A smile of recognition spread across her face. "Yes, you're—"

"Hot guy!" The young woman's eyes widened.

"The calendar! Remember, Susan?" Ben excitedly pointed to the one on the wall. "You asked about him. Here he is!"

Dammit, Ben. Although great at his job, the kid had the social awareness of a turtle. "Yes, here I am."

"As am I." Susan chewed on her bottom lip.

"I thought you weren't due for another few days."

Her eyes sparkled at his comment. "Yes, I told you that, but my Albuquerque assignment ended early. Surprise."

After texting and talking for months, he spent countless

hours debating their perfect, official introduction. None of his scenarios included him standing near that damned fundraising calendar, where he looked arrogant as hell while bare-chested, oiled up, and standing in front of a helicopter.

On the upside, the project did exceed fundraising goals.

"That photo of you is amazing." Still holding her phone up, the girl next rocked sideways, cupping her belly as she slowly blew out through her mouth and inhaled through her nose.

Uh-oh. "Thank you? Are you in labor?"

"I'm between contractions presently. Susan's been a lifesaver. Literally."

"Yes, she is." *How did she keep her cool facing that guy?*

"She's amazing. Gonna make a great mom one day." The comment appeared to pink Susan's cheeks.

"I have no doubt."

"She's single, you know." The girl gave him a wink.

Never looking toward his beefcake picture, Susan nodded. "It's good to meet you in person finally, Reynolds."

"Same." He extended his hand, hoping to appear confident, but the moment the warmth of her touch hit his palm, Reynolds's intelligent words stuck to his tongue like peanut butter. "Your ... your ... siblings told me ... um ... about you."

"Don't believe any of it." Her smile reached her eyes.

"Not even the good stuff?" Not that he ever brought up the subject of Susan with his colleagues, aka her brothers and sister. As far as Reynolds knew, Susan had yet to mention their long-term communications, and he certainly wasn't going to unilaterally offer the information before her arrival.

"Depends on what the good stuff is." Her cheeks flushed a deeper pink as if her mind sat south of her belly button.

And she liked it.

The drink machines hummed as the clunk of the snack wheel rotated while they appeared to be stuck in each other's tractor beams. *For the love of everything, don't be an idiot.*

"This meet-cute is all great rom-com material and shit." The girl grimaced while she pointed at Reynolds. "That calendar doesn't do you justice. In real life, you look like Loki from his TV series. You have great hair by the way."

Without taking her eyes off him, Susan agreed.

"That's quite a compliment." Being compared to the god of mischief happened frequently, and the way Susan took him in, he wondered how mischievous she'd like him to be. *Get your shit together, man!*

She turned to Susan. "You remind me of … who is it, Ben?"

He prairie-dogged his head from behind aisle three. "The TV Wonder Woman."

"Lynda Carter?" Susan ran her fingers through her hair. "I'm humbled."

During their get-to-know-each-other time, Susan's knowledge of superheroes, sci-fi, movie quotes, and fantasy pop culture impressed him. And she did resemble the classic Wonder Woman. *If she has a golden lasso, I'm a goner.* "I can see it."

The young woman rested her hands on her thighs, her phone still firmly in her grip. "And … as much as … I'd love ... to talk about ... what ... an amazing power couple ... you two ... will be ... I ... need ... this ... badass nurse ... right now."

Susan gasped. "I'm so sorry, Bernie. Phased out there. Not enough coffee this morning."

"You say that, Susan, but you ... seem to ... phase out when ... that ... dude ... or his calendar ... is in front of you."

The moment Susan pulled away, Reynolds realized they'd been shaking hands that entire time. *Strong work, Rey. Now she knows you're a creepy, hand-hogging weirdo.*

Bernie clenched her fists. "Holy shit! *I wanna push! Push so hard!*"

Instantly, Susan's demeanor easily morphed into caregiver mode. She removed the phone from Bernie's hand and placed it on the counter. "Can you stand for a few more minutes, sweetie?"

"Lean on me, kid." Reynolds held his arms out, and Bernie stepped into his protection as that catchy, annoying "Happy" song played somewhere overhead.

Reynolds tucked his phone in his hoodie pocket and placed his coat on the candy display. Next to it was a monitor with a view of the back door.

Reynolds motioned as Bernie snatched up her phone, holding it with a white-knuckle grip. "That's how you saw me."

"It was risky, but I knew you'd be a game changer, Dr. June." Bernie gave a thumbs-up before pounding the counter with her fist. "Ouch. *Ouch. Ouch!* Susan!"

Quickly, Susan cleared wayward merchandise out of their workspace. "Ben!"

He popped up on aisle four. "What?"

"I need you to get my medical bag out of the front passenger side and the bin labeled towels and blankets on the back seat." She tossed him her keys, and he caught them midair but hesitated.

"You're not going to ask me to deliver, are you?" His eyes widened more through his prescription lenses.

This kid! Reynolds stabbed toward the front door. "Ben! I'm a doctor. She's a midwife. You don't have to deliver anyone."

"But you're helping, Ben." Susan's tone left no room for discussion.

Within a minute, the kid returned with everything Susan requested. "Thanks, now get me some paper towels, a boxes of garbage bags and gloves, hand sanitizer, a bottled water, a Gatorade, and a beer."

Ben paused and Reynolds knew why. "I'll pay for it."

"What?" She continued to work.

"Anyone who visits the store knows Ben's catchphrase." With his foot, he pushed Susan's medical bag closer to her.

Snatching the money out of Reynolds's hand, Ben placed the bills in the register. "On it! But I can't sell you the beer until after eight. It's the law."

As the teen ran around the store, Susan prepared a large area with layers of absorbent pads, garbage bags, and towels before topping with a large homemade blanket.

"Hang tight, Bernie. I'm making a pallet for you to lie

on. It'll be a cleaner place where you can have the baby."

"We're not going to the hospital?" Tears stained the girl's face as she rested her head against Reynolds's chest and gripped a fistful of his hoodie.

"We don't have time, and the weather isn't cooperating. I don't want to risk us getting stuck in a snowbank somewhere."

"Keep leaning on me, kid." Reynolds watched Susan work. "When that's done, what else do you need?"

"I need a mega-sized coffee with tons of cream. Fold some of those paper towels and dampen them for forehead compresses. Gatorade for a few calories and hydration. Beer for afterward."

Bernie reached for Susan, who grabbed the girl's hand, mimicking Bernie's breathing. "I'll. Pay. You. Back. After. This."

Bernie momentarily smirked through her pain. "Hot. Guy. Badass Nurse. You. Should. Ride. Him. Hard."

Reynolds wasn't sure whether to laugh or thank the girl for her endorsement.

Susan squeaked on her next exhale but recovered quickly as Bernie wrapped her arms around Susan's waist.

Holding back a laugh, Reynolds rolled up his sleeves. "What can I do to help?"

Susan's forehead furrowed as she slowly rocked herself and her patient side to side. "You don't want to deliver this baby?"

"Nope. You've delivered *a lot* more than I have."

"That's true." When her lips thinned, he understood

why.

She fully expected him to pull the *I'm the doctor* card and disregard her experience. No doubt it happened to her before, but her expertise in this field far exceeded his.

Reynolds's ego didn't depend on whether or not he delivered this child. Mom's and baby's health were top priorities. "Susan, I'm glad to deliver if you want me to."

"I've got her. In my bag, there are more thick, absorbent pads. Please place several garbage bags down and top with another layer of the pads, all on the blanket."

"You got it. Ben, come here." The men worked quickly as Bernie continued her Lamaze breathing. They finished up and Reynolds scooped Bernie up and laid her on the makeshift birthing area, kneeling next to her. "There you go, kiddo."

She slid down, resting on her side, placing her phone by her belly. "This is lovely. You two are amazing. I'm so tired."

"Get in whatever position works for you, Bernie. You've got room to move." Susan mouthed *Thank you* to Reynolds.

A warmth spread across his cheeks as Susan dialed 9-1-1. While she gave a report, Bernie tapped his knee.

"You're blushing, Dr. June."

"Yeah. Yeah, I am." He appreciated the girl's candor and quick observation. "Kind of hard not to, meeting her in person. But we've got you. Okay?"

"That's sweet you're so smitten. She said all you've done is talk and text."

"She mentioned me?" That sent his heart racing.

"When I noticed your calendar." She grimaced but her

tone remained upbeat. "No sexting?"

"Nope. It would complicate things." Not that he hadn't been tempted, but hearing Susan planned to relocate to Marietta, and she was his boss's sister, kept his common sense in check. It didn't mean she didn't visit him during his alone time or star in some of his dirty fantasies.

Bernie sighed, "I hope you complicate things soon. Labor hurts like a sonofabitch."

"That's my understanding." He held out his hand for her to take, and Bernie immediately accepted.

Calmly, Susan explained each move as she lifted Bernie's skirt. "I'm looking first, checking for anything obvious, we'll see how far along you are, but I'll need to remove your panties."

"I'm commando." Bernie sighed.

"Well, that saves time."

Bernie whimpered, "Are you staying, Dr. June?"

He planned to step away, give the girl the privacy she deserved, but he simply pivoted so his focus was on her face. "I'll stay if you want, Bernie."

"Please."

"Susan, I'll take care of the baby when it arrives. Until then, what can I do to help, Wonder Nurse?"

"Unless you can make a huge double mocha with whip on top, I'm good. Everything looks good so far, Bernie."

"We'll save a mocha for another day, but I can get you that coffee. Anything else?"

When she began to answer, her eyebrows hit her hairline. "You can take care of him!"

Chapter Three

T HE ACRID SMELLS of nicotine and sweat hit Reynolds's
nose two seconds after Susan's warning.

A quick move to the left put Reynolds out of the strike
zone and encouraged his wild-eyed attacker to follow.

Stumbling, the man sloppily threw punches like a great
dumb beast. "Quit movinnnnnnng! I'm ... kick your assth."

"Words slurred. Probably concussed." Reynolds avoided
each clumsy swing, leading them in the opposite direction of
Susan and Bernie. "Probably won't remember any of this
later."

"Kick his ass ... Dr. June." Bernie grabbed her phone.

"I don't want to hit him in the head." He ducked as
Carl's arm swung wide. "Cause brain damage."

"Carl's already ... a dumbass. No one ... would know ...
the difference."

"Get out of there, Reynolds!" Susan gasped. "Bernie, why
are you filming this?"

The bright blue of Ben's magnified eyes peeked over the
magazine rack on aisle one before disappearing and then
popping up again farther down the row.

The kid bounced around more than a jackrabbit. A cold,

hard wall slammed against his back, stopping Reynolds in his tracks.

Susan picked up a can and Reynolds's heart skipped a beat at her concern, but things were under control despite appearances.

"Don't worry ... he's ... got this." Bernie grabbed Susan's arm.

"I'm gonna kill you." Carl cocked his hand back and let loose, but Reynolds stepped sideways, and Carl's hand crunched against the sheetrock.

Everyone flinched as he howled like a wounded animal.

Reynolds pinned Carl's arm behind his back and shoved his face against the now-damaged wall. "Calm down."

Carl screamed, "My hand! Fucking hurts!"

"It's over. We're done. Got it?"

"I hate you." Carl slid to the floor like a boneless chicken and immediately farted.

"Is he out?" Susan craned her lovely neck.

A loud snore interrupted the cautious quiet before Reynolds checked and then dragged the unconscious gunman to the front of the store. "Yep. He's out. Ben! Tape!"

From aisle two, a roll of duct tape shot across the room and Reynolds caught it one-handed. With the quickness of a calf roper, Reynolds bound Carl's hands behind his back and his legs together before securing him to a large wire display of chips and crackers.

He added a couple of the dented cans and a twelve-pack of drinks for weight before throwing his hands up. "Done. Now if he moves, we'll hear him. Getting your order."

Susan opened her mouth, but nothing came out.

Guess I made a good impression.

Bernie used one of her many shirts to wipe her face. "Wonder Nurse is speechless. Good work, Dr. June."

If a wash of crimson hadn't colored Susan's cheeks, Reynolds wouldn't have believed it.

Clearing her throat, Susan gently lifted her patient's skirt. "Ready, Bernie?"

The first bits of daylight faded the darkness of night. The waves of snow continued, making the outside world look like a very shaken snow globe.

From the drink machines, Reynolds eyeballed the shaggy attacker. The sooner the cops took him away, the better. *If I could get away with it, I'd dump his ass outside in the snow.*

After getting her coffee, he settled next to her, eyeing the water bottle and paper towels nearby. "The storm's gonna slow EMS down."

Susan happily accepted the caffeine in a cup. "I'm not worried. With you and me here ... we've got this."

"Damn straight." Reynolds wet the towels and positioned himself next to the patient.

"Bernie, I don't see a cord or a foot. I see a hint of the top of the baby's head. Starting off with all good things."

Only after she mentioned the word *cord*, did that horrible scenario process. If the child's lifeline were compromised, there would be little they could do to save it. "Very good things."

Susan took a long drink of her coffee and moaned happily, making him extremely jealous of that cup. "Good?"

"Amazing."

"You two are perfect for each other." A tired smile spread across Bernie's face as she turned her phone over. "This … this is like the opening of a real-life rom-com. You two … meet-cute over … baby being born. You get together. Fall in love. Become a family. Drink, please."

If it were only that easy. Reynolds filled the cap with Gatorade and held it to her cracked lips. "Just a sip."

"That would be wild, huh? But I can see it," Ben answered from somewhere near the magazines.

"Very wild." *And ridiculous.* Still, Reynolds didn't hate the idea. Although his medical school marriage hadn't worked out, becoming a father was a top priority since his teens. Pursuing that latter title was what brought him to this moment, meeting Susan Davidson far sooner than he expected in a situation he never could have imagined.

As he watched her work, that want of happily ever after pinched his heart. *I'd sure like to be a husband again, too.*

"Rom-coms are fun movie and book escapes, but they aren't reality." Susan sounded like a Hallmark heroine who'd all but given up on the idea of love.

After sipping, Bernie licked her lips. "Rom-com meet-cutes aren't supposed to be a reality, Susan. They're about hope. Hope in forever love and good people and sweet babies and cute dogs."

"And towns that always look like Christmas," Ben added.

"And Christmas! Valentines. Holiday baking."

"And always finding a great parking spot."

"And bookstores." Susan momentarily closed her eyes. "I

love the smell of books."

"Take note. She loves books." Bernie winked at Reynolds.

"Don't worry. I'll remember." He had to give it to her. Despite her pain, the kid had incredible skills of observation. And matchmaking.

"Bernie was my co-valedictorian," Ben proudly announced. "She's super smart. Always has a book in her hand."

Bernie rolled her eyes. "Right, I'm so brilliant I'm not married and having my baby on the floor of a convenience store. Genius-level dumbass more like it."

The corner of Susan's mouth twitched. "No one's perfect, sweetie. Maybe we all need a bit more hope in the world."

"You two give me hope." Bernie nodded. "A lot of it."

After obtaining Bernie's blood pressure, Susan put her purple stethoscope back in her purse before removing her hair tie from her wrist. She pulled her long, dark locks back as she set her jaw with that confidence that says shit was about to get real and she had it well under control.

Labor and delivery were never Reynolds's strong suits, but he loved watching midwives and obstetricians work their magic.

Reynolds delivered plenty of babies in his emergency room residency and at work. Yet, he didn't have the finesse of those who practiced regularly, like Susan and his OB/GYN brother, Nate. With such a tenuous situation like this, Reynolds happily left it to the experts.

Susan's elegant fingers organized her work area with a routine she probably perfected long ago and could do blindfolded.

Blindfolded. That could be fun. His gut clenched and he hoped his stupid, Susan Davidson–focused libido hadn't spoken for him.

Reynolds dabbed Bernie's forehead with a wet towel and dried one of her tears with his thumb before giving her a comforting wink. His heart worried for her because he understood childbirth hurt like a bitch. "We're here for you."

"That means the world to me." Closing her eyes, Bernie placed one hand on her belly. The other stabilized her phone.

With a tender touch, Susan moved a sweaty lock out of the girl's face. "Your blood pressure is perfect. No signs of eclampsia. No issues I can see."

"Another good sign," Reynolds agreed.

As the girl rested, he and Susan turned at the same time and locked eyes. His entire mouth went dry as his heart thumped against his ribs.

Months ago, his boss and her sister, Lucy Davidson, introduced Susan to the ER staff over a FaceTime call. A few days later when he answered the work phone, it was Susan. Her strained voice concerned him, and he asked if he could check on her later. A simple conversation opened a constant texting and phone dialogue between them, which led to thoughts about Susan multiple times a day. So much so, he worried he would make a total idiot out of himself upon her arrival. Then fate allowed him to take out a gunman and assist her in delivering a baby.

Now, as neither of them looked away, he fought with his better nature not to lean in and kiss her senseless. "Susan, I—"

The clunk of Bernie's hard case hitting the floor broke their eye-sex foreplay.

"Meet-cute over. Oh. *Oh!* Here comes another one. I hope my screen didn't crack." Bernie checked her phone as her body tightened. "No crack. Is it out yet?"

Immediately, Susan blinked herself back to the present, and Reynolds relaxed, since his lizard brain hadn't erased common sense. "What do you need me to do?"

"Get these off me." Sitting up, Bernie peeled off all her button-down shirts, then slid back down to her side and handed Reynolds her phone.

He laid it within her reach before making a pillow out of her shirts and placed it where she requested. Her oversized cartoon-themed tank top caught his attention. "You like Dino the Dinosaur?"

Bernie patted it. "It's the father's. Loves Dino. *The Flintstones* is his favorite cartoon, which makes sense since he's a total caveman."

"He's not as smart as a caveman." Ben rolled his eyes.

"Dino was my sister's favorite character, too." Reynolds hoped no sadness laced his response speaking of his sweet Audrey. There was already enough worry in the air.

"Then I guess we were destined to meet, Dr. June."

Reynolds appreciated the girl's upbeat mood despite her

trauma. He gave Bernie's hand a tender squeeze as he hoped to offer good comfort and decent distraction. "I'm surprised he knows the cartoon. How old is he?"

"He's our age." She motioned to her and Ben. "He's even got a tattoo of it on his arm. Loves that stupid dinosaur. Said anyone who likes Dino is good by him."

"Dino's fun." In honor of their late sister, Reynolds and his brother, Nate, were each inked with Dino tattoos. "Keep breathing, kiddo. You're doing great."

Despite her fatigue, she smiled at him. "You have nice eyes. Really handsome. Labor hurts so fucking bad."

"I'm sorry. More towel?" When she nodded, he pressed the cool compress to her forehead, and hoped his nurturing response offered comfort. "Labor pain sucks."

He failed spectacularly.

"How the fuck would you know what it feels like?" Bernie snapped, then apologized, followed by more cursing. And then an apology as she yanked on her skirt. "I get you're trying to help me, but I'm in pain. I'm tired. I haven't seen my bikini line in, like, five months. I pride myself on a nice bikini line. It's gotta be insane down there, right?"

Panic punched him in the gut, but he kept his eyes laser-focused on her face. "I haven't looked. Sip of water? Towel?"

Amazing what patients worried about in situations like this, but he understood it. In complicated times, the simplest things were the easiest to grab on to.

"Drugs. I need drugs." She gasped as her belly tensed.

"It's too late for drugs, Bernie. You can have a beer when we're done." After a long drink of her coffee, Susan placed it on the counter and out of the way.

Ben poked Carl's foot with the broom handle. "She likes fruity beers."

"I'd rather have a shot of tequila." The girl's face distorted in dread as her body pummeled itself.

Susan agreed, "We'll make it so."

"Did you just quote Picard?" Reynolds's eyebrows hit his hairline.

"Indeed." Her voice dropped an octave, sounding like a popular character from a long-running sci-fi series.

I'm gonna marry this woman and wife her so hard.

Susan cleared her throat. "This time, I need to check your cervix, and see how far along you are."

"Then we're close?" Sadness washed across Bernie's face.

"Yes."

"Contact my social worker, Lori Ramon, please,"

The mention of his friend sent Reynolds mentally sideways. "Lori? I can text her."

"She's helping me find the perfect family for the baby."

Reynolds's mouth went dry. "What about your family?"

"They're terrible people. I don't want my baby near them." Bernie's chest bobbed as tears ran freely.

"That's true." With a broom in hand, Ben stood guard next to an unconscious Carl.

She covered her eyes with her hand. "Parents kicked me out when I started to show. The dad's parents told me to get lost. That passed-out idiot promised to take care of me. Now look at where I am. Yeah, I'm such a genius."

Anger grated around Reynolds's brain. *Why do irresponsi-*

ble pricks get the privilege of fathering a baby and I don't?

Yesterday, Reynolds came to meet a prospective birth mother who never showed. He stayed for hours with Lori at her office, hoping the mother would arrive. But the longer he waited, the dimmer his last opportunity to be a father became.

The early arrival of this winter storm derailed his plans to drive back to Marietta. He grabbed a hotel room to wait it out, but his annoyance at a paperwork-heavy system that made it damned near impossible for a good, single man to adopt robbed him from decent sleep.

Frustrated, he arrogantly decided to drive home anyway. It took about a mile before the stupidity of his decision kicked in.

As soon as the familiar sign came into view, he pulled into the convenience store and planned to wait out the worst of the storm. He came in the back door only to end up thwarting a robbery and finally meeting a long-distance friend, Susan Davidson.

At least his first two impressions were good.

"Bernie, after the baby's born, we'll call her." Reynolds patted the girl's shoulder.

"How long will that be?" She sniffed.

Placing a large glob of lubricant on her gloved fingers, Susan rubbed them together before examining her patient. "Very, very soon."

Reynolds hated he could do little to nothing to help.

As if Susan could read his mind, she said, "I'm so glad you're here."

"Thanks. Trying to help where I can."

"You two better get together after this or there's something very wrong in the world." Bernie held on to Reynolds's hand as if his presence prevented her from falling into a million pieces. "It hurts. So bad. How do you know Lori?"

"She's been my friend since high school." Reynolds didn't plan to confess anything, especially not in front of the woman who occupied his mind twenty-four-seven. Yet, his frustration came out anyway. "She's helping me with the adoption process."

"You're planning to adopt?" Susan's eyes went wide with curiosity.

Nausea twisted his gut. He and Susan had never discussed his desire to become a dad. After a year of great conversations, was he about to ruin everything? "Yes, but there's been issues."

"Issues? Why?"

His eyes darted between the two women before answering. "I'm not married."

Bernie's eyes narrowed. "That doesn't seem … fair."

"No, it doesn't." Susan chewed on her bottom lip. "So, if you were married—"

Bernie gasped. "A single dad? Lori said…" Her body tensed as she panted, "Was I supposed to … meet you … yesterday?"

Chapter Four

"**M**EET ME?" WAS Bernie the no-show birth mom? *This was a potential meet-cute on steroids.*

"It's starting again!" The fear in Bernie's eyes punched him in the chest. "Stay with me."

Sandwiching Bernie's hands between his own, he swallowed his concerns. "Bernie, we're here for you. You're in good hands with Susan."

"I sure hope so, because it's gonna get real personal."

"You're fully dilated, plus one, head presentation." Susan pulled off her gloves before donning a new pair.

"What does that even mean?" Ben craned his neck.

"The baby is starting down the birth canal just like it's supposed to. Bernie, you're on your side. Is this the position you want to stay in?"

"I think so." She gritted her teeth.

Respectfully moving Bernie's skirt up to her belly button, Susan explained, "You can lie on your side, on your back, be on all fours, child's pose, whatever you're the most comfortable being. You deliver in any position. Change as needed."

The thick smells of sweat, labor, coffee, and whatever was in that machine behind the counter with dancing pepper on the side mixed in the air around them, but Reynolds held on to the memory of Susan's sweet-scented shampoo.

"Doesn't she have to lie on her back?" Ben watched from across the room, intermittently pausing to check a still-unconscious Carl.

"We do what's comfortable for the mother." Susan readied for Bernie's next contraction. "You're almost there."

Bernie wearily pushed herself up on her elbow. "It's almost over?"

Joyful anticipation filled Reynolds's chest at the child's arrival, especially hearing it wasn't a breach or face-first presentation. "This is one of my favorite things."

Bernie frowned at him. "Glad you're having fun, *Fräulein* Maria, but having my crazy-haired hooch out for the world to see on the cold, hard floor of this pit isn't gonna make me sing happy, annoying-as-shit tunes."

"I'm sorry. What can I do to help?"

"Go away." She held his hand tighter, and he stayed put.

"Whatever you need."

"I don't want to do this alone."

"You won't."

Without warning, she grabbed Susan's hand and placed it with hers and Reynolds's. "I don't want my baby to be alone."

The pain in the girl's voice pierced his resolve. "We won't let that happen."

"You won't?" Bernie whimpered as another wave of winds rattled the front doors.

What are you doing? You can't promise her anything.

Yet, before he could correct himself, Susan gave their hand pile a gentle squeeze. "We won't."

Again, Reynolds took the brunette in. A confident calm emulated from her, a necessary quality for a midwife. Yet, when she looked at him, her eyes swam with … hope.

Guess my adoption plan didn't scare her away. "Susan's right. We won't."

Through tears, Bernie pounded her fist on the floor. "Now that stupid fucking song's stuck in my head. 'My Favorite Things' are hard, heavy-beat, powerful Broadway songs."

"Think of 'Defying Gravity' or 'All That Jazz.' Anything from *Kinky Boots* or *Six*?" Ben interjected, which only made Bernie growl at him. "What about *Hamilton*?"

"Bernie. I know you're scared, but I'm here. Reynolds is here. Ben is here. For you and your baby." Susan's gentle words radiated from her like the noonday sun, bringing down the entire stress level of the room.

As her bottom lip quivered, the mum-to-be's eyes darted back and forth between Reynolds and Susan. "You're going to be amazing parents. A perfect family."

The kind comment pinched his ego to the point of pain. Reynolds forced a smile because it wasn't her fault the foster adoption system made the process so damned difficult for a single man who wanted to adopt. "That's a nice thing to say, Bernie."

"It's true. I can see it."

"Hopefully, one day." But if it stayed up to the state, he had little faith.

"I hope the best thing possible happens for you, Reynolds." Susan sucked on her bottom lip. "I truly do."

Bernie's forehead furrowed. "Wait. Is your name Dr. Reynolds Reynolds?"

He chuckled when he realized what she asked. "No, my first name is Thomas, but there are a lot of Thomases, so people call me by my last name. Avoids confusion."

"Got it." When the next contraction kicked in, Bernie squeezed the hell out of his hand.

A line of sweat ran down Susan's cheek as she enthusiastically coached, "That's it, Bernie. Bear down. Doing great."

The smell of caffeine and old fast-food snacks drifted around him as Bernie attempted to break his fingers. "Holy crap, kid. You're strong."

"She is. Glad you're here, Reynolds. Much safer with both of us attending."

As Bernie momentarily drained the blood from his bones, it hit him. Susan planned to handle a gunman, deliver this baby, and care for the mom, all on her own.

She is Wonder Woman.

Susan wiped the sweat from her lip with the shoulder of her shirt. "Strong work, Bernie. The baby is moving like it should."

"It is?" Ben craned his neck.

As her body tensed, Bernie requested, "Wet towel. Please."

"Of course." Reynolds dabbed her forehead.

During her next contraction, Bernie grabbed a handful of Reynolds's hoodie, yanking him forward. She rested her head against his knee and curled up in a sideways crunch, holding her upper leg out of the way and screaming many, many four-letter words, specifically about the absent bio dad.

"That's it, Bernie. You've got it. Great job." Susan guided Bernie through each moment of her pain.

As soon as it was done, Bernie collapsed. "I can't. I can't. No more."

"I've got ya, kiddo. You're almost there." Reynolds cautiously slid his hands under her shoulders. "Lean on me."

With an appreciative nod, Susan patted Bernie's knee. "A few more pushes, okay? Reynolds, that's good. Let her brace against you. Can you hold her leg up?"

"I can do it." Before the contraction began, Ben stepped in. "I want to."

"Um, Bernie?"

Bernie frantically nodded, and quickly, Ben took Reynolds's place behind his friend. As the young man supported her both physically and emotionally, the girl burst into tears, grabbed Ben's hand, and held it to her chest. "Thank you. Thank you."

Reynolds moved next to Susan to assist while Bernie asked Ben to pick up her phone and start recording.

Between contractions, Susan expertly explained each next step while working her midwife magic. "Push, Bernie! Push!"

At the end of the contraction, Bernie collapsed against Ben. "I'm done. I can't."

"Bernie. You've been perfect!" Susan's calm, but badass instructions helped coach a terrified woman in incredible pain.

Susan's siblings spoke volumes of their fierce sister who ran on routine and predictability. After the devastating accident that killed their father, and disabled their mom, Susan saved them all from falling into a sea of despair.

The woman did everything with purpose, practicality, and passion, and Reynolds was in awe of her.

A few moments later, Susan coached Bernie to effectively push the baby's head out.

A wild-eyed fear replaced Bernie's exhaustion. "This next one's gonna hurt like a bitch. Like I'm shitting a watermelon."

"Get past the shoulders, and you're home free," Susan's easy instructions were like audible Xanax. "I promise."

As he nervously opened and closed his fists, Reynolds's heart sat in his throat like he needed to swallow an orange.

"Take a moment, Bernie." Susan's steely composure rivaled that of a Super Bowl quarterback about to be hiked a ball for the last play of a tie game. "Ready?"

Donning a pair of gloves to decrease infection risk, Reynolds exhaled, "Ready."

After placing an extra pad under Bernie's bottom, Susan's eyes went wide. "Wait."

"What? What do you need?"

"I don't have anything to wrap the baby in."

Despite having only a Henley underneath, Reynolds shed his Captain America hoodie and laid it flat. "I've got you covered."

"Thank you for being here." Her appreciation shot into his heart like an arrow.

"You're welcome."

"Dammit! Get a room! It's happening!" With a guttural growl, the mother-to-be's cheeks turned to beet red.

"The next contraction you bear down. Hard." Susan blew a piece of wayward hair out of her face.

"You fucking keep saying that!"

"Give me one hard, strong push and your baby will be out."

A constant stream of tears flowed down Bernie's cheeks as the blue and red lights flashed across the front windows. "Now? Those assholes get here now?"

Ben didn't flinch, but his blanched fingers indicated they were void of blood. "Push! Get it out! My hand!"

The newborn slid into Susan's awaiting hands, and she quickly cleared its airway. "Baby's out. You did it, Bernie!"

Oxygen painfully lodged in Reynolds's chest at the perfect, pink newborn. "Boy or girl?"

"Ten fingers, ten toes. It's a girl!" Susan clamped and cut the cord, before tapping the bottom of the baby's foot. "Wake up, sweet baby."

The child remained motionless. *No. No. Don't do this.*

Before concern took hold, the stomping of heavy boots preceded a hard blast of frigid air whipping through the store.

"What the fuck?" Carl groggily yelled as he gazed up in the faces of the local authorities.

Leaning into Susan, Reynolds placed his body between the chill and the child, but the quick temperature drop slammed into everyone.

Suddenly, the newborn opened her eyes and wailed.

The gloomy daylight highlighted the storm's strength, but everyone momentarily forgot the weather as the first lusty cries of a new life came into the world like a lighthouse in the darkness.

When the sound hit his ears, Reynolds's vision momentarily blurred as Susan placed the precious package on his hoodie.

With tender strength, he swaddled the infant in the thickness of his clothes as tears fell freely. "I am an expert baby wrapper, Bernie. Don't worry."

"If she's with you two, I'll never worry again, Dr. June." Bernie smiled through sobs.

"Neither will I." Ben continued to hold up the phone and shook out his other hand.

She faced Ben and whispered, "Did you get all that?"

He nodded as paramedics approached and aided Susan as she coached Bernie through her final part of childbirth.

"Is that the placenta?" Cheery Ben immediately turned a light shade of green and put the phone down.

Afterward, Bernie rolled to her side and buried her face in Ben's lap. "Thank you for being here for me, Ben. You really are my best friend."

"I got you, Bernie." He rocked her and kissed the top of her head. "You're safe now."

Giving the paramedics a place next to Susan, Reynolds held the baby against the warmth of his chest and moved to the farthest corner of the store.

"She's beautiful, Bernie." The child gazed into his eyes

with innocent wonder. Her hand reached up and he instinctively leaned in as she touched his nose. Reynolds didn't hide the chest-crushing happiness. He shouldn't be this euphoric for a baby that would never be his, but for a moment, he basked in the beauty of her safe arrival.

Susan wrapped her arm around his waist. "She's perfect."

"She is." When he turned, Susan grabbed his shirt and pressed her lips to his.

He froze until the soft coaxing of her lips triggered him to return to the same intensity, and for a blissful second, his world fell perfectly into place.

When Susan pulled back, she released her hold. "I'm … I'm … I'm so sorry."

Her subtle berry scent drifted around him as she stuttered through her apology. "It's okay. I'm okay. You okay?"

A sweet pink stained her cheeks. "Such an emotional morning. I'm so sorry to complicate things. No idea what I was thinking."

"I'm not sorry." Was this the practical, rational sister the Davidson siblings spoke volumes about? The one who never allowed emotions to get out of hand? Who always kept a level head?

Swallowing hard, she waved off her actions. "That was … I'm … just … th-thank you."

"For what?"

"Standing by me … while I delivered the baby." With trembling fingers, she touched her lips as if he'd branded her.

And she liked it.

Her flustered state amused him, but her comment didn't.

"Who didn't stand by you?"

"No one of consequence."

Did she just quote Princess Bride*?* "I must know."

A slow, sexy smirk spread across her face. A smirk that spoke louder than any sext. "I'm going to like *officially* getting to know you, Dr. Reynolds."

As much as he appreciated the rational Susan, this impulsive, movie-quoting, superhero-loving one always piqued his interest far more. And she was finally here in Montana. "As you wish."

"You are an adorable couple. The baby's perfect adoptive parents." Bernie pulled the EMS blanket up to her chin.

"You're adopting her? How cool! I'm adopted." One of the paramedics gave a thumbs-up as the police pulled Carl to his feet and out the door.

"Parents?" Susan's pretty forehead furrowed. "Wait. What?"

Reynolds shook his head. "Adoption?"

"I've already texted Lori. Sent her the videos. I'll sign the papers when I get to the hospital." When the girl nodded, Reynolds's breath caught in his chest.

After being passed over by multiple birth mothers, he had to be sure he understood her correctly. "Bernie, what are you saying?"

"Susan wants to be a mom. You want to be a dad. You two are the perfect power couple, so it seems obvious what I need to do."

"Wait, wait. I never said—" Panic swam in Susan's eyes.

"But you did, Susan. Remember when you said you

couldn't—"

"Yes, of course, I do," Susan snapped, then exhaled before gaining his gaze. "Do you? With me?"

"He does." Snuggling into the heavy blanket provided by the paramedics, Bernie beamed in the post-partum hormone glow.

Before they wheeled her away, Reynolds asked again, "To be clear, Bernie. You want Susan *and* me to raise your baby?"

"I told you. She's your meet-cute." Bernie waved without looking back. "Now, go be a rom-com, book-loving, superhero, happily-ever-after kind of family."

Chapter Five

"ARE YOU SURE about this?"

Not at all. Susan drummed her fingers against the ceramic mug as the events from the last several hours mentally tumbled like socks in a dryer. "Pretty sure."

The gorgeous, dark-haired woman sitting across the desk raised an eyebrow. "Why?"

"Bernie asked us and I ... we promised." The dry answer didn't even convince Susan of their good intentions.

Social worker Lori Ramon shook her head, her lips thinning as if she were holding in expletives. "Adopted a lot of your patients' babies, have you?"

Despite Lori's spot-on observation, frustration spoke first. "What the hell do you want me to say, Ms. Ramon?"

Reynolds threw his hands up in surrender. "Come on, Lori. Hear us out."

With a set to her jaw, Lori locked her arms across her chest. "Fine. I'm listening."

Reynolds shed his jacket, laying it on the back of the chair next to Susan. Since he wrapped the baby in his thick hoodie, the dark blue Henley probably didn't offer him much warmth, but damn if he didn't look good wearing it.

She bet he looked even better out of it. *Focus!*

"I ... we can't walk away from this opportunity." Instead of sitting, he slowly paced. A wave of his citrus-scented whatever-he-used washed over Susan with each pass, making it difficult for her to concentrate.

"You? No. *Her?*" Lori tilted her head, her deep brown eyes narrowing. "I don't even know her. And neither do you."

"Yes, I do." Taking a seat, he rested his forearms on the desk between them.

Lori mimicked his body language. "You said you met today."

After months of long-distance correspondence, Susan's grip on her mug blanched her fingernails as the reality of him sitting right next to her sunk in. "Officially."

"What does that mean? Officially?"

Ever since that first video call, his lopsided smirk lit up her computer screen and libido. Too many times, his rich voice caressed her eardrums. Now *officially* meeting him, he was *so* much sexier live than she anticipated.

Every cell of her rational brain banded together to hold her thoughts above her belly button and keep her hands to herself. "I mean, in person."

Rubbing the bridge of her nose, Lori looked one unacceptable response away from going nuclear. "In person?"

"Please, let me explain. When my sister, Lucy, first started at the ER in Marietta, she Face Timed me around the unit. Introduced me to all the staff. She'd call, text, or FaceTime daily. A few days later, she didn't answer her cell. I

got worried. I called the hospital. Reynolds answered."
Thinking of that day threatened to derail Susan's composure.

The day the love of her life gave her an unreasonable ultimatum, broke her heart, and shattered their perfectly planned future. After canceling her third engagement in ten years, Susan needed to hear comforting words from her younger sister.

"She sounded upset. I asked if I could check on her later." Reynolds casually rested his arm across the back of her chair, and before she realized it, Susan instinctively leaned toward his gesture.

It was unnerving how quickly she found comfort in his presence. She fought the urge to crawl into his lap and snuggle against his broad chest.

Instead, subtly she shifted away. "I didn't think he'd actually call."

The corner of Lori's mouth twitched as if she were holding back an all-knowing smile. "But he kept his word, didn't he?"

"He did." When her skin warmed from the sweet memory, Susan giggled, then tried to play it off as she cleared her throat. She doubted she fooled anyone.

"And we've talked or texted every day since. Sometimes it's the best part of my day." Reynolds winked at her, causing her ovaries to quiver.

"Really?" she managed to squeak.

"*Reeeeally?*" Lori tapped her pen on her neatly organized desk without disturbing the stacks of folders on each corner.

"Yes, really, Lori." His relaxed posture indicated he felt

far more comfortable in this situation than Susan did, but his bouncing knee told her otherwise.

As her eyes darted back and forth between them, Lori pursed her pink-stained lips. "This is insane. You know this, right?"

"No more insane than me being passed over as an adoptive dad because I'm a single man."

"You mentioned that this morning." Susan took his hand in hers, hoping to offer comfort.

His fingers tenderly curled around hers. "It doesn't matter that I have a solid job, strong finances, a ton of good references, and a legit reason for wanting to adopt. Not have bio kids."

Now that last bit of information certainly shifted Susan's focus above her beltline. "You don't want bio kids?"

A momentary clench to his jaw before he answered. "I don't want to pass a genetic anomaly. Cystic fibrosis killed my sister, Audrey. I appreciate that there are a lot more treatment options now than twenty or so years ago, but there are different severities. No one can know how effectively treatments will work. She never had a chance to be a kid."

"It was rough for her," Lori agreed.

"But there's genetic testing you can do." *If you can have a bio child, you might not want me anymore.* The fear of another rejection terrified Susan more than she'd admit.

He sadly shook his head. "Nope. I'm a homogeneous carrier, so I'll pass on the gene no matter what. I won't burden a child with being a carrier or having the disease. Dating is hard enough without worrying about genetics in normal circumstances."

During their many discussions, not once was family biology discussed, but to be fair, that was a pretty niche and deep topic. They mostly stuck to movies, books, TV shows, superhero trivia, food, and general things about their days. He told her about Montana and she, Florida then Albuquerque. She gave an abridged version of her trauma from the car accident, and he said little about his parents and sister. Neither of them pushed the other for more information, wanting to stick to positive topics.

Not until he mentioned adoption back at the convenience store, Susan had no idea if he even wanted kids. Now, understanding that he did want to adopt *and* not have bio children weirdly comforted her. "I respect your decision, although it couldn't have been an easy one."

"A single woman who wanted to adopt and had the same situation wouldn't have her intentions questioned the way I have." He roughly ran his fingers through his thick chestnut hair, messing it up in perfect disarray.

Lori tossed her pen on the desk and leaned back. "You're not wrong, but she'd still be pressured to get pregnant anyway."

"It's a lot of pressure."

It is. Susan swallowed hard as her former fiancé's cruel words slammed into her brain.

What do you mean you can't get pregnant?
Get the corrective surgery so you can!
Why would I marry your broken ass now?
Adoption? You've got to be fucking kidding me.

"Susan, you okay?" Concern washed across Lori's sweet face. "You spaced out there. Something you want to tell us?"

The woman was far too perceptive. Confessing her own infertility might satisfy Lori's concerns about why Susan agreed to this insanity, but the words froze.

If Reynolds knew, would he still want to adopt with her?

Or would he shun her? Hate her for not being *perfect enough* despite *his* choice not to father a child?

If so, how could she stay in Marietta long-term without the pain of seeing him regularly?

She'd have to leave her siblings and live somewhere alone.

And she was so tired of being alone.

Pulling at the collar of her hoodie, Susan focused on preventing the *what if* part of her brain from spiraling out of control.

When his hand rested over hers, it provided a much-needed distraction. "Grip that coffee mug any tighter Susan, it'll shatter."

His awareness of her worry mainlined relief through her veins, triggering a few decompressive tears. "Thinking about your decision. I didn't know any of that."

"You didn't know about him wanting to adopt?" With a flick of her wrist, Lori silenced her phone.

"Not until he mentioned it this morning." *And surprised the hell out of me.*

"All this must be overwhelming, then. Hard to think straight. Make a rational decision." Narrowing her brown-eyed gaze, Lori's body tensed like a cat that was about to jump over the table and attack. "Don't you think?"

Careful, Susan. "It could be if we'd never met, but we've talked about a lot of things. Fun, friendly conversations. Found so many common interests. Our futures weren't a main topic, but it certainly would have come up once I got to Marietta."

"I'm sure of it," Reynolds agreed.

"Friendly? For almost a year? *No* sexting? Like none at all?" Lori raised an eyebrow like she didn't quite believe them.

"Why do people keep asking that?" Reynolds chuckled. "We kept things platonic for several reasons."

"Which are?"

Suddenly, the hem of her hoodie became fascinating. Susan twisted the fabric between her fingers so hard, she'd probably break the thread if she wasn't careful. "Mainly because we'd work together."

"And her sister is my boss," he added as his thumb slowly moved up and down the back of her hand, sending her thoughts somewhere way outside the realm of platonic.

"Those are good reasons. I guess you still have a lot to learn about each other. Give me a second." Lori's fingers sailed across her phone screen before she placed it back on her desk.

Even with the single-digit temperatures outside, a steady stream of people walked by the office and waved Lori a good-morning hello as they shed their snow-peppered coats.

Drinking back whatever she had in her tumbler, Lori continued, "Rey, when you asked me to help you navigate the foster system to adopt, I explained you being single would make it more difficult to get a placement. Especially a baby."

"Just yesterday, you said a mother choosing me was unlikely. Well, a mother chose me. The mother I waited around to meet."

Lori's one-window office indicated how little government resources prioritized caring for those who advocated for the voiceless. With multiple small shelves behind her, Lori made good use of the space, adding color by way of pop culture figurines, personal photos, and a bookshelf crammed full of books from different reading levels. "Yes, you're right, but it's a package deal, Reynolds. *Both* of you have to agree to this."

Both of us. More times than she could count, Susan imagined many delicious scenarios with the man sitting beside her, but none of them included them raising a baby together.

Especially when she couldn't have a child.

Then fate stepped in. *This is insane.* Susan emptied her mug as if she were taking tequila shots. "Where do we go from here?"

"Go? I'm still trying to understand *why*, Susan."

Because this might be my only shot to have a child. The words fought in her throat, wanting to escape. After discovering her inability to get pregnant and the fallout that followed, Susan sought a second opinion from a GYN friend who specialized in cases like hers. Twenty-four hours ago, her infertility was verified. The finality of it still hadn't gelled in her brain, but her grieving heart told a different story.

"I ... um ... it's..."

"Susan? Can I get something for you? Do you need to sleep before we decide anything?" His hair sat wildly on his scalp, indicating the chaos of the morning. Yet, he still radiated the nerdish sensuality she'd come to admire when gazing at his image.

"No, no. I'm tired but sane, I promise. Been on the road for several days. Since my midwife assignment ended early, I added Utah to my schedule." With a tissue, she dried the tears that already stained her shirt.

"Utah? That's not a direct route from Albuquerque." Lori removed the clip from her hair and allowed her locks to fall about her shoulders.

"True, but since I was a kid, I wanted to visit the Dinosaur National Monument and Yellowstone. Our dad always promised to take us, but ... he never got the chance."

"It's a cool place."

Fatigue set in and Susan rolled her head from side to side, hoping to loosen the knots in her shoulders. "I built in a few days of exploring before my siblings expected me. Hiked around. Took some amazing pictures, but I got tired of traveling. Being alone. I left a few days early and ended up here."

"Then your siblings don't know anything?"

"No. Not yet." *And they will go mental when they hear it.* She could already anticipate her older brother Peter's unsolicited words of wisdom.

And with one of his coworkers, no less. "They don't even know Reynolds and I have been in communication."

"Interesting. Your side stops sound like great adventures. Plus, who doesn't love dinosaurs, right?" The corner of Lori's mouth twitched before her eyes darted to Reynolds, who nodded.

For a moment, Susan felt like she was the subject of a conversation in a language she didn't understand. "We good?"

He kissed the inside of her wrist. "It's perfect."

The moment his lips touched her skin, her body buzzed from anticipation of more. *What. Is. Happening?*

Never in all of Susan's practical existence had a man so unnerved her in all the right ways. Not to say she hadn't experienced lust before, but not like this all-consuming passion for someone and certainly not for a man she'd never actually met.

The moment she opened that fundraising calendar to his picture, he permanently resided in her brain, and she had no logical explanation for it.

Now, after finally meeting him, she didn't want one.

Clearing her throat, Lori disrupted the moment. "Since you've talked extensively before today, I'm guessing something is going on here."

Susan's foot tapped in nervous tempo against the carpet. "Something? I guess so." But what, she had no idea, and she certainly didn't want to emotionally overstep her first day here. *Things were so much easier to process when he wasn't sitting* right there.

"And you liked what you saw?" Lori cocked her eyebrow.

"What the hell kind of question is that, Lori?" Reynolds

snapped before Susan's voice could find oxygen.

"It's a question another social worker or a judge might ask, Reynolds."

"You're not going to handle our case? You have so far."

"I might ask someone else to head the case since I don't want to risk anything being used to overturn an adoption if there's an appeal. Of course, we're so short-staffed, they may not have anyone else." Lori rubbed the bridge of her nose. "As much as I want this for you, I want it to stick. Saying you planned to start a family with some random woman you've never met, while your best friend runs the adoption, doesn't work in your favor if anyone contests it."

When his jaw clenched, the worry radiated from him. "Fine. What do you suggest?"

With a long exhale, Lori rested her hands flat on her desk. "Let's try this again. You talked before yesterday."

Susan and Reynolds nodded.

"And did you like what you saw? Learned?"

Without looking at her, Reynolds swallowed hard. "Very much."

Some sort of relationship chemistry brewed between them, but to hear him say it kicked her heart rate into overdrive. "I did. I do."

"You do, huh?" Lori's fingers danced across the keyboard and the hum of the printer momentarily broke the awkward tension. "Speaking of I dos, what's the plan?"

"Plan?" Panic bitterly danced along the back of her tongue. Susan always had a plan, but being near him scattered her common sense.

The window to their left offered a limited view of the snowy parking lot and the gray, overcast sky. In the distance, the mountains with their white-capped peaks sat tall against the horizon. As much as Susan prepped and planned for her move here from the sunny coast of Florida, nothing prepared her for this magnificent natural beauty, the bitter cold in spring, or the possibility of becoming an instant mother.

In all her thirty-plus years, Susan did everything with great logic and purpose. She had to, especially after the brutal car accident that changed her world forever.

Otherwise her entire family would have drowned.

Today, she sat so far out of her practical element, she couldn't be sure of anything except her long-held desire to become a mother might come true.

Oh, and that Thomas Reynolds had to be the sexiest man she ever met.

After snatching the paper off the printer, Lori laid it facedown in front of her and interlaced her elegant fingers. "If you two *promise* to honor Bernie's wishes and raise this baby together, how do you see it playing out? I'm all ears."

With a chuckle, Reynolds rested his forearms on his thighs. "To be honest, I, we hadn't thought that far ahead, Lori. It all happened so fast, just damn glad to have a shot at fatherhood."

"Well, my friend. You have just under seventy-two hours to decide how this will play out with you two."

"That's an interestingly specific amount of time." Susan rested her hands on the edge of Lori's desk, hoping not to disturb her organized stacks of papers.

"The mother can't sign the relinquishment papers until the seventy-two hours after the child's birth."

"Then the adoption happening is not for sure."

"Nope. Not yet." When their eyes met, a flicker of worry danced across his.

Susan's heart dropped to her feet. "How long have you wanted to be a father?"

His broad shoulders relaxed as a sweet smile lit up his rugged face. "Since I was a kid."

"You pretty much raised Nate and Audrey before your grandparents stepped in." Lori checked her buzzing phone, then wrote something on the large desk planner in front of her.

Sounds familiar. "I had to help a lot after our father died." That was an understatement. Her mother appointed Susan the foundation to keep their family from falling apart.

"How old were you when your father passed?" Lori rolled a blue pen between her fingers.

"Fourteen. Car accident. A drunk driver hit us head-on."

"Oh God. How traumatic. So it was quick. Not an illness?"

"No, it was ... instantaneous." A knot of sorrow pinched her, causing Susan to flinch.

For a second, Lori appeared to be processing something. "Wait, you said us."

"Yes, my brothers, sister, parents, and I were in the car." Even though more than two decades passed since that awful day, the details were vivid. The song on the radio. The smell of the ocean. The blue of her father's suit. The sound of the glass shattering and her being violently thrown sideways before waking in the ER. "It's amazing that only our father died. Mom was permanently disabled. We almost lost Lucy, but she made a full recovery."

"And your mother?" The quick tapping of the keyboard indicated the social worker typed seriously fast.

Susan willed herself not to react to the angry memories of their mother giving up. Dumping all responsibilities on a teenage Susan. Treating her differently when the other kids weren't looking. *No time for sad backstories.* "She was never the same. Held on for several years before she died. My stepfather, Charlie, was a great help her last few years."

"Peter, Edmund, and Lucy have mentioned Charlie. Sounds like a good guy." Reynolds drummed his fingers on his thigh before sitting back in the chair. His shoulders relaxed. His hair still in sexy disarray.

There would never be enough words of gratitude in the English language for what Charlie did. Once he stepped in, Susan could relax for the first time in years. "He is. He was a news anchor at a local TV station. A drunk driver killed his brother. When the guy who hit us was up for parole, Charlie wanted to do a follow-up piece on us, see how we were doing."

"Doesn't sound very ethical."

"I thought that at first, but he wanted the public involved, to make sure the guy stayed in jail for his full sentence. He promised to be respectful about how he presented us, and he was. I was shocked when my mother agreed to talk to him." It never ceased to amaze Susan how her mother brightened up after talking to Charlie that day. For years, her mother walked under a storm cloud of sadness only for her to find the sunshine again in his presence.

"How did it play out?" Lori asked as snow peppered the windows.

"He didn't run the piece. Said we shouldn't have to re-live it, but instead aired one about drunk drivers getting out early from their sentences. He talked about his brother's death and used our case as one of many. It got state and local officials involved and laws changed for the better."

"Sounds like a good guy."

"He is. He fell in love with my mother and took care of her until the day she died. He helped us each get scholarships for college, med schools, my master's so we graduated with little to no debt." But what Susan appreciated the most was he gave her back her freedom. No longer was she her mother's primary caregiver, maid, or verbal punching bag.

"I'd like to meet him. Let's get him out here soon." It should have been criminal how good Thomas Reynolds looked after the morning they had, but when he smiled at her, Susan's stomach flip-flopped.

"I'd like that." Before she processed it, Susan rested her head on Reynolds's shoulder. This time, she did not attempt to move away when reality set in.

He offered a comfort she hadn't expected, but now, didn't want to give up.

"Thank you for sharing, Susan." A lopsided smile spread across Lori's face as she typed away on her computer.

"You're welcome."

After he kissed the top of her head, Reynolds added, "You've met her siblings, Lori. At my house."

For some reason, that bit of information bothered her, but Susan refused to ask about their history. It served no point.

As if reading her mind, Lori pointed to a framed photo on her bookshelf. "Nate, Reynolds, and I grew up together in Marietta. Graduated high school."

"Is that you in the middle?" Susan bit back comedic commentary about Lori's hairstyle in the photo.

An eye-roll replaced Lori's earlier stoicism. "High school graduation. Mom insisted a bouffant would really make my graduation memorable. A bouffant. In the twenty-first century."

"Unusual choice, sure, but you have an amazing smile."

"Well played." The heat of his breath on her ear caused Susan to shiver.

"Indeed. My parents worked all the time, so I spent a lot of time at Rey and Nate's grandparents' house since we rented the house next door. Nate lives there now, and Reynolds got his grandparents' house. You'll love it there."

"There?" Susan's tongue threatened to lodge in her throat.

"You're going to live together, right?"

Susan's foot quickly bounced as the thought of him living in the same house.

Right across the hall.

Naked. "We hadn't really discussed anything like this."

"That's a big ask." When his hand rested on her knee,

she wasn't sure if it was to offer comfort or prevent her from running out of the building.

"So is adopting a baby, but you've been married before Rey. Sharing space with someone isn't new." Lori shrugged.

A quick throat-clearing later, Reynolds rubbed his free hand on one of his perfect, jean-covered thighs. "True, I've been married before. Thanks for casually bringing that up, Lori."

"You're welcome." She obviously regretted nothing.

A snort escaped Susan at their playful banter that sounded so much like her and her three siblings. *I think I'm going to like Lori.* "You mentioned before you were married. How long?"

He shifted in his chair. "Two years. Amicable divorce. Different life goals that we simply couldn't work through."

"What about you, Susan?" Her phone buzzed again, but Lori silenced it without looking.

"Married? No. Engaged?" How she hated answering this question, but she swallowed her embarrassment since Lori would for sure ask why. "Three times since college."

"You mentioned that a few months ago." At this point, Reynolds's knee stopped bouncing.

Without a hint of judgment, Lori continued her inquiry. "Three, huh? Any particular reasons why you called them off?"

Subtly, Reynolds turned his body toward hers, but she felt his eyes on her all the same as she focused on Lori.

"After an engagement, some people show their true colors. Become who they actually are. They want something other than what they previously professed. So, I canceled."

The hard edge Lori held as soon as they walked into her office relaxed as a slow nod of understanding replaced it. "People hide all sorts of things from each other."

"They do." To prevent more sad memories from spilling out, she took a drink from her now-empty mug.

Not even her siblings completely understood why she hadn't followed through with I dos, especially this last one. To date, they'd respected her privacy, but that would last only so long. Especially now that she'd see at least one of them daily.

Still, the words sat largely on her tongue. If she allowed herself the privilege of confessing it all to Reynolds and Lori, she might never stop talking. And he might call this entire situation off. "Just your typical sad backstory. That's all."

"We all have breakup stories, but could it be that you haven't found the right guy yet?" It didn't go unnoticed that Lori's eyes momentarily darted to her friend, who leaned over and gave Susan a soft kiss on her cheek.

"Or that." Soaking in his tender attentions, Susan wondered why she hadn't considered moving to Montana sooner. The idea of the right guy sitting next to her should've rattled Susan's cage something fierce, but only calm settled in every muscle.

And lust.

A whole lotta of lust.

Lori's fingers played with the corner of the paper on her desk. "You'll appreciate the love and care put into Reynolds's home. Three bedrooms, two and a half baths."

As the practical and lizard parts of Susan's brain fought for dominance, Lori and Reynolds spoke fondly about his late grandparents, mentioning how his grandfather could build anything imaginable and how his grandmother's ability to re-create Scandinavian family treats like lingonberry jam, *Aebleskivers*—Danish donuts—and *Ris a la Malta*—rice pudding.

Many times over the past year, he shared stories about his grandparents and his brother, Nate. Their fishing trips, hiking expeditions, national park adventures, and trips to the Pacific Coast. The boys learned basic home repairs, survival skills, and their ways around a kitchen.

From time to time, he'd share sweet stories about his late sister, Audrey. She was crafty and creative, loved dinosaurs, books, and classic cartoons. She passed after Nate, she, and Reynolds moved to Marietta.

On the flip side, he revealed little about his parents, but the sadness in his voice indicated their impacts on his life lay heavy.

Continuing, Lori bragged like a proud friend about how Reynolds excelled in baseball and academics throughout high school and beyond. He completed an emergency room residency, followed by several years at a big-city trauma center as a flight doctor before returning to Marietta.

From their multiple discussions, Susan knew all this but loved watching him turn five shades of red as Lori continued to list his good quality traits.

He was an avid reader.

Loved movies.

Cared for an aging, one-eyed cat named Odin.

Had a fully stocked toolbox and knew how to use every single item.

Could dance a decent waltz and always kept a bottle of his grandfather's favorite whiskey in his kitchen.

"And finally." She opened a desk drawer and held up the calendar to his photo. "A hot model."

A lusty laugh escaped Susan. "Amen!"

Covering his face, he slouched in the chair. "When are people going to forget that thing?"

"The answer is never, sir. Ne-ver." She flipped through it and noted a few months she'd like to meet before tucking the embarrassing material back into the safety of her desk. "What do you think, Susan?"

"I think I'm getting the better end of the deal." The answer seemed to appease Lori and embarrassed Reynolds.

A twofer. And as much fun as this was, did she know him well enough to adopt a baby with him?

Could he be hiding a cruel core, like her former fiancés?

Watching him blush from his well-earned accolades, Susan couldn't imagine him viciously berating her for refusing to do what they silently expected from a wife.

The man was too humble. And he cared for an old, cranky, mono-optical feline named after a Norse god who looked like Anthony Hopkins.

What she did know, she liked. *A lot.*

And she wanted to learn more.

So. Much. More.

But would he be as interested in her when he discovered

all of her sad backstory? Why she moved here? Her imperfections?

Coming to Marietta gave Susan the chance to start over, to get away from all those who always saw the girl who survived that brutal car accident that killed her father, disabled her mother, and forever changed her life.

At some point, she had to tell Reynolds *everything*. Even with him choosing not to biologically father a baby didn't mean he couldn't or wouldn't change his mind later.

Yet, the idea of him rejecting her this morning hurt too much to even consider.

Still, she didn't drive all this way to lie. A baby's world depended on it.

Be logical, Susan. Like you've always been.

She blinked back tears.

Being logical sucks.

"Does that work for you?" Lori's voice yanked Susan out of her worry.

"What?"

"That you, the baby, and Reynolds live at his house?"

"That does make the most sense. Less confusion for the baby." Before her fear got the better of her, Reynolds sandwiched Susan's hand between his. The warmth of his touch offered immediate strength.

"Susan, we can live together, or—"

Tapping her finger on her desk, Lori adamantly shook her head. "There's no *or* here. You're going to have to present a united front. An actual couple. Even with Bernie giving you designated custody and you two having this digital pen pal situation, not everyone is as open-minded about two single people faking a relationship just to get a baby."

"We're not faking—" Susan blurted, then shifted in her chair to reorganize her response. "I mean, there's obvious interest here. Yes?"

Reynolds nodded as his eyes brightened.

Seeing a bit of his sparkle tugged the corners of her lips up. "We are a *we* in some form or fashion. No faking."

"And what about becoming a we plus one?" The tapping of Lori's pen increased its tempo.

To think, only twenty-four hours ago, Susan learned she'd never become a mother, biologically. Now, she was one honest answer away from earning the title of Mommy. And maybe becoming a hot calendar model's girlfriend. "Reynolds—"

In one loving move, he tucked their interlaced hands to his chest. The hard thud of his pulse vibrated against her skin. "Susan, please don't feel pressured to do this out of obligation. I like you. A lot. But if you want to back out, if this is all too overwhelming, please tell me now."

The scent of his citrus whatever he used mixed with his closeness and overwhelmed her libido. She struggled to find coherent words. "I ... um ... well..."

"What I don't want is someone who thinks motherhood sounds good, loves the good times, but bails when the reality sets in and the hard work starts." The subtle edge to his words made Susan wonder if that was why he and his siblings ended up living with their grandparents.

How heartbreaking. "I more than appreciate that motherhood is work. A lot of work. That part doesn't bother me."

"What part are you worried about?" His handsome brow furrowed as his thumb gently caressed her wrist, almost making her sigh with contentment.

Focus. "Us."

"Us?"

"What if *we* don't work? What if we're not compatible?" *Just had to throw practicality into the mix, didn't you, Susan?* But in all fairness, someone had to ask the question.

"Yeah, I don't see that being an issue." Lori tapped the rim of her mug with her thumb.

"Thank you for the endorsement." For a long moment, he stared at Susan as if reality and chaos fought in his head. "We start off simple."

"What?" *What does he mean?*

Lori's eyes went wide. "What does simple mean?"

Without looking away, Reynolds cleared his throat. "We take it slow. Build our relationship and friendship. No different than if we met and started dating. We can decide how fast or slow we want to proceed. How involved we want to get."

"According to the two of you, you've known each other a year. I think you're further along in the relationship game than just starting out." Lori's eyebrow cocked.

"Lori. I want Susan to stay. Don't scare her off, please."

"Fine, but just saying. You're further along than most ever get."

They were, but things could easily go sideways if they

weren't practical. Susan cleared her throat. "What do you think of starting with a platonic co-parenting arrangement?"

"If that's where you want to begin." Lori shrugged.

It made more sense than anything. They'd been able to easily establish a digital friendship. An in-person situation for half that time could easily work. "Plenty of people have raised children together with less emotional entanglements."

"A very practical approach, Susan." Lori raised her travel mug in approval.

"Yes. Practical." But there was one complication. The constant influxes of naughty thoughts whenever he was around. Seeing him on-screen was one thing but being able to actually reach out and touch him ... well, that was a whole other set of restraint skills.

Restraints. I wonder if he'd let me ... Stop it!

As the noises of the busy offices stirred in the background, and the winds howled outside, Susan zoned in on the man sitting next to her.

As she rested her forehead against his, she closed her eyes and inhaled him. For the first time in Susan Davidson's tumultuous love life, there were no doubts.

No worries. No fears. No hesitation.

And it scared the ever-living shit out of her, but not enough to say no and certainly not enough to walk away. "I'm in."

The tapping stopped. "You sure?"

"As sure as I can be on this short notice."

With a tilt of his head, Reynolds gazed into Susan's eyes. "Can I kiss you?"

"Please." Considering the importance of the situation, she expected his touch to be fiery, but when his lips lovingly touched hers, Susan's ovaries damn near exploded.

The kiss lasted no more than a few seconds, but the buzz from it easily seared into every fiber of her being.

"Thank you." He brushed his lips over hers before sitting back, the pulse point of his neck rapidly beating.

"You're welcome."

"A platonic co-parenting arrangement, huh? I give you two months before it's physical. Physical!" She sang a few bars from the top-forty hit for good measure.

"You and I are gonna be great friends." Even with fatigue hanging heavy in her bones, Susan appreciated Lori's humor.

"Thanks for your endorsement, Lori." Reynolds ran his fingers through his hair, only making it sexier.

"You're two consenting adults who've agreed to raise a baby together. Who am I to say otherwise?" With a flick of her wrist, Lori handed over a few thick folders and rattled off a laundry list of instructions before flipping over the facedown paper that she'd been tapping her pen against. "Once Bernie relinquishes her rights, then we can breathe a little easier."

They both nodded, Susan's body still tingling from Reynolds's thank-you-for-adopting-with-me kiss. "And the father?"

"He can sign anytime. It's finding him is the issue." For a few seconds, Lori sucked on her bottom lip like she was coming up with a plan. "But you let me worry about that part. Your jobs are to take care of this baby and not worry until there's something to worry about."

A yawn escaped Susan as her sleepless nights started catching up with her. "Sorry. Been up all night."

"I won't keep you much longer, so I'll make this short." She handed Reynolds the paper from her desk. "I strongly suggest you consider this. Get it done as soon as possible."

It took a moment for Susan to absorb the words, and when she did, her eyebrows hit her hairline. "Are you serious?"

"As a heart attack."

Reynolds's forehead furrowed and he shoved it back. "Lori, I can't ask Susan—"

"You didn't. I did. Changing both single statuses only increases the chances of this adoption being approved. You two have agreed to be a couple, no matter how you want to define what that is. Platonic. Simple. Physical. Complicated. A love match. Meet-cute. Whatever."

The absurd suggestion should have propelled Susan straight out the door. "I mean, it makes sense. We've known each other for a year so we're not total strangers. People do this by proxy all the time."

For a moment, Reynolds's deer-in-headlights stare had Susan believing he'd bolt. "Um ... well."

Bracing herself against her desk, Lori tilted her chin toward the paper. "So guys? Are you in or not?"

The moment Susan crossed the Montana state line, she drove straight into a blizzard, faced a gunman, delivered a baby, met her calendar model, and had the chance to become a mother, and it hadn't even been twelve hours.

It took only a second for his self-confidence to be replaced by defeat. "Susan, you don't have to do this."

As if she couldn't like him more. A good, intelligent, geek-gorgeous man who wanted to be a father. Don't even get her started on how the man could kiss.

Her girly bits quivered at the idea of what else he could do. And how well.

Nothing had been logical or practical, planned or prepped. And it felt exhilarating.

Besides, what could one more piece of pandemonium hurt?

Taking a rare leap of faith, Susan squared her shoulders and looked him straight in the eyes. "Like Lori said, we're two consenting adults who want to raise a baby together. This seems like the obvious next step. So, Reynolds? Want to get married?"

Chapter Six

"ARE YOU CRAZY? Married?" The hard rip of the box emphasized how well his brother, Nate, took the news.

Despite Nate's outburst, Reynolds smirked as they moved several boxes of nursery items into the recently cleared room. "Easy. We went in, filled out the paperwork, said a few of our own vows to each other, went back to the county clerk. She asked us some questions and gave us our marriage license."

"I love this state for the nature, but legalities? That's something else. Where is the hardware in this stupid box?" Nate stomped around the room that shared a bathroom with Reynolds and across from where Susan slept. Last night.

Alone.

Knowing she slept under his roof, probably not wearing much, had Reynolds tossing and turning. When he finally took matters into his own hand and decompressed, sleep found him.

The first morning light sent him out the door on a long, much-needed run. Upon his return, the house smelled of coffee and vanilla. He found her in his kitchen, making pancakes as Odin, the old cat, happily ate canned tuna out of his bowl.

When Susan smiled at him, Reynolds let out a breath he hadn't realized he'd been holding.

None of this should feel normal like this had been their routine forever, but it did.

And it terrified him that it could all end any moment.

"You in there, brother?"

The rip of another box pulled Reynolds out of his worry and back to the present. "Yeah. Where were we?"

Until yesterday afternoon, Nate's former room was used for storage of assorted items and keepsakes. Susan and Reynolds spent most of their wedding night clearing the space and moving things upstairs to the loft.

"Who knew getting married here could be simpler than Vegas? Did you know Montana is the only double proxy marriage state in the US?" Reynolds pushed a dresser-changing-table combo he and Susan put together this morning against the far wall. On top of it, he placed his toolbox and a leveler.

"Why do you even know that?" Nate tore off the flap of the crib's box, causing the main contents to collapse against the hardwood.

"The county clerk told us yesterday. Careful, Nate. I don't want to lose any pieces."

His brother angrily snatched up the instructions. "A crib. Double proxy? Do you even hear yourself right now?"

"Yes, and I hear *you*, too."

Stepping closer, Nate lowered his voice. "You told me

you'd never get married again."

The truth bomb hit without warning, but he should have expected it from his glass-half-empty brother. "I did, but this is different. Susan is different."

No truer words had been spoken, but Nate rolled his eyes. "Yeah, okay. And what if this adoption doesn't stick? Are you going to stay married?"

Reynolds pinched his lips together because he honestly didn't know. *Would they?* Or would she leave to be with someone who could give her a biological baby?

Dammit. Why does he have to make sense? "I don't know."

"Maybe you should ask her."

"Probably, but not today." As gentle footsteps approached, Reynolds waved off Nate and eyeballed the spot where the crib should fit, next to the dresser. Away from the window, but closer to the door.

That way they'd hear the child when she needed them.

Them. Child. Our child. The impact of the last twenty-four hours' events suddenly gelled, and for a moment, Reynolds convinced himself he dreamed all of it.

The dream where, despite all the shit that happened in his life, love found him, he married the woman of his dreams, and they had a sweet little family.

The scent of her strawberry shampoo hit his nose, verifying his reality. "Going okay? My siblings are on the way."

Before Reynolds answered, Nate scoffed. "Sure. It's great, Susan. My brother went off and married some women he never met."

"In person." She smiled like a woman who had no regrets.

"Yeah, yeah. They might bring a baby home in a few days. And now I've got in-laws. Again. Ever have something like that happen to you, Susan?"

"Sort of. My brother Peter and his kids Zoomed me right before Christmas last year." She winked at Reynolds, and he silently said thanks that his hoodie covered the front of his jeans.

"How is that like this situation?"

"Peter didn't know he had any kids."

The oldest Davidson discovering he was a dad of twins, a boy, and a girl, certainly caught their family by surprise last Christmas, but she said it so nonchalantly that Nate stared at her without blinking for a few beats.

"I remember that. I guess it fits. Do they include a screwdriver to fit this shit?" With a hard yank, Nate ripped the bag of hardware in half, sending pieces clanging all over the hardwood floor.

Before he could pick up any of the items, a flash of orange shot across the room, slapping some of the bolts rebounding off the wall.

"Knock it off, Odin." Reynolds's attempts to shoo the cat out of the room earned him an indifferent glare and *screw you* tail flip.

"I can't believe he's still alive. He's got to be close to twenty." Nate crawled around, searching for the runaway pieces.

"He was your grandparents' cat, then?" Immediately, Susan collected a few small items that Odin batted away, but when she came close to him, he stretched his neck for her to scratch.

Amazing how quickly she brought peace to any space she occupied. *And she's my wife. Platonically speaking.* "The back door was open one summer and while *Mormor* worked in the kitchen, the cat walked in and never left."

"*Mormor?*"

"Swedish for paternal grandmother. *Farmor* is for grand-father."

"Understood. How did he lose his eye? There's one by your foot, Reynolds."

"Squirrel got the better of him one day."

"After the stitches came out, he got the better of the squirrel." Nate snatched the bolt before Reynolds could.

Immediately, the cat jumped up on the dresser and flicked his tail like, *Yeah, I did.*

With a quick scan of the room, Reynolds nodded. "I think we got them all."

"We'll find out soon enough," Nate grumbled as he set up his work area exactly how he wanted it.

Typical surgeon.

Susan handed over some hardware. "Here's the rachet you need. It's included. Need help? I'm pretty good with—"

"I got it! I don't need … but thanks." Even when his brother attempted civility, he always came across like an asshole.

Without a hint of frustration, she put her elegant hands up in surrender and backed away. "I'll go do something else, then."

The doorbell rang and immediately, Susan offered to get it, and Odin followed like they were besties.

The moment she was out of earshot, Reynolds snapped, "What the hell, Nate?"

"What the hell to you, Rey! I've been up all night delivering babies and you called me two hours ago. You almost got shot. Then got hitched. Had a kid."

Loud, happy voices of the reunited Davidson siblings filled their awkward tension.

To an outsider, the entire story must sound like an insanely written rom-com, but to Reynolds it felt as natural as breathing. *That's because of Susan.* "You know how long I've waited for the chance to adopt? To become a dad?"

Nate's lips thinned as his thick dark hair sat in disarray. A sure indicator he didn't even bother to brush it before running over from next door. "I do. That's why I'm here. Why I'm helping, but I'm worried you're jumping into something because it's easy."

Not once had Nate questioned Reynolds's adoption plans, but that didn't mean he'd get a free pass. "Easy? I've been waiting three years for a chance like this. Been passed over multiple times because some bureaucratic asshole decided something must be grossly wrong with me to want to adopt *and* be a single man."

"Shit. I didn't know all that. That sucks."

"I appreciate your concern, and I know this is way out of my normal, but trust me. Please. Nothing about this has been easy."

As happy as he was that Susan agreed to this parenthood

plan so far, angst knotted in his chest at the thought of her changing her mind like their mother did when the kids became actual work and lost their cute factors.

For the love of everything, please don't change your mind.

Nate rested his hand on Reynolds's shoulder. "Look, I love you, but fuck, all this is a lot before noon. And I worry about you. That you're too focused on the parenting part and not thinking enough about the marriage part."

"I learned my lesson last time." *At least, I hope I did.*

"Good. And at least have breakfast next time you spring something like this on me."

Even as kids, Nate's demeanor always improved with the promise of good food. "Fair enough, brother. I think we still have pancakes."

"She made you pancakes? Shit. If this doesn't work out for you, I might ask her out."

"Don't even think about it." They bro-hugged it out as multiple footsteps approached.

"Just be careful."

Susan entered with her three siblings in tow. "This will be her room. We'll put those shelves there. The bathroom connects to Reynolds's room."

Reynolds gave them a nod. "This used to be Nate's room."

Before it was his, it was Audrey's.

With a flick of her wrist, Susan opened her bedroom door. "I'm in here."

"Across the hall. By yourself," Peter grunted.

Lucy's, Peter's, and Edmund Davidson's faces swam with

questions as Nate cursed, "Some assembly required my ass."

Reynolds expected no less from her siblings. He worked with each of them for well over a year, but as the three *physicians* listened to Susan about the plans for the nursery, it hit him.

She was the only one without MD after her name.

Why didn't she go to medical school?

Not that her midwife career path deserved any less respect. She was a damned good nurse and fierce patient advocate as he personally witnessed yesterday.

No doubt, she possessed the discipline, intellect, and personality to survive and succeed at physician's training. Yet, until she stood with her brothers and sister, the question never even crossed his mind.

But now, his curiosity was piqued by all the questions bounding around his cranium. Had she been held to a different set of rules?

What's your whole story, Susan Davidson?

As his now in-laws set him in their sights, Reynolds swallowed back his queries. "I appreciate all of you for coming. I'm sure this is all very confusing to you."

"You think?" Peter, the oldest of the four, unzipped his coat with a hard yank. He still wore his scrubs from last night's shift that ended this morning and a scowl that said he hadn't slept yet.

Lucy, the youngest of the four and the first to come to Marietta wore an oversized dark blue coat with a Disney T-shirt, mismatched sweats, and boots. She stabbed her hips with her fists. "Before you begin to explain all *this*, Susan, why are you here?"

Susan's brilliant smile faltered. "What do you mean? I accepted a job—"

Lucy stepped back, and her signature red ponytail bobbled loosely on her head as if she'd thrown her hair up in a hurry. "No. You told us you'd be here on Friday. It's Tuesday. Did something happen? I mean, something happened for you to deviate from your preplanned schedule. Otherwise, we wouldn't be here at Reynolds's place."

Did she snark when she said preplanned? *Was Susan not allowed the freedom of change? Aren't they happy she's here?*

Questions continued accumulating as did his underlying annoyance until a smiling Edmund put down his travel mug and hugged Susan. "Don't listen to her. I was supposed to be here on a Friday and arrived on Tuesday."

"That's true. You did." Lucy sucked on her bottom lip. "Rescued a dog on your way in, if I recall."

"Then Susan ups the ante and rescues a baby. Figures."

His bride's cheeks flushed. "I just know how to make a better entrance."

"You sure do, sis." Peter typed something on his phone before tucking it back in his pocket.

"You're here early. Now, *why* are you at Reynolds's place?"

Susan started with a strained laugh. "Funny story."

"How do you two even know each other? How long has this been going on?" With each question, Lucy's words sharpened, a hard change from her normally smooth demeanor.

"Breathe, Luce. Breathe." Susan placed her hands on her younger sister's shoulders. "This is all easily explained."

"Need help?" Edmund, the third in age of the siblings, casually took a long pull from his Miami Heat travel mug, but Reynolds knew him well enough. Despite his laid-back exterior, the tallest of the group absorbed every tiny detail around him.

Thankfully, Nate stopped cursing at the crib long enough to accept the offer.

While the two brothers silently worked, Susan smoothly interlaced her fingers with Reynolds. Her touch sent shock waves through him. *Keeping this a platonic co-parenting situation is going to be hard as hell.*

As anxious as he was for him and Susan to have a proper wedding night, he had to admit that Nate was right. He had to put as much effort into being a husband as he would a father. Jumping into a physical relationship with his wife too early would only muddy thoughts and wound hearts.

Still, it was a strangely comforting transition from long-term conversationalists to an in-person couple. A married couple no less. It still hadn't quite processed, but his heart told him to quit second-guessing his good fortune. At least for the moment.

She took a deep breath before beginning. "I'm sure you're wondering what we're doing—"

"We weren't aware you two were a *we*." The youngest locked her arms across her chest. "Something you *need* to tell us?"

Tilting her chin up an inch, Susan answered with the

same intensity. "Need to? No. Want to? Sure. I'm glad to share."

The honest response only made him like Susan more. *My God, she's amazing.*

"It happened organically."

Her sister's eyes narrowed. "How? Last year, you still lived in Jupiter. Then you suddenly sell your house and take a nursing assignment to Albuquerque? Now you're here? You've never even met Reynolds. Had you? Oh God, please don't tell me you met through some lame dating app or weird cult website."

"Not sure if I should be offended or amused," Reynolds joked, but only Edmund chuckled.

"And what if we did? Why should that worry you?" The lighthearted song to Susan's voice lowered.

"Cults have crappy snacks at meetings, so you'll never catch Reynolds there," Nate interjected without slowing his attempts to put that stupid crib together.

Edmund snorted. "I mean, raisins in the potato salad? Who does that?"

Although the two brothers found temporary amusement, Peter leaned against the doorframe with the same angry body language as the youngest Davidson.

Their normally friendly personalities were now gone. Something he never directly experienced. That sent Reynolds's blood pressure climbing. *This is not the way I thought this would go.*

Squaring her shoulders, Susan replied, "Lucy, remember when you introduced me to everyone on the staff on

FaceTime?"

Lucy's eyes widened. "That was over a year ago, Susan! You're telling me you've been seeing each other all this time?"

"Not in the traditional way, no."

"In what way, then, Susan?"

As Susan explained how she and Reynolds started their long-distance friendship shifting to in-person friends and then spouses, her siblings' body language morphed from slack-jawed shock to clenched jaws hard enough to break their own tooth enamel.

"Why didn't you tell us about all this?" The quiet fury in Peter's eyes told Reynolds he had about five seconds to keep his new brother-in-law from losing his shit.

Susan waved her doubters off. "Oh, I don't know. Maybe because I didn't need your approval to talk to or see anyone."

"I'm not asking for a detailed itinerary, Susan, but damn. We work with him."

"I'm your sister. And you work with each other's partners. Why am I held to a different set of rules? Again."

"You're not, Suze. It's ... you've been engaged before. And—You always break it off. Eventually." Peter opened his mouth to continue but shut it as though he knew he'd gone too far.

"Are you done casting judgment?"

The corner of Lucy's mouth twitched. "Calling us out. Good to see some things never change."

As much as he appreciated the balanced discussion, Peter's words bothered him. *You always break it off. Eventually.*

When Susan's expression didn't change, it only added more questions to his list.

"She hasn't even gotten to the crazy part yet." Nate pointed to a piece behind Edmund, who handed it over.

"None of this is the crazy part? I think you put that on upside down, Nate." Lucy motioned as Peter popped back a mint he produced from his coat pocket and chewed like someone with murder on his mind.

"Hell no. Susan almost got herself shot and my hero brother here took the guy out with a can of pork and beans. Shit, it is upside down."

All three Davidson siblings stilled for several beats until Edmund jumped to his feet. "What. The. Fuck, Susan!"

"Thank you for the summation, Nate." To the average person, Susan remained unfazed by her brother's concern, but the rapid tap of her thumb on the back of his hand said otherwise.

Again, his brother's attempt to positively add to the conversation crashed and burned. If Susan walked away at this moment, Reynolds wouldn't blame her one damn bit.

"A gunman?" A gasp from his boss.

Peter rubbed his jaw and momentarily turned his back to the room. "We almost lost you before you even got here, Suze?"

Susan's lovely lips thinned. "I guess it could have ended up that way."

In a protective gesture, Reynolds slid his arm around her waist. It shocked him how much he already liked having her so close. "But it didn't."

"No. It didn't."

Edmund's forehead furrowed. "Pork and beans? Now I gotta know the entire story."

Over the next few minutes, Reynolds and Susan rapid-fire explained the events that brought them to this moment in time. In retrospect, the ease at which they each wove their experiences into their evenly balanced explanations should have been a huge green flag to their compatibility.

But at the time, Reynolds only processed his appreciation that she stayed with him this far. "And right as the cops took that piece of shit out, Bernie announced she wanted us to adopt her baby. She already texted Lori about it."

"Who's Lori again?" Lucy stocked the changing table with a few supplies, her anger sliding to cautious acceptance.

"The social worker who's been helping … us." As confident as she'd been, it didn't go unnoticed to Reynolds that Susan stumbled over that last word.

He tried not to focus on it, but to be fair, if she didn't have second thoughts, he'd worry. Of course, this entire situation could collapse with a phone call. "Lori's been a friend of ours for years."

"She's great at what she does." Nate gave his brother a sideways glance. "Don't tell her I said that, or I'll never hear the end of it."

By now, Peter grabbed the leveler and a pencil. "That's the most insane situation I've ever heard. Is this where you want the shelves, sis?"

A general round of agreement filled the room before

awkward silence chilled the space faster than the blustering arctic winds outside the window.

"You really took him out with one can?" Lucy handed Peter the screw anchors.

"I did." Before yesterday, it had been a hot minute since Reynolds threw anything remotely resembling a baseball.

"He played shortstop in high school, but he also subbed for the pitcher when the guy had his community service requirements." Nate stacked the flattened boxes in the hallway.

"Well, that settles it."

"Settles what, Lucy?" Susan organized the books alphabetically while Peter secured the first shelf.

"I need you on our softball team. We play the ICU for the July Fourth charity game. You'll play?" Although it came out as a question, his new sister-in-law's words sounded more like a statement.

A common thread. Reynolds nodded. "I'll be there."

They all worked a bit more as Peter installed the additional shelves and the rest organized and straightened up.

"Did you want to save a box for the cat?" Lucy asked.

"What cat?" Edmund glanced over his shoulder. "That's a cat?"

In the doorway, Odin sat, shoulders squared, his one eye narrowed as if to say, *Who the hell are you people?* and *Of course I want a box!*

"That is the oldest cat I've ever seen. Does he have one eye?" Lucy placed a large diaper box on its side just inside the room and immediately Odin took possession.

"Yep." Nate slid the front of the crib up and down, clicking it into place and verifying it worked.

The anger emanating from the Davidson siblings now waned as everyone worked for a common cause.

A baby that could be part of their family.

And finally, Nate quit cursing the crib manufacturer.

Once the bed found its place against the wall and the basics were unpacked, Susan broke the quiet. "Thank you for your help and understanding."

"It's a pretty vanilla room, Susan. You sure you don't have more for us to do?" Lucy opened and closed drawers, most of which were empty.

"To be honest, Lucy, we're waiting to order more stuff after the bio mom signs the papers. Don't want to get too ahead of ourselves." The sad truth, a split-second decision or one upsetting phone call could end this journey, but Reynolds didn't want to think about it. He also didn't want to jinx it.

"Right. Of course. Positive thoughts."

Susan hugged her sister before pointing toward the door. "Now, if you'll follow us to the kitchen, we'll explain the rest of this. I made pancakes and bacon."

"Hell yes!" Nate beat them all out of the room, the pace of his footsteps the same as when he ran across these floors when they were teens.

"There's more?" Peter yawned as he followed the crowd.

"The plan is to adopt her, right?" Edmund carried the trash bag to the kitchen, placing it near the back door. "How long does that take?"

"A minimum of six months. The bio mother designated us as legal guardians, which makes this process easier." Even though Bernie would willingly sign her baby over, Reynolds couldn't allow blind hope to reign supreme. The bio dad or a relative could come forward at any time.

Lori told him to expect the worst and hope for the best.

"When will she be here?" His boss chose a purple mug, a color she had multiple scrubs in.

"Lori will bring the baby on Friday, provided the mother signs off on everything."

"And if she doesn't?"

Then I'm done. The idea of this falling apart cut him deeply, but he had to believe this time it would stick. "I'm not going to think about that right now. If everything goes as planned, she'll legally be ours by Christmas."

"Yours? Meaning, yours and Susan's?" Lucy grabbed some food and took a seat next to Susan, giving her sister a shoulder nudge before her first bite.

Since Susan worried all yesterday about how her siblings would take the news, the siblings' positive interaction more than likely comforted her.

Other than some initial animosity and death glares, Reynolds felt it had gone well. So far.

Then Peter spoke. "Married, huh? How's that going to work?"

"What do you mean, Peter?" Susan raised an eyebrow, almost challenging him to continue.

The tight set to his jaw indicated the oldest Davidson debated on asking more at the risk of his life. "Um…"

"Choose wisely, man." Without a hint of humor, Edmund poured a healthy amount of syrup on his five-high stack of pancakes.

"These pancakes look amazing, Susan." Peter shoved food in his mouth and gave a thumbs-up, which sent Lucy into a fit of laughter. That triggered everyone into a lighter mood.

For the next several minutes, general small talk took over and the anxiety all but vanished.

Until...

"You're married? Like married, married?" Peter cringed as though the words left his mouth before his brain processed the shit he just stirred.

"What do you want to know, brother? I slept across the hall in my own room if that's what you're asking, but I may not tonight. That's up to us to decide, right, *husband*?"

Instantly, Reynolds's mouth went dry, and his pants became uncomfortable. "Right?"

"Reynolds? You okay?"

"The door has a lock and its own bathroom. She was safe." The words poured out of his mouth like some teen boy who stood in front of an unhappy, gun-toting father.

"She better be." Lucy raised an eyebrow, which said she knew how to kill him and make it look like an accident.

Susan wasn't amused. "Hey. I've never asked any of you about your relationships so quit acting like I'm some innocent virgin that needs to be protected. Because you all know, I'm nowhere close to that."

The clank of a fork hitting a plate caused Reynolds to

jump. It took a second to realize it was he who dropped it.

"I know you're not a virgin, Susan. You've always had a healthy sex life, but you've just met him."

How healthy are we talking here? The words balanced on the tip of his tongue, but Reynolds shoved a piece of bacon in his mouth to keep them from falling out.

"Get off your high horse, Lucy. You were having sex with Thomas within a week of your first date." Edmund wagged his finger at her and then at Peter. "And you arrived right before Christmas and had sex with Shelly before New Year's."

Lucy's lower jaw jutted forward. "You and Jade had us beat, Edmund. Less than five days from meeting until they started messing around."

"We did a lot more than mess around. And we have nearly every day since." Edmund reclined back with his hands behind his head and a shameless smile.

This was a side of the Davidsons Reynolds never anticipated. It almost sounded like a bunch of guilty kids tattling on each other while one regretted nothing.

Rolling her eyes, Susan shrugged. "What's the worry, Lucy?"

"Hear me out." Lucy put her hands up.

"This is not gonna be good." Edmund headed to the sink to wash his dishes.

Standing, Susan braced her hands on the table. "Your confusion is understandable, but I have a plan."

"You always have a plan," Peter mumbled behind his coffee mug before taking a healthy gulp.

I'm glad she does. It suddenly hit Reynolds that he hadn't prepared anything past getting the nursery set up and their siblings informed. *Good lord, what is the plan?*

"Guys, I need you to trust me. Please."

The unexpected pain in her *please* unnerved him. *What is going on?*

Exhaling a long breath, Lucy squared her shoulders. "We love you, Susan, and always want the best for you, but you have to admit, you've not been the best at picking boyfriends."

"Are you kidding me right now? This is what this is about? Me canceling my weddings? You know, I had other boyfriends that I never wanted to marry besides those guys."

Lucy's perfectly sculpted brows pinched together. "Some of your previous relationships didn't work out great."

"Not great? You make it sound like I could only have one boyfriend and since I didn't marry him, I'm what? Cursed? Ancient? Damaged? A spinster." The hurt in her voice had Reynolds clenching his fists under the table.

"Not at all, but we worry that this time, you made an impetuous choice. So unlike you."

"And?"

"Your first engagement you canceled almost immediately. The second, you called it off a few months before the event."

"He cheated on me. As soon as I knew, I was done." She moved to the counter and refilled her almost-full coffee mug.

Exasperation filled her every syllable, which only pissed Reynolds off, but he hesitated pushing back against his sister-in-law, who was also his boss. Plus, hearing about Susan's engagement history started to concern him.

"I was proud of you for canceling, but this last engagement. It was within a month, deposits were made, invitations were about to go out, and you suddenly called it off. You two seemed perfect for each other, and then bam! No explanation. No warning," Lucy coaxed, but Susan looked away, only to catch his gaze.

The pain in her eyes cut him to the core as her words played in his head and fell out of his mouth. "After an engagement, some people finally show their true colors. Become who they actually are."

"Facts." Edmund snatched up another piece of bacon.

"Sure, I guess they can." Lucy cocked her head.

Susan rested her hand over her heart as a tear ran down her cheek. She mouthed *Thank you* before retaking her seat.

What did that guy do to her? Because whatever it was, she hadn't told them.

Susan dried her face with her napkin. "Guys, trust me. It was the right decision."

Lucy tapped her thumb on the handle of her cup. "For sure, but each time you pushed it a little further. This time you actually got married? You barely know him. No offense, Reynolds."

"No offense to you, Lucy, but Susan and I know each other more than you understand." At least, Reynolds hoped he understood her. What he did know, he liked. A lot, but damn. These last few minutes threw an entirely new list of concerns his way.

Lori was right. They still had a lot to learn about each other.

His boss looked less than amused at his interference, but she quietly took her plate to the sink and washed it.

Peter pushed his empty plate aside. "I don't understand any of this."

Crossing her arms, Susan faced off without hesitation. "You don't have to, Peter. I'm a grown woman. I can make good choices for myself."

"But this time, a baby is involved. A marriage. Kids complicate things. Makes it more heartbreaking if it doesn't work out."

Her brother wasn't wrong about that, and he would know. Discovering he fathered twins a decade ago, but only after their mother died in a car accident, would send anyone's life sideways.

Susan clenched her jaw, her words trembling with anger. "I made all sorts of choices for all of us after Dad died. When Mom wouldn't even get out of bed. I navigated all of us through all that insanity. I went to school and worked and took care of all of you and her. You trusted me to do all that when I was a teenager. Now that I'm an adult, I'm not trustworthy?"

Lucy and Peter leaned back in their chairs as if an epiphany slammed into each of their faces.

Edmund raised an eyebrow. "I told you she's fine."

Peter scoffed. "No, you didn't, Ed. You said she probably had a good reason for all this."

"She'll explain it when she wants to. I work at noon." He

tapped his watch before shaking Nate's and Reynolds's hands and kissing Susan on the cheek. "Glad you're here, sis."

"Thanks, Ed."

The front door clicked closed, and the hum of the refrigerator filled the momentary silence. Vanilla and sugar still lingered in the air.

Susan interrupted the quiet. "Understand, a young woman who trusted almost no one trusted Reynolds and me to raise her baby."

"But Susan—" Lucy interrupted, only for Susan to cut her off.

"No. No, I don't want to hear anything about it, Lucy. Reynolds and I are adults. We've got a plan."

Peter chuckled. "There gonna be addendums to this one?"

"What do you mean addendums?" Reynolds nervously chuckled as he learned more about his bride.

"Susan isn't so unbending that she doesn't calculate change in any project she takes on. There's always wiggle room."

"Life doesn't move in a straight line. One should always be prepared for adjustments. Addendums." Answering with the intensity of a schoolmarm, she stacked the empty plates in front of her. "It's just the practical thing to do."

"Practical. Logical. Responsible." The way her brother sang those words triggered a memory as Nate finished off the last six pancakes.

Sunshine poured in through the windows, giving the room a cheery feel despite the tension as Susan exhaled.

"Okay, listen, you two. Am I or am I not one of the most logical, responsible, practical people you know?"

The corner of his mouth twitched up at her quirky question.

"You are. Usually." Peter drummed his fingers on the table.

Lucy sucked her bottom lip before jumping in. "Yes, you saved us all, but this ... this isn't any of those things. This is impulsive, incompetent, and unreasonable."

"And it's *my* life." Susan's fingers blanched as she gripped the edge of the table.

Reynolds did not like seeing her this frustrated.

With a mouth full of food, Nate furrowed his brows. "Logical. Responsible. Practical? Aren't those lyrics to a song?"

"It's from Supertramp's 'Logical Song.'"

"Is there a reason you used those particular adjectives?" Nate slid the last piece of pancake around to soak up the syrup. "Fuck me, these are good."

"Thank you, Nate."

The oldest Davidson patted his stomach. "Dad swore the reason Susan is so levelheaded is because she was conceived when that song played on their bedside radio."

"Thank you for announcing the sex secrets of our parents, Peter. I'm sure Reynolds and Nate are thrilled to have learned such intimate details about our family." Lucy pinched her lips together as her shoulders began to bob.

A low round of laughter rumbled through the room, starting with Reynolds. It quickly spread to Lucy, Susan,

Peter, and finally Nate, who blurted, "Explains a lot."

"That is an amazing story." Reynolds grabbed Susan's hand and kissed her inner wrist.

She immediately blushed and scooted closer. "You sure you don't want to run for the hills after hearing us fight and learn I was created during a popular seventies tune about a kid's boarding school experiences?"

Tucking a lock of hair behind her ear, Reynolds soaked in her beauty. "If anything, all of it makes you more interesting."

"Thanks."

When Reynolds glanced back at his new in-laws, gone were their creased foreheads and hints of skepticism. Instead, twinkles of amusement danced in their eyes.

What is happening? "Peter? You okay?"

"It's good, Reynolds. Look, I don't know what you're doing, Susan. I may not agree with it all, but you're right. You made it work when our family hit rock bottom." Peter lifted his mug in toast. "I'll support whatever this is, but I reserve the right to ask questions later."

"Agreed." Lucy nodded, her eyes glistening with ... were those tears?

As the Davidson siblings appeared to have established a truce and his brother patted his pancake-filled belly, Reynolds hoped this would be one of many happy memories they'd make in this house.

For many years to come.

All they had to do was make it over the first hurdle.

Please, Bernie. Sign those papers.

Chapter Seven

D R. PEYTON GREY tapped her impeccably neat desk with a shiny gold pen. "Trauma nurse. Labor and delivery, then midwife? A lot of experience in fifteen years. We're lucky to have you."

"Thank you for considering me." Susan beamed at Peyton's compliments while marveling at her incredible sense of style.

Considering the construction in the hall, Peyton managed to keep her office neat as a pin. Minimalist décor with calming colors created a welcoming space, but on the bookshelves, windowsills, and side tables, small Pixar figurines added the perfect touch of whimsy.

After a crazy few days of paperwork, initial foster care classes, and multiple trips to the hospital nursery, sitting in the medical environment helped Susan find her footing again. "It's serendipitous that you planned to open the birthing center when I needed a professional change."

"It was meant to be. I've enjoyed working with your *doctor* siblings. I do have to ask."

Here it comes. "What's that?"

"Why did you become a nurse when the rest of your siblings went to medical school?" Peyton held a pen between her long, elegant fingers as though she were planning to write down what Susan confessed.

"Because I'm the smartest, most rational one." Susan forced a laugh as her knee bounced to a quick beat.

Peyton smirked, but her amusement didn't quite reach her eyes. Her future boss either didn't believe her or she didn't appreciate Susan's humor.

Starting off with a bang. "I liked more of a hands-on position when it comes to patient care. More procedures-based brain. More direct interaction. Time to teach."

Peyton's beautifully sculpted eyebrows arched in understanding. "Not everyone is geared for direct bedside care."

"That's true. I mostly love the patient education. Teaching people how to self-advocate."

The theme from *The Incredibles* blared out of Peyton's phone. "That does take a special patience. Hold on."

"Take your time." Susan re-gathered her thoughts as she scanned the decor.

Although everything she said about becoming a nurse was true, Susan omitted that her role as caregiver didn't stop when Peter left, and she prepared for college.

To ensure they stayed financially stable, always practical Susan plotted out the fastest completion to a medical-related degree. One that kept Edmund, Lucy, and their mother fed, clothed, and sheltered.

Since nursing solidly fell into that category, Susan started classes in high school, graduating with a bachelor's in nursing just short of her twenty-first birthday.

The lawsuit from the car accident and initial community fundraising paid for their undergraduate degrees to state schools and only lasted so long with monthly expenses.

Acceptance to a medical program could take her across the country or even a state away. She couldn't risk the change and refused to take Edmund and Lucy away from their friends or their mother away from her doctors.

It was hard enough just getting her mother out of bed to go to appointments. Changing physicians would have given her the perfect excuse to never go.

Plus, there was no telling how expensive it would be to live in some other place, and the medical school hours alone were grueling.

By the time their stepfather, Charlie, came into the picture and took over care of their mom until her death, Susan had already applied for her master's in nursing, and Lucy and Edmund were off to college and focused on med school.

"Sorry, a staffing crisis I had to fix." Peyton tucked her phone away in her Pixar-themed scrub pocket.

Susan pointed to a popular movie poster on the wall behind the desk. "Is that signed?"

"Yes. My previous practice was in Northern California. Took care of some of the people at the studio." She tapped her pen on the desk before letting it drop. "Great group."

The pounding of hammers and the footsteps of workers echoed outside the office. The faint smell of paint mixed with the crisp chill of the morning.

Susan pulled her coat tighter around her and wondered if she'd get to wear shorts again.

Extending her hand, Peyton gave Susan a quick shake and handed her a thick folder with COPPER MOUNTAIN GYNECOLOGICAL AND ASSISTED REPRODUCTION CENTER printed across it. "Let me show you around. Then you can go home and fill out all this paperwork."

Home. After this, she'd head to back Reynolds's house, where she'd live with him and a newborn for the next few months.

She appreciated his input with their road to adoption plan, but the topic that remained unanswered was just how long they wanted to keep their co-parenting platonic.

It seemed jumping right into bed with him rushed things, but to be fair, they had known each other a year, and they were legally married.

"Susan? You in there?" Peyton's forehead furrowed as she pushed her chair back, readying to stand.

"Yes. Sorry. Time changes. Crazy week."

"With the emergency pitstop in Bozeman, I understand."

"You understand correctly." Nothing like meeting your boss for the first time and asking for adjustments on a schedule to accommodate a new baby. "How did you find out?"

"While standing at the nurses' station, Dr. Nate received that initial call from his brother. He expressed his thoughts quite loudly."

"Nate's certainly outspoken on the subject, but I think he'll be okay." *At least I hope so.*

Even now, she wasn't sure her own siblings were completely on board with this arrangement, but she didn't doubt they'd show up if she needed them.

Peyton smoothed out her blouse. "Dr. Rey stopped by this morning on his way out the door. Told me you were brilliant with that entire crazy situation."

Her cheeks warmed at the mention of his name. "An over exaggeration. I delivered a baby like I'd done hundreds of times before."

Leaning forward, Peyton braced her hands on her desk, her red lips thinned. "You know that's an understatement. You delivered a baby under dire conditions in a dirty environment while coaching a scared, first-time mom through a quick delivery with minimal tearing. All while making sure a newborn baby arrived in a clean situation. And you confronted a gunman."

"That does make me sound pretty amazing, Dr. Grey." *Like Wonder Woman.*

"It's Peyton. From what I can tell, you are."

Susan's stomach flip-flopped with her recent good deeds. Her usual MO of flying under the radar wasn't going to take here. "It'll be hard to live up to all that if that's where the bar begins."

"You're good. Is the baby doing okay?"

"She is." No issues or glitches from Lori so no reason to think otherwise.

Still. Her nervous fingers tapped her watch to check for missed messages. Nothing.

"You're the kind of midwife I want. Thinks on her feet, improvises when she needs to, and doesn't put up with bullshit." Before she walked around the desk, Peyton opened the sheer decorative curtains behind her. An uninterrupted view of the snow-capped mountain range that overlooked the town appeared.

Susan gasped at its beauty. "This is gonna take some getting used to."

"What's that?"

"Not seeing the beach every day."

"Grew up on the West Coast, but the mountains have their magic. It's one of the reasons I moved my practice here." Her thumb rubbed her bare ring finger, telling Susan a broken heart might have also been involved.

"Fresh air. Less pollution and traffic. Stress. Thought it might increase the chances of women having healthier pregnancies."

"I've lived next to the beach pretty much my entire life, so this is very different."

"You'll do fine."

"At least I won't have to worry about hurricanes. Or the humidity." She ran her fingers through her hair.

"So true."

"It's been quite a learning curve since I crossed the Montana state line." *That's an understatement.*

Peyton sat on the edge of her desk in front of Susan. "What's this I hear about you and Dr. Rey being designated custodians of this baby?"

The mention of his name instantly raised the temperature of the room twenty degrees. "It's a ludicrous, but endearing situation. The birth mother designated custody to us right after the baby was born. She's supposed to have signed the relinquishment papers by now."

"And then what?"

"The social worker will bring the child this afternoon. She'll be in our care until the adoption is finalized. Hopefully."

"Plan for the worst. Hope for the best."

"What do you mean?" Susan's knee began to bounce again.

Peyton shrugged. "Sometimes adoptions don't work out for whatever reason but hold tight to the fact you're providing a safe, nurturing place for her to be. Especially in these critical months."

"Right. Of course. Reynolds and I have decided to take it one day at a time." As practical as her boss's advice was, Susan's heart grew fonder of the idea of becoming a mother for the long term. *And co-parenting with Reynolds was an added bonus.*

"Your siblings explained you do everything with great passion and commitment. You stepping into a permanent caregiver role doesn't surprise me."

Really? "Thanks, but it's happening so fast."

"It is, but sometimes that's what life throws at us, so we don't overthink the obvious. We do the best with what we have."

"We do." *The general outlook about life choices is sure different here in Marietta.* Every day she spent here, it became increasingly difficult to deny her love for the place.

For the people.

For one particular person.

Love? No, a like for certain. A whole lot of lust, but love? *Talk about irrational.*

Peyton snapped her fingers. "Which reminds me, we'll have a full-time social worker to help parents navigate any paperwork for WIC, Medicare/Medicaid, and any foster/adoption questions."

"That's amazing." Every month after the accident, Susan spent hours filling out supplemental paperwork to get the basic needs and government assistance for her, her siblings, and their mom. She often wondered how anyone with less than a high school education completed any of it.

"I've also hired an amazing geneticist and a pediatrician, both of whom will be here in the next few weeks." Peyton handed over a brochure with a brightly colored DNA double helix on the front.

"A geneticist? Here? You have that many babies in Marietta to support a specialist?"

Peyton flipped the brochure over and tapped the photo. "Because of the internet, consultations can be done from anywhere. Labs are drawn where the patients live. Grace Harper, my friend, has a *huge* client list. Plus, she wants to transition to the lecture circuit and write books. Wants more of a homelife. A family."

In her photo, Dr. Grace Harper smiled like someone who hated having her picture taken. "She looks nice."

"She's very pragmatic, sometimes prickly, but has a great attention to detail." Peyton touched her perfectly placed ponytail as her grin highlighted her amazingly white teeth.

"She's moving here with her family?" Outside the window, a group of moms with strollers power-walked by. Susan's heart pinched at the possibility of that being her one day.

Sooner than expected.

"She wants to start one. I think Dr. Nate went to medical school with her."

"Small world." Susan twisted the strap of her purse between her fingers at how much was at stake for her to fit in here. Then she wondered if she'd taken on too much.

"Keep me posted. We can figure out what work you can do from home versus your clinic hours. I'll do my best to keep you on a set schedule, but of course, any babies that are due will arrive when they want to."

"That's extremely generous of you, Peyton. My siblings have offered to help with any babysitting needs." Butterflies danced in Susan's chest at how quickly things came together.

This could work.

"Shelly, your brother's fiancée, she's got a couple of amazing kids. I bet they'd help out in a pinch."

Yesterday, Susan met Peter's beloved, Shelly Westbrook, and her son, Freddie, and niece, Tia. She also officially met her niece and nephew, Polly and Diggory.

Peter still wasn't totally on the same page as Susan, but that didn't stop them from being family. "Shelly's kids are amazing. They get along great with Peter. Looking forward to getting to know them all more."

"Polly and Diggory are a blast. I see them riding their bikes all the time." After a bit of awkward silence, Peyton added, "Understand, all this is an entirely selfish gesture."

"How so?"

With a shrug, Peyton tilted her head. "I figure if I solidly reel you in, you'll stay for a good long time, put down roots. Like your siblings have."

"Shrewd business tactic." *Now I get why she's not questioning what I'm doing.*

"But effective. So, you and Dr. Rey?" While she casually motioned to the door, Peyton's simple question was anything but. "How is that going to play out?"

"You get right to the meat of the matter, don't you?" The *how is it gonna work with Dr. Rey* question constantly tumbled through Susan's head like socks in a dryer.

Platonic. Physical. Platonic. Physical.

There were moments when her interest in him sat this side of feral. Then a bit of rational thinking made her wonder if her intense attraction to him muddied common sense.

What if her willingness to go down this matrimonial-parenting road was grounded in a fairy tale? The one where she aimlessly chased the happily ever after that always eluded her.

So, why would it be any different this time?

Sadness threatened to derail her hope, but she shook it off because in about thirty minutes she was due back at Reynolds's … their house. She and Reynolds. Reynolds and she.

It's different this time because of him. Right? "Um, it's a work in progress."

"This isn't the ER." Wearing a local college T-shirt and

high school letterman's jacket, a teen shifted his weight as his body took up the majority of the doorway.

"Can I help you?" Peyton approached.

He held up his sadly bandaged hand. The frayed edges of the gauze and poorly placed tape indicated he tried to bandage with his nondominant hand or someone helped him and had no idea what they were doing. "Came to get some stitches out."

"I'll show you the way." As Peyton stepped into the hallway with the kid, Susan tucked her purse away, but before she joined Peyton, a face caught her attention.

On a short bookshelf to the left of Peyton's desk, tucked between two sets of larger medical books, rested that first responder fundraising calendar. After looking through it many times, Susan memorized every man of the month.

Seeing a shirtless Officer Rob Shaw dangling a pair of handcuffs wasn't anything new. *Good to know my boss appreciates local law enforcement.*

Peyton and Susan watched the stitches kid lumber down the back ER hallway where Lucy waited.

Her sister's smile lit up the morning, and she waved to Susan before escorting the patient to an exam room.

"Must be nice to be with your siblings again." Peyton motioned toward an exam room.

"We're a pretty tight unit. Always have been." Life was always easier when talking to people who understood why brothers and sisters were close.

"How do they feel about the adoption?"

Susan wavered between annoyance and relief that Peyton

shot from the hip. "Peter has questions every time I talk to him. More than Lucy and Edmund."

"I can see that."

"Reynolds and I have a plan." Seemed as good of an answer as any.

"He's a good man. There have been more than a few people in town who hoped to catch his eye."

The man could easily tempt the most celibate of townsfolk. "No pressure, then."

"None whatsoever. Okay, before I send you home with the binders full of exciting reading like our mission statement, OSHA requirements, etcetera, let me show you around."

"I'll brew a big pot of coffee for all that excitement."

"Only one pot?"

"Smartass." She was going to like working with Peyton. The woman had a sharp wit and a take-no-bullshit personality.

A brisk breeze ebbed and flowed through the wide-open, front double doors. Even in April, Montana's morning air held a strong chill. Far different from Jupiter, Florida, where the humidity and the temperatures climbed well over eighty by this time of day.

Susan pulled her coat tighter around her as Peyton spoke. "We're a little behind on construction. Going to delay the opening by about a week. We're set for the Tuesday after Memorial Day. Let me show you what we have so far."

The calming color scheme and themed birthing rooms offered a hint of distraction without being overwhelming.

Wide doorways would allow easy passage of wheelchairs or stretchers. Large windows brought in natural light as the view of the mountains sat in the background.

Susan visualized a happy family in here, waiting for the birth of a girl or boy. She soaked in the Zen of it all, but an ache nestled in her chest, for the experience she'd never have.

The truth punched her lungs hard enough that she had to hide a gasp.

You have to tell him before this gets too far.

Angst twisted her stomach as Susan tried to construct her words to explain why she wanted to go through with this adoption and give him a chance to back out.

She glanced at her watch.

And she had twenty-three minutes to figure out what to say.

Chapter Eight

"STEINBECK. HILLERMAN. ROBB. Childs." Susan's eyes slid along each spine of the neatly arranged books she had just now had the chance to scan. "García-Márquez. Clancy."

Heavy hardbacks about everything from the American West to espionage to Latin American classics sat upright in two of the four built-in sections.

But the other sections of floor-to-ceiling shelves including well-worn paperbacks from authors like Austen, Roberts, Devereaux, Gabaldon, Jackson, Jenkins, McNaught, and Quinn caught her attention more.

The corner of Susan's mouth curled up as she ran her fingers along the spines' creases. "I've read almost all of these. Many more than once."

"You mean all of these?" Reynolds tilted his chin to the paperbacks.

"No." Susan motioned to the entire unit.

"You *do* love books." With a bit of bedhead, Reynolds handed her an oversized mug and smiled like she hung the moon. "Your mocha, madam."

"You spoil me ... husband."

"You should be spoiled ... wife."

"Careful, Reynolds. You keep treating me like this, I'll never leave," she laughed.

"And that's a bad thing?"

A mischievous twinkle in his eye sent her brain into Dirtyworld. "I guess not."

"Please." He motioned toward the oversized chair and took a seat on the couch. His attempts to appear alert were undermined by the wrinkles in his rich blue button-down.

A button-down she could easily rip open and get her hands on that chiseled body of his. The body she dirty-dreamed about last night. Again.

While he slept across the hall.

Alone.

And probably naked.

Good grief, go sit in a snowbank, Susan.

"The paperbacks were my grandmother's. She loved reading." For a moment, a sad smile sat on his lips.

He misses her. That tugged on her heartstrings. "Looks like both of your grandparents did. The spines are creased in different places." She inhaled the sweet aroma from her mug and went cross-eyed. "Perfect."

"*Mormor* read everything on that shelf at least half a dozen times. Kept reading long after she got sick." He placed his cup on the coffee table between them, the pain of her death cutting far deeper than Susan guessed he planned to reveal today.

Before she knew it, Susan sat next to him on the couch and sandwiched his hand between hers. A calm comfort settled between them. "She sounds amazing."

"When *Farmor*, Nate, or I took her to her chemo treatments in Bozeman, we'd stop at the bookstore before returning. Tell her to pick whatever she wanted. She'd get a stack of books."

"What a lovely gesture." His commitment to family lessened her angst at this whole absurd situation. A situation Lucy, Peter, and Edmund texted gentle concerns last night after Reynolds went to sleep.

"Books helped her escape."

"Books are amazing inventions. I've spent many weekends sitting outside reading. Learning ... things."

"What kind of things?" He rested his forearms on his thick thighs. He probably meant it as an innocent question, but Susan swore it held a hint of seductive inquiry.

"All sorts of things." *Naughty things.*

He swallowed hard. "I bet."

Not even a good night's sleep quelled her lust for him. If anything, her desire gained momentum, especially when he looked at her with sultry promises and wicked thoughts.

Or it's all wishful, complicated, non-platonic thinking on my part. "Thank you for the drink. It's perfect."

"You're welcome."

Out of the corner of her eye, she noticed a smaller bookshelf, tucked in the corner as though it were too special to donate. "May I?"

Reynolds thinned his lips. "Sure."

Middle-grade and young adult classics filled the upper two shelves. The bottom three were packed with books about dinosaurs. Susan tapped several spines. She smiled at the thick layer of dinosaur decals, specifically, Dino from the Flintstones cartoon that decorated the outside of the shelf along with multiple stickers with the name AUDREY.

"That's ... was my sister's," he answered before she asked.

Heartbreaking. Considering the highest reading level books were for middle grade, she wondered how old his sister was when she passed.

"You read all those, too?" Although he smiled, it didn't erase the sadness in his eyes.

"Not all, but most. Some of these I haven't seen before." A bit of sorrow tucked under her breastbone. As close as they'd come to losing Lucy after the accident, Susan couldn't imagine his grief. "Audrey sure liked dinosaurs."

"And the Flintstones."

"Well, who doesn't love the caveman version of *I Love Lucy*?" If someone told Susan a year ago she'd now be married to a handsome calendar model who appreciated classic animation and pop culture references, she never would have believed it.

"The Ricardos had no pets. The Flintstones have Dino." With a single-shoulder shrug, he gave her a wink.

"It would be difficult to fit a snorkasaurus in a New York City walk-up."

"Remind me never to challenge you to a TV trivia game." The pulse point on his neck increased as he outstretched his hand, palm up. "Can I show you something?"

"Of course." It didn't go unnoticed that his fingers trembled, making her wonder what she said to illicit his reaction.

"Since you're eyeing my bookshelves."

That's not all I'm eyeing. The moment his hand touched hers, all of Susan's thoughts turned unapologetically carnal.

This kind of unrelenting passion never once consumed her so completely, but every time she stood near him, all her thoughts went straight south of her belly button.

We need to get some addendums on that plan. Or not.

He led her to a small phone cubby under the stairs. "Very few people know about this."

"Then I'm humbled."

A mischievous smile crossed his handsome, unshaved face as he pulled on a well-hidden handle.

When the cubby wall swung out, Susan placed her coffee mug on the side table before it slipped from her fingers. "A hidden door? What's in there?"

"Take a look."

She paused. "You're not going to lock me in some weird basement situation, are you?"

"Only if you want me to." He playfully shrugged.

Annnnnnd my panties instantly disappeared. "Platonically speaking, of course."

"Of course." A hint of pink colored his cheeks. "*Mormor*'s chemo made it difficult for her to concentrate, even sleep, so we built her a quiet hideaway. Sometimes Audrey used it."

He flipped on the light. "Even after my grandma added Audible and e-books, we hit the bookstore in Bozeman for her to browse."

For a minute, Susan thought she imagined the room. Floor-to-ceiling shelves covered the tallest wall and went farther back than she thought possible. "So many books."

"You like it?"

"My first bookgasm."

Reynolds's lusty laugh filled the space. "Bookgasm. I've never heard that before, but ... um ... glad to be your first."

Without thinking, she leaned in to smother him with appreciative kisses, but stopped short and gave him a simple peck on the cheek. "May I look?"

He grandly stepped out of her way. "Be my guest."

"*Merci*, Lumiere." To her right, a built-in desk with a sewing machine on top. Under it, a plastic bin filled with brightly colored material and a pattern for a dinosaur plush.

Above the machine's small workspace were several black-and-white photos of people she faintly recognized. Something about their smiles tugged on her heart.

An oversized futon chair and two multi-head standing floor lights sat on each side. A small side table with a charging station and speaker added to a perfect hideaway reading place.

She turned her attention back to the shelves filled with the literary bounty as twinkling fairy lights covered the ceiling. "A secret library."

A hardy laugh escaped him. "Okay, Belle."

"I've always wanted a little room like this." Susan knelt, then crawled as she scanned the titles, her excitement escalating with each spine.

Again, alphabetically and genre-arranged, it held more

books than she could possibly read in a year. "A secret library under the stairs. Be still my heart." Under the far wall, a light. "Is that a door?"

"Yes." He leaned against the doorframe.

"Where does it go?"

"Go find out." Amusement danced in his eyes, cranking his sexy factor up to dangerous levels.

Breathe, Susan. Standing, she pushed the door and peeked around it. "The kitchen? This goes all the way through?"

"It does."

The scent of oranges and spices signaled his approach. She greedily inhaled, allowing the flavors to feed her secret thoughts. Crossing her arms, she subdued the overwhelming urge to pin him against the wall and perform salacious things on him with her tongue. Things she dreamed about doing last night.

The mountain air must have pheromones in it. "What a huge project."

"It was. Took several months. We reinforced the beams and stairs since we raised the ceiling. Ran new lighting." When he guided her back through the passageway, his hand rested on the small of her back.

His touch sent her thoughts carnal. How she wished he'd ravish her on that oversized chair. Or against the door. Or pretty much anywhere in general.

Focus, Susan. "A cupboard under the stairs and secret passageway. It's like Harry Potter and Narnia had a baby."

"You like it, then?"

"It's amazing. Your grandpa was quite the handyman."

"He taught me, Nate, and Audrey everything about house repairs." The hidden latch clicked and locked in place.

"If this doctor thing doesn't work out for you, you've got a backup plan." A vivid image of Reynolds wearing nothing more than a tool belt ticker-taped through her brain.

"After difficult shifts, it's tempting to start my own side business. I like working with my hands."

I bet you do. "Medicine would be lesser if you left it."

A healthy flush of color stained his cheeks as he handed back her coffee and motioned to the kitchen. "Shall we?"

They walked in tandem to the kitchen table and turned their chairs to face each other.

To keep from staring at his beautiful features, Susan scanned the kitchen, taking in the custom details. The thick butcher block table sat in the middle surrounded by a dozen Windsor back chairs in different colors.

Across the room, a double oven and five-burner gas stovetop with a pot-filler faucet. The blue-tiled heart design on the backsplash tugged the corners of her mouth up. "Did you help with that?"

His eyes lit up. "Took us all afternoon and a lot of cussing, but Nate, *Farmor*, and I built the backsplash to include the heart. A perfect touch to my grandmother's dream kitchen."

"And I bet she loved every inch of it." A few handmade items indicated Reynolds, Nate, and Audrey spent a lot of time here and their grandparents cared for them dearly.

The amount of work put into this place pulled on her

heartstrings as much as it antagonized her worries about messing this up for him. For them. "Your grandparents' home, your home, is lovely."

"Thank you, but it's our home now."

For whatever reason, that froze her perfectly prepared breakfast in her stomach. "Our. Home?"

His forehead furrowed. "Yes. We're both here so—"

"Right. Of course. Yes. Ours. But it was your grandparents'."

"Yes. They were good people. Made me and Nate who we are today." His index finger tapped on his mug.

"Then I'm sorry I won't get to meet them. To thank them for who you are." Despite her nerves twisting her gut to the point of nausea, Susan gently tapped her mug against his. "To your grandparents. And Audrey."

He smiled at her so brightly, her ovaries quivered. "Yes. And to *our* new adventure."

"To new adventures." She hoped her voice didn't sound as stressed as she felt. Susan took two large gulps, hoping the whipped cream, sugar, and caffeine would calm her.

"Um … you've got—" He hesitated before he pointed.

"What?" She set her mug down.

"Your mouth." His body leaned forward but he immediately pulled back, touching his face. "You've got whipped cream."

Without thinking, she scooted to the edge of her chair, turning her cheek toward him. "Where?"

With trembling fingers, he slid his thumb along her top lip to the corner of her mouth. "There. All better."

The gentleness of his touch set her body on fire and short-circuited her brain.

"So much better." Again, her eyes zeroed in on his lips, and before she knew it, the space between them disappeared.

Chapter Nine

M ANY TIMES, HER siblings spoke of Susan's unwavering composure, intelligent nature, and practical planning.

This was especially true last night when she presented their adoption plan that would increase their chances of success.

Bullet points included having a crib in each of their bedrooms along with the one in the baby's nursery.

Setting up a care and feeding schedule so each of them could get a break but also have time with the three of them.

A PowerPoint slide simply labeled *Physical* had a bolded TBD right in the middle.

"Thinking a slow, getting-to-know-you situation would keep emotional factors in check," she insisted this morning. But as she passionately embraced him right now, that TBD could easily transition to JBF.

She kissed him like Aragorn kissed Arwen at the end of *The Return of the King*. *Get your head in the game. No nerd references, Reynolds!*

His mind wandered to what else she might be adventurous about, which made him truly thankful he wasn't wearing sweatpants.

When they came up for air, he brushed his lips against hers and appreciated the taste of chocolate and whipped cream from her drink. "If this is starting slow, I'm all for it because I wanted to kiss you today."

Her eyes sparkled. "Had you hoped to kiss me like this before I got here?"

"Many. Many times." *So many times.*

As the sunshine poured in, she licked her lips as though she were debating kissing him again. "Really?"

Tucking a wayward lock of hair behind her ear, Reynolds nodded. "The moment I met you on that first FaceTime call, I couldn't stop thinking about you. Then you let me check on you. The more I learned about you, the more I wanted to know."

For a moment, she wide-eyed stared as though she didn't truly believe him. "I made that much of an impression?"

"You've haunted my dreams more times than I can count." *Dammit, I sound like a lame version of a Jane Austen novel.*

"You know how to deliciously complicate things, sir."

"Thanks." *Maybe she likes lame versions of Jane Austen novels?*

"Guess we need to work on the specifics of that Physical slide. I mean, because people who date kiss, right?"

He wasn't sure who she wanted to convince more. Him or herself. "They do, but these are special circumstances."

Her eyes lit up like the Fourth of July. "That's true. We're married so ... are we dating? We've done this all so backward. I don't even know what the protocol is."

"The protocol is whatever we decide it is. As long as we understand the ground rules." This was certainly uncharted territory for him. Granted, he'd been married before, but a year of dating did occur before the I dos. He could generally predict how to navigate the emotional cycles of a relationship. Here, everything was brand-new.

"So, kissing is okay with you?"

Was it ever. If he started kissing her, he might never stop. "We're married. Seems a logical thing married people do."

"Logical, huh? Now you're just teasing me." She playfully pouted.

"I am, but I am serious about understanding our protocol."

"That's fair. The best chance of success is when we understand the rules. Present a united front for the adoption. For us. Right?"

Gently, he placed his hands on the curve of her waist, relishing her closeness. "Please know, I'm not only interested in you because of a box on an adoption application and your great organizational skills."

"I know that."

"I'd understand if you wanted to back out—"

"No way." Her cute nose crimped. "Do you?"

"No, but it would be easy to be caught up in the moment."

"I'm not caught up in anything. I know exactly what I'm doing." A sultry tone now replaced her playfulness.

Don't screw this up, man. "Susan, I appreciate you having this much faith in us. Me."

"But?"

"No buts. Just worry."

"About?"

Shit. He didn't plan to tell his backstory today, but he walked right into this one. "Worry we won't stick because I work too much. It'll bother you when I'm distracted by a patient's diagnosis. Go to the hospital when they need help. You'll be annoyed about my weird shift work. Sleep schedule. When I don't want to go out and be social. When I fall asleep before eight."

She threaded her fingers through his hair as if to calm him. "I get all that."

"You would, wouldn't you?" With them both being in the medical field, it erased the stress of explaining every time a patient kept him late. Or if he was at the hospital at all.

"Is that what happened with your marriage?"

The woman was too observant for her own good. "I was in medical school, and she loved the idea of being married to a doctor. Hated that I was barely home because I was studying, in class, or at clinicals. When I was home, I was exhausted."

"Didn't she understand what you did for a living?"

"She loved the status. Hated the reality. Loved the potential for what I'd make. Hated the loans I had to pay off. Loved having crazy sex. Was mad when I was too exhausted. Up. Down. On. Off. Love. Hate." When her fingernails lovingly grazed his scalp, he almost purred.

"It's a lot of work what we each do. It takes a tremendous amount of time to learn. Some patients deserve more of our attention." The soothing cadence of her voice almost lulled him into a drunk stupor. "That's why you want to know the ground rules? You need consistency."

"I don't want to screw this up."

"You won't. I have faith in you. In us working together."

It was as though she reached into his brain and plucked out his fears. Before he could reply, his phone buzzed a unique pattern. "That's work. Give me a moment?"

"Yes. Take your time."

After a quick update on a patient, he returned to find Susan splashing water on her face and giving herself a quiet pep talk. "Breathe, Susan. It's going to be okay. You're doing a good thing here."

Doing a good thing? His heart stopped. The last thing he wanted was for her to be a part of this due to obligation. Hell, for three years he tried to get this far in the adoption process, and this entire adventure terrified him. He rubbed the back of his neck as she took deep, cleansing breaths before grabbing the sink sprayer and rinsing an already clean surface.

As drawn to her as he was, he wouldn't bind her to this because of an impulsive promise to a distressed young woman. Or to rescue him. Right as he decided to give Susan an out, she discreetly sobbed, "What if ... what if he wants more? I can't give him ... because I'm broken?"

"Did someone say that to you?" he blurted, obviously scaring her because she spun around with the handheld sprayer still in her grip.

Cold water immediately drenched the front of his clothes.

"Oh, shit!" She scrambled to turn off the faucet before frantically opening and closing drawers. "Shit! Shit! Shit! I needed some cold water ... there's a towel here somewhere."

Biting back a laugh, he opened a drawer and pulled out two towels, handing one over. "Easily fixed."

Chagrin stained her cheeks as she patted herself, then the counter and floor, dry. "Sorry. I didn't think you'd be back that fast."

He appreciated her attempts to constantly be composed, but she didn't have to put on such a brave face for him.

She placed the perfectly folded towel on the counter. "I'm so sorry about the water."

"It's water. What do you mean you're broken?"

"What?" She ran her fingers through her hair, slicking it back, giving him a full view of her makeup-free face.

Then he had to remind himself to breathe.

No photograph could ever do you justice, Susan Davidson. Most of her thick, dark hair remained restrained in the hair clip, but a few escaped strands drifted about her cheeks.

The deep green of her eyes reminded him of the polished sea glass he, Nate, and their sister, Audrey, collected on trips to the California beaches with their grandparents.

During the trips he stood on the sand as the ocean called to him like a siren's song, luring him closer to uncertainty. He always fought the urge to give in to such desires, but today, he desperately wanted to drown in them. "Why would you be broken?"

"You heard that?"

"I did. And why would anyone say that to you?" *Whose*

ass do I need to kick?

Squaring her shoulders, she locked her arms across her chest. "There's a reason I broke off that third engagement."

She didn't answer my question. "Anyone who doesn't think you're anything but amazing isn't worthy of you."

The compliment had her shifting her weight. "That's kind of you to say."

"It's not kindness if it's the truth. But why would he say you're broken?"

"Because he's a jerk." Her lips slowly parted as she seemed to study him. Her eyes full of questions as they settled on his mouth.

After several moments of her stare, he couldn't help but ask, "Thinking about that kiss, aren't you?"

Because I know I am. In fact, that memory would never leave his brain anytime soon.

"I'll admit, it was an impulsive decision. I apologize if it made you uncomfortable. Complicated things."

"I think you're putting too much emphasis on a Power-Point slide."

"Probably."

"And I don't think you mind complicating things." Despite her cool exterior, he wished he could read her mind. *The sultry,* learned *thoughts tumbling in that brain of yours, Ms. Davidson.* He could almost see them popping over her head in dialogue bubbles like in the comics he read.

"You're right. I don't, because married people, even people who are dating, have some sort of physical contact. Attraction. And I'm very attracted to you."

"Good." *Really, dude? A gorgeous woman tells you she's attracted to you and all you can manage is "good"?* "I mean, yes. Great. I'm attracted to you, too."

She let out a nervous laugh as she ran her fingers through her hair. "But I also don't want to mess this up for you. For me. For us. All three of us. Is everything okay with work?"

The powers of deflection are strong with this one. Dammit, Reynolds. No nerd references! "Patient returned for stitches removal. They let me know since I wasn't sure if he would."

She returned to the table, her fingers immediately fiddling with her coffee mug handle. "If it's who I think it is, he came in the wrong entrance, and ended up in the clinic."

Inhaling the wake of the sweet scent of her shampoo, he followed and joined her. "The kid's not the brightest bulb. Cut his hand on a beer bottle last week. Before then he dislocated his thumb during house repairs, jammed his toe when he kicked a cinderblock, and burned his eyebrows off when he added too much lighter fluid to the outdoor grill."

"Sounds like quite a character. I've treated a few of those patients in my time."

Reynolds drummed his fingers on the table for a few beats. *Say something clever.* "Tell me about yourself, Susan. Something that doesn't involve you being a nurse."

"Born in Florida. I'm the oldest girl—"

"Or a Davidson sibling." When excitement sparkled in her eyes, Reynolds understood her a little better.

She truly loved her siblings like he loved his, but after the heated discussion about her previous suitors, it was painfully obvious Susan needed to be someone more than their nurse sister. More than the woman who took care of everyone after that accident.

Or the bride who canceled her wedding for all the right reasons.

And he greedily anticipated discovering who *that* Susan was.

A smile spread across her face. "I like superheroes."

They'd spoken about movies and superhero franchises many times, never totally agreeing on which reigned supreme. "Marvel or DC?"

"You're ready to have *that* conversation again?" Instantly, her eyebrow cocked as she leaned forward, almost daring him to continue.

Shit. I'm a dead man. "It's probably too early to revisit *that* discussion." However, he hoped she'd initiate it because it thrilled him that she could name the three different men who donned the Blue Beetle costume and explain how the 1967 Captain Marvel was not the present-day DC Shazam.

"It's *never* too early to discuss such important matters. If we're going to go on this baby adventure together, we need to know where we begin."

You really are a dream come true. "Correct. Speaking of baby adventures, did you always want to adopt?"

"Yes."

"Why?" He hoped she wanted to adopt for the right reasons because so many didn't.

A sweet smile spread across her makeup-free face. "I had this great friend in school, Chloe. She and her brothers were adopted, and her parents were amazing. Fun, loving family."

"She sounds nice."

"They were. No matter what, they were there for each other, you know? Kept wondering what it took to step up to care for a child who needed an advocate. A safe place to be. Love them unconditionally. Forever."

"You mean people who aren't family?"

"Biologically speaking, but they are still family."

She gets it. So often, he talked to people about adoption, only to hear things like *But what about their real family?* or *How can you care for a child that's not really yours?*

"After the accident, when Lucy was in the ICU and our mom was so beaten up, I kept wondering who would step up for us. For Peter, Edmund, and me." Her finger traced the rim of the Flintstone-themed mug. "Dad was gone. Mom couldn't, wouldn't, get out of bed. Peter was too young to be deemed our guardian. I worried constantly about us being separated like so many other foster sibling groups."

"No family? Of any kind?" Despite her matter-of-fact tone, the idea of having no one to help sliced him deep.

"My mother and her parents had a big falling out about a year before the accident. My father's parents died before I was ten. Neither were close to any cousins or siblings. The day Peter turned eighteen, I breathed a sigh of relief since he could be our guardian if need be."

"Oh shit, you're right. I didn't think about that."

"I did. Every day." She took a long swig from her mug and licked the whipped cream from her lips.

"I bet you did." Even at their most desperate times, Reynolds never doubted his grandparents could be there for them. He couldn't imagine being a fourteen-year-old without a safety net and strapped with a whole lot of responsibilities.

"During all that, I decided I would adopt one day so a child would never have to worry about who'd step up for him or her. Even if I wasn't there, I had my siblings so there would never be a moment where that baby had to worry about such uncertainty." The steady tempo of her fingers drumming on the table indicated she might not quite be done telling her story. "But not everyone is interested in adoption. Finds it an acceptable option. No matter why I wanted to."

No matter why she wanted to?

"Is that why you broke off the last engagement?" He berated his speak-before-thinking mode.

The drumming stopped. "He refused to consider it. Only wanted bio babies. That was a deal-breaker for me."

Was that why he called her broken? Although he understood it, Reynolds held little sympathy for a man who allowed a woman like Susan Davidson to slip through his fingers. "His loss. My gain."

"And mine. Ours." She swept her arm out and pulled her gaze from his. "This is a beautiful kitchen. Love the colors."

Deflection. "Blue. Grandma's favorite. She ran a little baking business out of here. Grandpa loved her, so he made her a dream kitchen."

She reached over and held his hand. Her thumb brushed the backs of his fingers. "Tell me more about them."

The same gentle gesture from earlier, but this time, her

touch felt more purposeful, more intimate. Or maybe he was simply increasingly aware of how close they were.

"Married over fifty years. Committed to each other. To family. Taught us how to cook, clean, fish, fix things." *If she keeps stroking the back of my hand like that, I'm going to have to excuse myself for a few minutes.*

"They sound like great role models."

"They were." Decades of love, laughter, and tears lived in these walls, and suddenly, the weight of this entire situation finally registered.

No matter how much becoming a father meant to him, if she had a sliver of doubt, he would not proceed with her. To bring a woman into this who loved only the idea of being a parent, but had no desire to do the work, would be soul-crushing.

Like his mother had.

Sadness uncomfortably churned his gut as he gently sandwiched her hand between his. "Susan, are you sure—"

"I like blue, too." After a quick kiss to his cheek, she re-filled her coffee.

"What?"

"It's true blue, so that's gotta be a good sign, right?" A mix of fear and curiosity swirled in her eyes, as though the rational and emotional sides of her brain fought for dominance.

"A true blue?"

"Wonder Woman blue. Add a bit of red and gold to represent Wonder Woman's outfit and the Lasso of Truth?" Despite her trembling fingers, her smile lit up his heart.

"I'd rather you just wore the costume and tied me—"
Horror filled his chest as he realized his lust went vocal. *Way to go letting your pants speak for you.*

Without a hint of embarrassment, the corner of her mouth curled up. "Guess I won't need to use the Lasso of Truth on you."

Swallowing hard, Reynolds squeaked, "Do you have those items?"

"Which items?" Fire danced in her eyes as she leaned back in her chair, her mug partially hiding her playful smirk.

"A lasso or an outfit?" *I can't believe I'm asking her this and she hasn't thrown hot coffee in my face.*

"Like Lori said, we still have a lot to learn about each other." Confidence radiated from her. She was a woman who owned her desires, her wants, her fantasies.

And she wants to raise a baby with me.

Leaning forward, he asked, "Where have you been all my life?"

She reduced the gap between them and played with the buttons on his shirt. "Florida."

The urge to kiss her reigned supreme, and as he leaned in, both of their phones pinged.

He greedily grabbed it when Lori's name popped up.

Papers signed. Heading to the nursery now.

"She signed." Every muscle in his body relaxed right as Susan threw her arms around his neck.

"She signed. Let's do this."

Chapter Ten

A FTER SO MANY rejections from the foster care powers that be, the opportunity to be a parent literally dropped into Reynolds's hands because he happened to walk in on a robbery.

It couldn't be that easy.

Waiting three years, filling out a thousand forms, taking annual foster care classes, having his finances and references searched with a fine-toothed comb, and being told *no* more times than he cared to mention had been far from *easy.*

Serendipitous? Maybe.

Now, standing over the crib his brother cursed while assembling, a perfect infant slept as an amazingly smart woman who loved sci-fi and superheroes and might have a sexy Wonder Woman costume at her disposal stood at his side.

Could this sexy meet-cute be the universe apologizing for his disastrous marriage? For the genetic roadblock, he chose not to pass on?

"She's beautiful." Susan interlaced their fingers.

Joy threatened to suffocate him, but he slowed his breathing while they watched the tiny being they helped into this world. "She is."

No matter how many times he imagined this moment, being present in it now overwhelmed him.

Years ago, his grandfather tried to explain how much he loved his grandchildren. "I love you so much it hurts," he'd say.

As a kid, that made no sense to Reynolds. *Why would anyone love until it hurts?*

But today, he understood all too well, and he had the brunette next to him to thank for getting him this far. For helping him become a father.

No matter her pain or her sad backstory, or what her stupid former fiancés ever said to her, Reynolds promised he'd help her heal. Hopefully, she'd let him.

And they would work for the long haul. "Hey. You hungry?"

"I could eat."

After grabbing the baby monitor, they turned to find Odin sitting in his box that he positioned right inside the nursery doorway.

"I thought we put that out in the living room." Susan scratched the cat under his chin.

"Guess he brought it back."

"Hello, Nanny Cat."

Odin responded with a meow and a loud purr.

They headed to the kitchen, and each prepared a plate from the Chinese takeout Lori brought with the baby.

"Do you have suggestions for her name?" Susan moved a slice of carrot around her plate before eating it.

"I'm surprised Bernie didn't name her." Best he understood, the moment those papers were signed, Lori stepped out to talk to the charge nurse. When she returned, Bernie had already left down the back stairs. "I hope she's doing okay."

"Me, too. Is that orange chicken?" She pointed with her wooden chopsticks.

The sunlight poured in, bringing flickers of colored light from the Flintstones suncatchers that hung in several of the windows. Blue, purple, and pink danced around the room as the sun played peekaboo with the clouds.

"I like the sparkly artwork. Adds character to the space." Susan pointed as a fat strip of purple floated on a cabinet door.

"My sister loved those kits where you put the tiny pieces of glass in the metal frames, then bake them." He hadn't thought about that for a long time. How Audrey sat at this very table, taking her sweet time picking up each piece of colored glass with tweezers and placing them exactly where she wanted it. "She wanted them perfect, but when the steroids caused her to shake too much to steady her hand, Nate or I would help."

"That's really sweet. I'm guessing you three were close."

"We were. Nate and I still are."

"It looked like my brothers and sister aren't, but we are. We all just haven't been around each other much these last few years, but if I needed a kidney, they'd be there."

"You'll find your groove." *But if they upset you like that again, we're gonna have words.*

"Thank you for understanding us." Susan put down

utensils, scooted her chair closer, and cupped his face before laying a gentle kiss on his lips. "I don't know why someone hadn't snatched you up before now, but I'm sure glad no one did."

A nervous chuckle escaped him at her compliment. Still, he buried his hope deep.

As attracted as they were to each other, he reined in his libidinous thoughts. One scenario included kissing her lips, then down her neck, and farther south. "Susan, let's back up."

She put her hands up in surrender, then rubbed them on her jeans. "Of course. Bullet points. Plans. Slides."

He was going to hate himself for asking this, especially if he got an answer he dreaded. "Susan, be honest. Do you have any doubts? Any that might make you want to break it off?"

Her lips thinned. "You worried about what Lucy and Peter said a few days ago?"

"How you always call it off eventually? I'd be lying if I said no." Since his mother took off before he turned thirteen, the discussion about Susan's previous dating history scared the shit out of him. Obviously not enough for him to call off this adventure, but still.

"Fair enough. Here's the thing, *husband*."

I love the way she says that.

"I may have been engaged to those guys, but I was never one hundred percent sure if it would work. There were a few reasons I called it off, which I won't go into right now."

I wish you would. "No?"

"No, but with you? Doubt never entered my mind." She took a large bite of her egg roll. "And you might have noticed, I married you. Not them."

Yeah, she did marry me. Suck that, crappy fiancés! "No doubt?"

"Nope."

He should bask in the glory of her words, but he had to ruin it. "You know I can't give you a biological child, right?"

She froze for a split second. "You've been very transparent about that."

"And that doesn't worry you?" The sharp smell of ginger emanated from one of the containers on the table, making his mouth water.

"I don't need to get pregnant to be happy. Have a family."

"You're sure?" In a normal situation, they would have already had this conversation, but since they'd done everything backward, he had no idea where they were regarding their journey.

Friendship?

Co-parenting-ship?

Starting mostly platonic with kissing with plans to get a glimpse of her wearing her secret Wonder Woman outfit. And then taking it off her.

"I'm completely sure. Why? Did *you* change your mind about wanting a bio baby?" Despite her confidence, her voice hitched on the word *bio*.

He tapped his bare foot against one of the table legs. "My sister was amazing, but she was also constantly sick, in pain, and missing out on most of her childhood. She never got to be a kid. Regularly go to school. Hang out with her friends. Had to be careful being in public. Around anyone who might be sick."

"It can be a rough disease."

"After med school, Nate referred me to a friend of his who specializes in genetics. Grace. I got tested."

She played with a random lock of her hair. "Then that's how you knew you're a homogeneous carrier."

As brave as he wanted to be, he couldn't keep the sadness out of his voice. "To be honest, Audrey isn't the only reason."

"Tell me, please." Susan turned to face him, but in her eagerness, he swore he noticed worry in her eyes.

"I mentioned I was married before."

"You did. And she didn't handle your medical school schedule very well."

"She desperately wanted a biological child, even with my genetic concerns." His attempts to be an analytical storyteller failed as regret strained his voice.

Leaning forward, she grabbed his hand, a comforting gesture she'd already mastered. "What happened?"

"She was insistent about having sex all the time."

"Sounds rough."

Hearing it out loud, it sounded absurd. "Let me qualify. She said she wanted to have sex all the time because we were newlyweds. The truth? She planned to get pregnant as soon as possible. It didn't matter that we agreed to wait until I was done with med school and residency. My concerns about passing on issues, she ignored."

"Sounds like you needed marriage counseling." Susan offered him the last of the orange chicken, then split it evenly between them. "Did she get pregnant?"

"She did and her water broke in her second trimester."

"How heartbreaking."

Odin wandered in and plopped down next to his bowl, his good eye sending demanding glares across the room.

"There were complications, but a one-in-twenty-five-thousand-risk type thing. Still, it was a wake-up call for me." He looked up at the ceiling for a few beats, not wanting to pull at the thread of his failed marriage but needing Susan to understand him sooner rather than later. "Her doctor explained another pregnancy would be just as risky. She wanted to try anyway. I pushed for adoption. Tried to convince her it would be safer. She refused. So that was that." *And I broke her heart.*

"That's a lot. Thank you for sharing that part of your life with me."

All he could manage for a response was a stiff smile because he had to confess it all. "Looking back, it's obvious I focused far more on potential fatherhood than being a good, present husband."

"What do you mean?" She rested her head in her hand as she fully faced him.

"I was constantly concerned she'd get pregnant. I wasn't sure about kids at the time, and I should have enjoyed the time for it to be just us. Maybe she would have calmed down about a family. Maybe things would have been different."

The guilt still lingered in the back of his brain for taking that choice away from his wife. And now he was doing it to Susan.

"That had to be a tough time for both of you."

"I lost Audrey and my grandmother because of genetic illnesses. I couldn't watch another woman in my life die or suffer because she wanted to risk it for something she thought she *needed* to give me. I didn't want to give a disease or the gene to my child for the sake of my DNA. Adoption worked just fine, but I could never convince her of it. I offered her a divorce. She accepted."

"That was noble of you, Reynolds."

As much as he appreciated her kindness, he shook his head. "Noble? Not even close. Some people would tell me I'm selfish for not having a bio child."

"Some people are not the issue here. It's only me and you. That's all that matters right now." She said it so strongly, he waited for her to take on the Wonder Woman stance.

He'd be done for if she did. "There are plenty of people out there who have CF, and survive a good long time. Treatments are better than twenty years ago, but no matter how you slice it, it's a lot to handle, and don't even get me started on the medical costs."

"I remember juggling all my mother's medical bills. Fighting with insurance companies. It's never-ending. And exhausting."

He pushed something around on the floor with his toe. "It's a lot to navigate."

"It is. Since we're digging deep today, how old was

Audrey when she passed?" She stacked their plates and tossed the empty cartons while he fed the cat.

Every detail of his sister's final day branded his mind. The way his brother and grandparents all sat at her bedside as she took her last breaths. "Twelve."

With tears in her eyes, she wrapped her arms around her waist, the confidence she held not moments ago suddenly vanished. "Not much older than Lucy when we had the accident. We weren't sure if she'd make it through that first night. That first week."

"Must've been tough for things to change so quickly. Audrey had been sick her entire life—"

"But that doesn't mean it didn't break your heart."

"No. You're right. It did. Still does." He marveled at how well they connected. Enough to keep him cautiously optimistic. Still, it didn't escape him that she didn't completely answer when he asked specifically about her being *broken.*

A tiny fuss from the baby monitor immediately rendered them mute, but the infant settled back down.

Susan let out a long exhale before she smiled. "That's gonna take some getting used to."

"She's probably going to be hungry soon."

"Order up." For the next several minutes, they cleaned the kitchen and Susan prepared a few bottles. The way she so effortlessly fell into the role of mother astounded him, a natural-born nurturer with a fierce mama-bear heart.

Am I robbing her of having her own baby by doing this?
"Susan?"

"I can hear you thinking from across the room."

"Am I that loud?" He unpacked the three bottle warmers they planned to set up in the kitchen and each of their bathrooms. "Tell me what you're thinking."

"You *want* to know what I'm thinking?"

"Yes."

"Without a filter?" She laughed before snatching a few pieces of chicken from one of the containers already tucked in the refrigerator.

"Why wouldn't I?" Who hadn't wanted to know what truly churned in that intelligent mind of hers? Maybe the same person who said she was broken? Now he was just pissed.

"You have no idea how nice it is for someone to ask me exactly what *I'm* thinking. I've carefully chosen my words for a good, long time."

"Why would you need to?"

The faint quiver of her bottom lip indicated whatever drifted through her mind hurt like hell to think about.

She leaned against the counter and crossed her arms. "I suppose it wasn't anyone's fault that it mostly fell to me after the crash. I had to be so careful about what I said around teachers or other well-meaning adults, because the last thing I wanted was Child Protective Services getting involved, separating us."

Oh shit. I never thought of that. He collapsed two of the bottle warmer boxes and placed one on the floor. "Would they have?"

Odin licked his lips as he finished his dinner and immediately headed to the new box. He tapped it with his paw before sticking his head inside and flipping it on its side.

"It was always possible someone would get worried about us. Especially if they knew how close to financial collapse we were most of the time. How our mother barely got out of bed. I didn't want that pitying look from classmates or boyfriends about our situation in general. As I got older, my mindfulness of words simply stuck."

Over the past year, each of her siblings explained this sweet sister. He marveled at how a fourteen-year-old girl saved her family. Then again, he was around that age when he had to do the same until his grandparents took over. The difference was that she had no one for backup other than a brother who was barely older than she was. He tugged on her hand, leading her back to the table and encouraging her to come sit on his lap. "This okay?"

"We'll call this addendum one A." Without pause, she loosely wrapped her arms around his neck.

"Talk to me."

The pain in her eyes told him it sat far deeper than her siblings ever understood. With gentle fingers, she played with his collar. "It's just a sad backstory, Reynolds. It doesn't change anything to talk about it."

Again. Deflection. As much as he didn't like how she handled those hard questions, she'd been here only a few days. Their year of lighthearted conversations rarely dug deeper than superficial. To hear her sorrow triggered his want to heal her wounds. "It might be nice to get it off your chest."

"Maybe. But not today. Not her first day here."

Instead, he savored her closeness, hoping to gain a bit more of her trust. "Susan. You don't have to be strong for everyone else anymore."

"I know." She touched her forehead to his.

A wayward lock of her hair tickled his nose.

"That includes me."

"I'll keep that in mind."

"Gotta be real honest with you about this platonic situation we talked about."

Locking green eyes with him, she traced the line of his jaw. "Oh yeah? What's that?"

Her touch almost sent him cross-eyed. He held on to his sanity with his fingertips, but if she kept touching him so intimately, he'd be hard-pressed not to kiss her again. Everywhere. "I'm going to try real hard to keep things not physical."

"Interesting that you put it that way."

It took a moment for him to process what she meant. And then he liked her even more. "Funny."

"I try." She ran her fingers through his hair. "I appreciate your concerns and honesty. I will, too, try *real hard* to keep things not physical until we're ready to move in that direction. Like a normal relationship."

"Day-by-day, right?"

"Yes. But we are married so I think we're allowed a faster timeline."

"We are?" Now that idea certainly made his jeans fit uncomfortably.

"I'm in it for the long haul, especially now that she's here. We need to come up with a really amazing girl name."

She was so good at turning a phrase. "Any suggestions?"

"Yes." She smiled at him like he could do no wrong.

God, I want to kiss you senseless. "You want to tell me?"

She repositioned, now straddling his lap but sitting on his midthigh.

He appreciated and regretted the distance between them.

Susan rested her forearms on his shoulders. "What about Audrey? After your sister."

If she'd punched him in the heart, it would have shocked him less. "I would love that."

"So would I."

"And I really l-like you, Susan."

She wrapped her arms around his neck and pulled him flush. "I really like you, too, Reynolds."

Chapter Eleven

"WHAT IN THE hell happened while we were gone?"
Standing in the doorway of Audrey's room, Susan and Reynolds discovered a completely decorated nursery.

"We were only gone a few hours to the doctor's." Reynolds could barely keep up with how quickly his world turned one hundred and eighty degrees and happily soared in the direction of happily ever after.

Maybe. Hopefully.

And to think, my only goal last week was to clean out and organize the upstairs loft.

"Who did this?" Susan held a sleeping Audrey to her shoulder. The baby traveled well to and from her one-week visit. She'd gained weight and recovered from the rough introduction into the world.

"'Everything you need to get a good start. Congratulations from everyone at Marietta Medical ER.' How sweet of them." Susan held a card up and handed it to him.

It didn't go unnoticed how effortlessly Susan cradled a baby with one hand and opened the card with the other. Something she probably did hundreds of times when caring for patients, but today, it was different.

She held their baby, who wore dinosaur-themed clothes.

A baby she asked to name after his sweet sister.

The joyous moment almost smothered the oxygen from his lungs, but he distracted himself by opening another envelope and pointing to the tall stack of boxes of wipes and diapers. "Your boss must really like you."

"I'll have to call her shortly and thank her."

Reynolds wouldn't lie. Finding a fully decorated and re-stocked nursery alleviated some of the stress because the kid could go through diapers like nobody's business.

For the past few days, he and Susan filled out endless paperwork, set Susan up for foster adoption classes, had her interviewed by Lori's bosses, organized their schedules, talked to attorneys, ordered a ton of baby supplies, and learned how to be functional on two to three hours of sleep at a time.

"This was what my siblings were up to." Susan's eyes glistened with tears.

Her comment pulled him out of his thoughts. "Who?"

"Lucy texted me a few too many times this morning be-fore we met for breakfast." She handed him the note and then patted Audrey on the back when she started to fuss.

The baby calmed right down and snuggled back in the crook of Susan's neck.

Way to set the comfort-the-baby bar high, Susan. "What do you mean?"

"Lucy can't keep a secret to save her life. She was too eva-sive at Main Street Diner."

Baskets of beautiful new and hand-me-down clothes had

been set in the corner of Audrey's new room next to her changing table.

The sofa-bed chair that was in the box when they left was now assembled and tucked in the corner.

"Someone thought ahead because there are different sizes of diapers and clothes. There's wipes, burp cloths. My gosh, how did they get all this stuff so quickly?" Susan turned to face him, her eyes went wide as she pointed. "Reynolds. Look."

Vivid moments in time captured on canvas decorated the wall above the crib. Marietta's four seasons, the Christmas stroll, snow sculptures, ice-skating, springtime flowers, hiking trails in the Copper Mountains, and the rodeo.

"The card says Edmund and Jade took these." Reynolds scanned the wall as each picture told a different story. Showed a different adventure he couldn't wait to take his girls on.

My girls? Even standing next to Susan and Audrey, Reynolds wondered if he imagined it all.

Candid family photos of all the siblings, their significant others, and their kids rounded out the collage. Included in those were photos of Susan and him from the past week.

"This is amazing." Susan tapped the moment that would never leave Reynolds's brain. When he and Susan held the baby for the first time. The moment life punched him right in the gut and settled in without pause or apologies.

The one next to it froze the instant where he and Susan looked at each other. It could easily be a Hallmark movie poster. Their hope-filled gazes. The endless possibilities and, dare he say it, love.

Even now, he remembered every detail of her face as she glowed with joy.

"Wait, who took those?"

Reynolds nodded at the moments captured in time. "Lori. Our siblings."

"She doesn't miss a beat."

"No, she doesn't." *And I'm damned grateful for it.*

"Wait, that one is at the convenience store." Susan pointed. "Did Bernie take that one?"

"She must have. And gave it to Lori. Wow."

"Reynolds. Are those your grandparents? Sister?"

Two photos in the middle of the mix caused his breath hitch. Reynolds's grandparents' wedding photo and the picture of the kids and Grandpa after a day of fishing. "I can't believe they got all this done so quickly."

"What does the card say?"

He picked up the card set on top of one of the dressers and exhaled. The words caught in his throat, and he had to force them out. "They all helped with the family photos."

She patted Audrey on the back and softly spoke. "This is your room, sweet girl. Look at all the love that's already here, just for you."

"Guess they are all on board."

A wave of oregano, rosemary, and tomatoes hit his nose. "Is something cooking?"

"Maybe." As they headed to the kitchen, they stopped when they realized a new pack-and-play was set up in the living room. Reynolds quickly checked each of their bedrooms to find similar setups. "Holy crap. What didn't they do while we were gone?"

Odin perched on the armrest of the couch, standing guard over the new item. The look on his face told them he planned to sleep in said new bed and there wasn't a damned thing they could do about it.

In the oven, a lasagna and a loaf of garlic bread on low heat. "Lucy made all this."

"You sure?"

Taking a deep inhale, Susan nodded. "Oh yeah. My sister's Italian food is second to none."

"And there's a card. A lot of cards." A stack of congratulatory cards from the kids of Harry's House, the after-school program funded by the first responders' calendar, sat in a basket on the kitchen table. Beside it, an assortment of different crackers, cheeses, and coffees.

Reynolds's heart warmed, knowing his brother had a big part in all this. "I guess people are excited for us."

"I guess so. Want anything?" She handed the baby over and Audrey quickly snuggled into his chest.

"Whatever you're having." Handwritten notes left on the table caught his attention as Reynolds settled in, holding his daughter against his shoulder.

Shelly Westbrook, Peter's fiancée, offered her son, Freddie, and her niece, Tia, as babysitters.

Brightly decorated cards from Peter's two children, Polly and Diggory, stated they would be willing to help with anything but changing diapers and vomit.

Jade and Edmund promised to bring dinner tomorrow.

He knew if he ever needed Nate, he'd be there in a heartbeat. No questions asked.

Closing his eyes, he hoped this wasn't some fever dream where none of this existed.

Worry hovered in the shadows of his mind as his happy family could be taken away with a phone call.

As of this morning, the father had yet to sign off on anything simply because they couldn't locate him. His parents refused to talk to CPS. They made it clear the next time Lori showed up on their lawn, they'd call the cops.

Then, a smiling Susan placed the mug of coffee in front of him and Reynolds shoved worry away, locking it up tight. He would not waste a single moment with *what if*. Not anymore.

"What should we do first, husband?" Susan took the chair across from him.

Damn, would his heart ever stop racing when she called him that? "Honestly, I don't want to do anything but sit here with you and Audrey."

"Soak it all in?" She leaned in and kissed the top of Audrey's practically bald head.

"Exactly."

"In case it changes." Her smile tightened, but her eyes remained hopeful. "But maybe it won't."

"Day by day, wife."

"Day by day, husband." She patted his hand before kissing his cheek. "When did Lori say she'd be over to visit again?"

"In a few days, but we can call her anytime."

Audrey stretched but didn't wake as she continued to sleep on Reynolds's chest.

"Guess I'm trapped." And Reynolds didn't mind it one bit.

Reynolds spent most of the day trapped with his daughter sleeping on his chest.

Since Nate had worked nonstop for the past several days, he hadn't met the new addition. As soon as they finished their dinner, Nate arrived with skepticism etched into his face.

To be fair, that was his normal expression.

Then, Susan placed the infant in his arms for the first time and told him his niece's name.

As soon as baby Audrey gazed at her uncle, his stoic brother cried happy tears. "Damn, you two."

Around the same time the Davidson siblings, along with their significant others, stopped in to check on all of them, including Odin.

Edmund brought a new box with cat toys inside, and Odin's one eye went so wide that Reynolds thought it would pop out of the cat's head.

Audrey's sweet face even managed to coax a few smiles out of Peter, despite his furrowed forehead.

By eight-thirty, Susan and Reynolds struggled to keep their eyes open. They fell asleep on the couch, with Audrey next to them in her pack-and-play.

Susan's head resting on his chest, his arm around her body, he drifted off to sleep to the sounds of the clock in the hallway and the scent of her body wash tickling his nose.

But the strong smell of fish rudely woke him a couple of hours later when Odin demanded to be fed, his furry face only inches from Reynolds as he protested. "Okay, cat."

Odin jumped off the couch and headed straight for the kitchen, but Reynolds took a moment to appreciate what his life had become.

Him passed out before ten on the couch with his beautiful wife beside him and their baby sleeping close by.

After all the time he pined for such a moment, it arrived, and he hardly understood how to absorb it all. But what he did absorb was how uncomfortable Susan looked sleeping sideways.

After feeding the cat and tucking Audrey into the crib set up in his room, he returned to encourage Susan to her bed.

Despite her awkward state, he hesitated to wake her. "Susan?"

"Hmmm?" A sleepy response.

"Susan? It's time for bed."

"Okay." Her arm reached out and slid around his neck, pulling him close. "Kiss me good-night, then."

He hesitated. Was she awake enough? Would she remember this tomorrow? "You want me to kiss you good night?"

A slow smile spread across her face as she slowly opened her eyes. "It's allowed under addendum one."

"It is." Cautiously, he touched his lips to hers. How he dreamed of kissing her good night, every night.

She nibbled on his lower lip before capturing his mouth with hers. "Kiss me, Reynolds."

How he wanted to get lost in her touch.

Her scent.

Her touch.

Her taste, but he had to keep a level head, even though his other one screamed for her attention.

Slowly, he pulled away. "I could get used to that."

"We need to decide on a timeline." She arched in a stretch.

"Do you want to wait until the adoption is finalized?" What the hell, man? *Why. Did. You. Ask. That. Question?*

"Six months minimum? We could." He took his hand in hers, and they walked together toward their bedrooms.

He stopped right outside her door, waiting for ... he didn't know what. Answers? "Do I want to wait? Hell no. Do I think we should? I'm on the fence about it all, especially with all the effort you put into the plan."

"The physical power point slide says TBD. To be determined."

"I remember." *And I love how you left it so vague.* Told him she struggled with this as much as she did.

"On the one hand, us not being physically involved does avoid emotional entanglements as it were." Her fingers fiddled with the buttons on his Henley.

How he wished she'd rip his shirt off and then throw caution to the wind, but this wasn't a normal situation. The answers would be obvious if they'd met a year ago, dated, and then their adoption opportunity came. "I care about you. About her. I want the best possible outcome for all of us."

"So do I." She ran her fingers through his hair, and he leaned into her touch. "But you worry, don't you?"

"Yes. Are you sure you don't want—"

She silenced him by pressing her fingers to his lips. "Reynolds. Please don't ask me again. I am very happy with our arrangement. Please, trust me."

That *please* was the same tone she used with her siblings. And it told him there was more to her story. "I trust you."

"Thank you. Good night. Sleep well."

"You, too." Secretly, he hoped she would invite him in, but relief flooded his veins when she closed the door behind her, leaving him with his thoughts and the need for a very cold shower.

Chapter Twelve

A S THEY NAVIGATED the next few weeks, he and Susan found a routine juggling Audrey's wake, sleep, poop, and eating patterns.

Lucy, who ran the ER, scheduled Reynolds's shifts consecutively, to give him long periods off.

Susan's foster parenting classes ran on four consecutive weekends while she managed her hospital and clinic orientation as well as completing mountains of paperwork for state-required midwife and nurse practitioner certifications.

Their siblings and coworkers helped by bringing food and providing short-term babysitting.

Even though Nate still voiced his concerns about the potentially disastrous outcome of all this, more than once Reynolds caught his brother reading to Audrey as he cradled her in his arms. All the while, Odin sat on the armrest of the couch, looking over his brother's shoulder.

You old softie.

Motherhood immediately agreed with Susan. She glowed as though she had birthed Audrey herself. Even on the nights when sleep eluded her, she navigated this new adventure, as she called it, with class and confidence.

Not that he expected anything else.

More than once, they ended up lying in one or the other's beds, fully clothed of course, as they spoke about their days and Audrey's most recent cuteness factor. Then, she'd fall asleep between them or in the bedside crib.

Even with the constant mutual simmering attraction, both managed to keep it about as uncomplicated as humanly possible.

And Reynolds was about to lose his mind.

"How's fatherhood?" Sue Westbrook, Shelly's aunt, asked during a steady shift on Memorial Day weekend.

"It's a hard learning curve, but we're figuring it out."

"It's always a learning curve. Even when they're teens." Sue chuckled while juggling five things at once at the central ER desk.

"Something to look forward to." *Hopefully.*

Pointing to room four, Shelly laughed, "Speaking of teens. Your frequent flyer is back."

"What did he do this time?" He didn't wait for an answer but walked in to find Ford Hanson sitting on the stretcher, his hand wrapped in a bloodied towel. Again. "Ford."

"Hey! Dr. Reynolds. How's it going?" Before he graduated high school, Ford played offensive line for one of the schools in Bozeman, taking them to the playoffs for the first time in decades. Since then, he seemed to spend more time in the ER than he did in class. "I was in the neighborhood. Visiting my grandma. Thought I'd come by."

"Thanks for that Ford, but you don't have to be injured

to see me. What's going on today?" He motioned for the teen to hold out his arm, and Reynolds slowly unwrapped it, revealing a bruised, bloodied, and, most certainly, broken hand.

"This friend of mine told me that he could hit a brick wall with his fist, and it wouldn't hurt. I said he was full of crap."

Well, I know where this is going. "And?"

"And I'm here."

"Short and sweet. Open and close your hand if you can."

With slow movements, Ford winced and pointed to the outer knuckles. "These two hurt the most."

"I bet they do. Your friend going to be my next patient?"

"He said he wouldn't get injured on account he takes some sort of karate shit and he didn't get hurt," Ford snarled.

Nodding, Reynolds smirked at Ford's youthful arrogance and invincibility. "Do you know why?"

"Why what?"

"Your friend probably didn't break anything?" Reynolds glanced at the clock. He had two hours left before he'd go home. For the first time in weeks, he'd be off for four days straight.

His heart beat a little faster as he thought about it.

"He scratched up his hand, but nothing was broken. Bastard." Ford pouted as his University of Wisconsin T-shirt appeared to be at its stretch limit. "It's probably because he's like half my size. Kind of wimpy."

Apparently, not so wimpy that he ended up in my ER. "It's

because of the way you each hit the wall."

Ford's eyebrows pinched. "What?"

"Usually, when people throw a punch, they come from the outside. Make an arch." Reynolds illustrated the move in slow motion. "But your friend, he probably hit it straight on."

"He did. He cheated!"

"No, he used the technique he learned in his classes. When you hit like you did, the smallest two fingers are going to get the biggest impact. But they have no support in the hand." He held up Ford's hand and pointed to the injured knuckles. "See, no support in your hand. Your friend hit straight on like they teach in many martial arts studies. The impact on these two knuckles but look. The support goes all the way down the forearm."

When Lucy walked by, her ears perked up. "Good evening, Dr. Reynolds. Did I hear you talking about martial arts techniques?"

"Yes, Dr. Davidson. I was."

Despite her size, Lucy could pack a serious punch since she studied kung fu and tai chi for years. First, as part of her rehab after the car accident, the Davidson siblings were in so long ago. Then as a way to stay in shape and not put up with anyone's crap. Essential skills for a female ER doctor.

"You know about marital arts?" Ford scoffed, obviously deciding her size offered him no threat.

"Third-degree black belt," she stated without a hint of playfulness.

Reynolds saw that same fierceness in her face that he

witnessed in Susan's when she took on Gunman Carl.

The fierce is strong with these women.

Then he silently laughed at his Star Wars reference.

"Wait! You're the doctor who wouldn't let me and my friends back last week. My friend fell off the truck, and broke stuff." His upbeat mood turned angry.

Ford reminded Reynolds of those cartoon characters who shoot steam out of their noses when they don't get exactly what they want.

Without a hint of concern, she stood as tall as an NBA all-star. "Your friend was in bad shape. We didn't need all of you back here, getting him worked up and getting in our way."

"But we're his friends. He needed us there."

"And I was his doctor. My job is to make sure he's stable and taken care of. Not entertain all of you."

"It was still a shit thing to do."

"Then you wanted to hold his hand while we cleaned up the blood shooting out of his elbow? When we reset his wrist?"

Immediately, the kid's face paled. "Not that part."

"Or be there for the IV insertion?"

"No, I don't like needles."

"Or when we put in the bladder catheter?"

The kid shielded his groin. "No thanks."

"Maybe keep his attention while I sewed up the lacerations on his face and chest?"

"All right! All right! I get it. You're a badass."

By now, she stood within arm's reach, totally unfazed

that this kid probably outweighed her four times over. "Thank you for noticing, Mr. Hanson. Do you have any other concerns about how I run this ER you wish to share today?"

Ford deflated as fast as the Barney the Dinosaur float did in the 1997 Macy's Thanksgiving Day parade. "No, ma'am. Thanks for taking care of my friend."

"It was my pleasure, Ford. I hope he's recovering well."

"Yes, ma'am. Good for you, about the martial arts, ma'am. Thanks, Dr. Reynolds. I'll remember to punch it straight on next time my friend challenges me."

"That's not what Dr. Reynolds said." Lucy leaned against the doorframe, a slight smirk to her face.

"I suggest *not* hitting a wall at all." Reynolds glanced at the clock and said a small thank-you he'd be home soon.

"What's the fun in that?" Ford rolled his eyes.

"There's not any."

"I'll leave you to it." Lucy gave a wave. "And, Ford?"

"Yes, ma'am?" His answer was more reactionary than respectful.

"Make sure to keep checking on your friend. He's got a long road of recovery ahead of him. He's likely to get pretty depressed about what he's missing."

The kid rested his hands in his lap and picked at his fingernail. "Yes, ma'am."

Reynolds smirked as Lucy exited. "You need an X-ray."

"Dude." Ford's thick shoulders slumped. The subtle smell of nicotine drifted around him. "That's my writing hand. How am I supposed to take my notes in class?"

Maybe you should have thought of that before you punched a brick wall. Long ago, Reynolds realized practical advice never made a damned bit of difference when it came to people who kept making dumb mistakes. "It's Memorial Day weekend. Aren't you out for the year?"

"My mom told me to stay at college because they're selling the house. Can you believe that? Right before college, I make one stupid mistake, come home one weekend, and there's a for-sale sign in the front yard." He rolled his eyes. "The only place I can stay is the dorms, but I gotta take classes. I ditched class today to come see my grandma. She does my laundry."

"Why not stay with your grandma in the summer?"

"My grandma is mean. And she smokes like a chimney. I'd rather stay in the dorms. The food is better. She only has ramen noodles and Cheez Whiz."

"But she's not so mean that you let her do your laundry?"

"She's meaner if I don't, but she makes my clothes smell like Marlboros. Gotta drive with the windows open to air them out."

At least your parents told you where they were moving. Even now, Reynolds and Nate have no idea where their parents set up residence since Nate graduated high school. "Well, maybe you can ask someone to share their notes."

Ford's face lit up. "Get a hot, smart girl, to take them for me. There are a couple in my classes. I like hot, smart girls."

So do I. "Sure, that works, too. As long as she's interested in sharing them."

For a moment, Ford stared blankly at Reynolds. "Are you talking about consent?"

"Not intentionally." Although, it was good to hear the kid heard the word before. Hopefully, he understood it.

"I wouldn't use any hot, smart girl's notes without her consent. It wouldn't be cool." He air-quoted *cool*.

The response reminded Reynolds of Joey from *Friends*, when the character kept using the same hand gestures incorrectly.

Of course, Joey wasn't six-five or two hundred and seventy pounds, but the comparison worked just the same. "None of the best people would ever use anyone's notes without their permission. Give me a second."

Leaving the room, Reynolds headed straight for the ER desk. "Sue, please order a right-hand X-ray to rule out a boxer's fracture."

"That kid is gonna meet his deductible before the summer is out." Lucy tilted her chin toward the room. "He came in with one of his friends last week."

"What happened?"

"Car surfing."

"I guess Ford wasn't the one surfing?" Reynolds checked for his pending rapid strep and a CBC in room five as the radiology tech took Ford for his films.

"Nope, but his friend was." Lucy exhaled. "That kid was such a mess."

"Where's the friend now? The strep for room five is positive. No drug allergies. Let's give the first antibiotic dose here, since the pharmacy doesn't open for a few hours."

"He's recovering in Bozeman. Then he'll go to long-term rehab." Lucy tapped the computer screen. "He won't make it to two-a-days come August. He'll be lucky to be out of a wheelchair by Labor Day. Laceration in room six."

"Damn. What did he break?" Reynolds rolled his neck from side to side, hoping he wouldn't completely pass out as soon as he got home.

"One hip and both arms. He's lucky he didn't break his neck, but he landed in a field instead of on pavement, but they were going pretty fast."

"I bet his parents were thrilled with that phone call."

"The driver's parents told him they were tired of his shit, and he should enlist or move out." With a shrug, Lucy moved the pens around her scrubs pocket.

"Sometimes the military is the best option for kids who have a whole lot of energy, no direction, and zero respect for the rules." Sue shook her head.

Lucy picked up an iPad. "For certain, Ms. Sue. Hopefully, he'll appreciate what the army will teach him. I'll be in room six. Dave, will you pull a suture kit and size seven gloves for me? When I get in there, I'll know what sutures I need."

"Be right there." Dave, the nurse, gave a thumbs-up and headed to the supply room.

Reynolds rested his elbows on the counter and closed his eyes for a few moments.

"The circus getting to you, Dr. Reynolds?" Sue Westbrook's fingers sailed across the keyboard after answering the ER line and texting something on her phone.

If energy were bottled, it would have Sue's photo on the label. She seamlessly kept every aspect of the unit running as smoothly as melted ice cream on a hot sidewalk.

She grabbed a stack of papers off the printer, sorted and stapled them, and set them on the counter in front of her. "Discharge instructions. You're off a few days, Dr. Reynolds. Got any interesting plans?"

"Four days off in a row. Gonna sleep when the baby sleeps."

"You've got to, otherwise you'll never get rest again."

Sue motioned to Shelly when she approached the desk. "When did Freddie sleep through the night?"

"What do you mean by sleep through the night? Six? Eight hours? Twelve?" Shelly finished entering something on the iPad and placed it in the charging rack.

"More than three straight." Reynolds pinched the bridge of his nose as the exhaustion of the last few weeks crept deeper into his bones. As prepared as he believed he was for the role of fatherhood, there was no way anyone could have prepared him for this level of exhaustion.

"Freddie started sleeping longer at night when he was about six months. The first time he slept from midnight to six, I remember waking up rested, but panicking that something was wrong. I ran to the bedside and he was simply staring at the world around him. Happy as could be." Shelly chuckled. "Baby not sleeping well?"

"She's fine. Doing what babies do. Susan's amazing, though. I swear, the woman thought of everything. She's taking care of the baby, finishing all the foster parenting classes, filling out the paperwork, helping schedule CPS visitation, and she's getting ready for the clinic to open this week." After all that, Reynolds wondered what the hell he was complaining about.

"Peyton's excited about the official opening of the birthing center on Tuesday. She's worked hard for this." Sue patted her chest, a serene smile on her face. "If all goes well, Marietta is about to experience one epic baby boom in the next few years."

Hopefully, Reynolds would make it through the next few hours without falling over from fatigue. "I planned to adopt as a single parent, but now, I wonder how I would have even pulled that off."

Shelly tapped her penlight on the counter. "Things sound doable before reality hits. Parenting's harder than it looks."

A loud ouch from room six as the patient's mom in room five stood in the doorway and shook her keys. The international gesture of annoyance and impatience, but one that did not make the ER staff move faster.

"How much longer before you can officially adopt?" Sue moved around the desk organizing between entering orders and answering the phone.

"We're at almost seven of twenty-four weeks." His heart thumped harder about the risk of Audrey leaving. He shoved the possibility away because obsessing about it didn't help. "Still no news from the dad."

"Twenty-five percent there." Shelly patted him on the back. "We're all rooting for you."

"That we are. Cannot wait to celebrate." Sue picked up the unit phone on the second ring.

"The Davidson siblings mentioned you and Susan are a good team."

The siblings. Even though Lucy, Edmund, Peter, and their significant others frequently helped out, Peter still hadn't warmed to Audrey as the others had. Plus, when they worked together, his demeanor turned stiff toward Reynolds.

Glancing behind him, Reynolds lowered his voice. "What's the general discussion between them about all this?"

Shelly raised an eyebrow, and her eyes darted from her aunt and back to Reynolds. "You want the truth?"

No. "Absolutely."

"Lucy and Edmund are concerned, but they say Susan looks happy so they're going to go with it until she says otherwise."

She looks happy? Guess my good impressions just keep on coming. "That's two. What about Peter?"

When her lips went flat, Reynolds already knew the answer. "That bad, huh?"

She glanced toward the closed door of room six. "I love Peter, I truly do, but he's having a very hard time. With him finding out about his kids in the past year and now Susan *not acting herself* as he puts it. He's frustrated."

"Why is Susan's behavior bothering him this much?" He entered the prescription for antibiotics into the iPad and hit send. The desk printer hummed to life. "She's an adult."

"You have to understand. When that accident made him the head of the household, Susan was his rock. His stability.

He said he would have lost his mind if it weren't for her rational approach to it all."

Over the past several weeks, Susan said little of that traumatic time in their lives, but Reynolds often wondered who her rock was during all that chaos. *Because it sounded like she had no one.* "I understand it was an awful time, but it's been years since that happened, Shelly."

"True, but the one person he could always set his watch to was Susan. Her practical, logical—"

"Responsible."

"Yes, responsible, consistent approach to life. She put her head down and got it done most efficiently. It got them through college and the three through medical school. Made sure their mother was cared for before Charlie took over."

The more Shelly told him, it hit him that out of the four of them, the only one who didn't go to med school was the main caregiver. "Sounds like Susan took care of everything for everyone else, made sure the other three succeeded, and got her shit done. Now she needs their support and he's angry?"

For a moment, Shelly stared at him, like she juggled her beloved's words in her mind before giving a thoughtful answer. "No, not angry. Confused. And Peter hates being confused. My love desperately needs to be in control of things life throws at him. He's learning he can't control everything. That he doesn't have to."

"True that. He was such a stick-in-the-mud when he got here, but a few falls on his ass ice-skating helped humble him right up." Sue laughed and placed the printed prescription on the counter. "He's learning to calm down, but he's got decades of that mindset to readjust. Give him time. He loves his sister. He loves she's happy. He'll come around."

"You keep taking care of Susan and Audrey. The rest will fall into place." Shelly patted his shoulder, and he appreciated his colleague's encouragement.

"Thanks, ladies. I'll keep all this in mind on my days off." *Four days off.* A trio of blessed words.

"You want me to give discharge instructions and meds for the strep throat?" Shelly held her hand out as Ford came back from X-ray.

"Thank you. I'll get Ford situated." Reynolds glanced at his watch. "Two more hours to go and—"

When the triage bell went off again, Reynolds felt a little bit of his soul die. "Why are people coming to the ER at four in the morning?"

Sue chuckled as her half-moon glasses perfectly balanced on the bridge of her nose. "Guess the circus is still open."

Chapter Thirteen

"HONEY, I'M HOME!" Scents of coffee and cinnamon bread attacked his nose the moment he walked in the front door.

Welcome greetings after a particularly chaotic Sunday shift of Memorial Day weekend.

The bright sun of the morning poured into the living area.

Perfect mornings like this tempted him to stay up as late as possible, to switch his body clock to sleep tonight.

Sitting on the couch, closest to the hearth, Odin opened his one eye up. Lying on a large pallet of blankets, the cat yawned, gave Reynolds an indifferent glare, and rolled on his back with his paws in the air, taking the form of a passed-out, inebriated college student.

No one was in the kitchen, but the scents of coffee and breakfast lingered. "Susan?"

"We're in here."

He followed her voice to her room.

Sitting in a rocker, Susan sported a messy twist on the top of her head. She wore a well-worn T-shirt and dark sleep shorts. Her long, shapely legs crossed as she cradled a very awake Audrey. A half-full bottle sat on the nightstand next to her.

With a tired smile, Susan simply said, "Good morning."

The picturesque scene punched him right in the heart, and he struggled for words that wouldn't make things *complicated*. "How'd it go?"

You look beautiful.

"She's been up since three and will only sleep if she's in my arms, so it's been kind of a rough night."

"I don't know how you'd sleep with all that in your way." He motioned to her bed.

A few large open binders with a neatly organized bin of highlighters sitting between them, two stacks of clinical nursing books, and several small piles of papers perpendicular to each other covered the neatly made bed. "I didn't get as much done as I'd hoped, but I think I've got it all organized like I want."

"Where did you sleep?" Reynolds peeled off his coat and tossed it into his room across the hall.

"I was too tired to put it all away, so I slept in the rocker." She rubbed the bridge of her nose. "I thought she'd sleep longer than she did."

When Audrey's hands came up, Susan gave the baby full access to her face. "But you didn't, did you? No, you stayed up and fussed."

"Sounds like a long night." As mundane as the moment might appear to some, Reynolds would never tire of it.

Despite her doubts and exhausted smile, motherhood agreed with Susan.

"It wasn't a total bust. We did discover she has a fondness for classic eighties tunes and loves Postmodern Jukebox."

"Interesting. Any particular groups? Songs?" He stood behind the rocking chair, and Audrey immediately noticed him. "Good morning, beautiful."

With wide-eyed wonder, she blinked at him, and his heart completely melted.

Susan yawned and pointed to her phone in the charging cradle. "So far, Hall and Oates, Lionel Richie, Pat Benatar, and PMJ's rendition of 'Juice' by Lizzo. And Supertramp."

"Of course, Supertramp. She has excellent taste." *Note to self, make playlists for possible late-night parenting issues.*

"She does. Now if she would sleep in her bed, I could get some work done. Yes. I'm talking to you, sweet girl."

"I can take over." As he greedily reached for the baby, Susan motioned at his scrubs.

"Do you mind cleaning up first?"

"Good idea. Saw a few cases of strep and RSV tonight. Give me five and I'll take over."

"Aren't you tired?" Susan stretched her arm overhead and arched her back. Her shirt lifted, revealing her curvy waist and smooth skin.

His mouth immediately went dry. *Do. Not. Go. There.*

With a quarter of their adoption journey completed, Reynolds promised himself he would not rush whatever their relationship was. "It wasn't busy. Grabbed a few hours of sleep around two. I'll nap later."

Reynolds lied. It had been horribly busy. After ordering a

cast for Ford, Reynolds treated a family of six for strep, a woman for chlamydia, three different patients for upper respiratory viruses, a man in his seventies for a head laceration, and a toddler who shoved a bean up his nose. "But I'm off four full days and you both are here."

"That's right. You're off and I start my job in two days." A melancholy smile replaced her exhaustion. "But we're making it work."

"We are. We don't have to go anywhere today, right?" That idea sent adrenaline through him faster than a double espresso.

"Right. I start Tuesday, so today and tomorrow, I'm getting all my paperwork ready." She motioned to her bed. "And maybe get some sleep."

"Never a dull day."

She snapped her fingers. "Doesn't Lori visit today?"

"I'll ask her." He quickly texted his friend.

"Thank you." She tried to get Audrey to take some more of her bottle, but the baby turned her head. "Well, that's a no."

"I'm glad to take over. Just … I'll be right back. Man, it's good to be home." *Home.* The word meant so much more now.

Lost in how much his life changed in the past several weeks, he absentmindedly removed his shirt as he walked away.

"Yeah, home is … great."

Her strained voice stopped him in his tracks. Glancing over his shoulder, he caught her heated gaze unapologetically roaming over him.

Damn. What he wouldn't give for her to look at him like that every day.

In every room of this house.

Multiple times.

He held his top in front of his scrubs to hide his immediate reaction to her visual appreciation.

A few beats before their eyes met and her eyebrows hit her hairline. The classic response to being caught with your hand in the cookie jar, although, Reynolds could pretty much guarantee cookies were not on Susan's mind.

She laid Audrey on her shoulder and gently rubbed the baby's back. "I like your tattoo. I hadn't seen it before."

He patted his right shoulder. "Thanks."

"I don't remember it from the calendar."

"They photoshopped it out. Licensing issues."

Red-faced and flustered, she cleared her throat. "Take your time cleaning up. We're not going anywhere."

While in the shower, Reynolds replayed Susan's heated gaze. That scented hair stuff she used always made his mouth water. He dreamed of burying his face in her hair as they shared his bed. Her bed. The table. The library and any other surface they wanted to try.

After he stroked himself to completion, his brain could focus on things other than naughty thoughts about Susan.

He threw on a wrinkled button-down and sweats before giving himself a pep talk to his reflection. "Don't screw this up."

Lori texted back that it was too early for him to be contacting her in any way, shape, or form, but she'd be over later today.

He followed the scents of fresh baked bread and cinnamon, then caught Susan mid-yawn as she filled her mug. "Coffee?"

"Sure. Let me take her." Scooping a still-fussy Audrey up, Reynolds opened his shirt and placed the baby against his bare chest. Although it wasn't his intention to seek Susan's admiration, he appreciated her gawking.

Another great impression made.

Clearing her throat, Susan settled on to one of the chairs and stirred her brew. "I don't know why she's so inconsolable. She's clean. I've burped her, rocked her, sang to her ... are you kidding me right now?"

$$-\sqrt{\Omega} 2 \sqrt{}-$$

As SOON THEIR daughter got skin-to-skin, she snuggled in and cooed contently.

Reynolds beamed, his hand gently patting Audrey's back. "You're making me look so good right now, kiddo."

"Well, that settles it. You are the baby whisperer." It took a conscious effort to pull her eyes away from the endearing sight of him comforting Audrey. But her mind had other ideas.

Reynolds comforting me as I rested on his bare chest ... sent Susan's lower bits into a tingling frenzy.

She shifted in her chair while a scenario of her on top of him, staring down at that naked, perfect body, played on a continuous loop. "You are so good at this."

"Nah, I'm who she wanted right now. She'll change her mind in a few minutes."

With lust ranging through her veins, Susan laughed, hoping it would give her cover. It became increasingly difficult to keep her hands to herself when he was around. The intensity of his visits to her dreams grew, but they'd been so busy, they hadn't revisited their physical plans. She wasn't sure where they were in their timeline.

Barely two months ago, her husband walked into her life and took out a gunman with a can of a popular side dish. His beautiful kindness only rivaled his fierceness for their new family, but after seeing him remove his shirt earlier, Reynolds shifted from beautiful to jaw-dropping amazing. How his body looked even better in person than in his calendar photo.

It seemed so very unfair ... to everyone else who didn't get to see him shirtless in person.

But I do. For seven weeks, she'd been good, kept her hands to herself, but getting a glimpse of what lay under those unironed shirts and dark blue scrubs sent sexual energy right down to the tips of her fingers.

She gripped the edge of her chair to keep her hands from reaching out and pulling him in to kiss his kissable mouth. *This is so unfair.*

How she managed to marry a great guy and have a baby, but hadn't properly touched said guy, only emphasized that Susan always had her unique way of doing things.

My own stupid, rational, noncomplicated ways.

When he smiled, Susan realized he caught her staring. Patting the table in front of her, she acted as though she hadn't noticed his panty-melting smirk. "Need anything?"

He cleared his throat, his hand tenderly patting a very content baby's back. "Coffee and a couple of slices of whatever that bread is you made."

"I'm not talented enough to create it. It's that cinnamon bread Gabby makes. Toasted?"

"Sure." Reynolds kept eye contact with Audrey while answering.

"You got it." As she quickly worked, Reynolds spoke softly to the baby about his shift, the people he worked with, and how many he saw. It became apparent that his night had been far busier than he let on, and yet, he acted more chipper than a properly caffeinated Ted Lasso.

And was just as sexy.

Deciding not to call his bluff, Susan placed his food in front of him and settled in her chair directly across from him. "Shift went okay?

"Your sister's been great about my schedule." He took a quick bite of his toast and Audrey continued to find him fascinating.

And so did Susan for entirely different reasons.

Susan pulled her knees to her chest and hoped to look casually comfortable despite his ability to make her skin warm.

"You can go get some sleep if you want." He tilted his head toward the door. "I've got her. Too awake from working to sleep. Lori said she'd be over this afternoon."

"Great. Hopefully, she'll have some news regarding the father." Fatigue settled deep in her bones, but she didn't want to leave. Watching him care for the baby made her ovaries quiver. Later they'd both catch a nap, and she could use one of her battery-operated friends to take the edge off.

Since her only conversations for the past few days were between her, Audrey, stacks of paperwork, and Odin, she needed to talk to another adult. "Let's talk. Haven't seen you much."

"Anything in particular you want to talk about?" A slight pinkening to his cheeks while he spoke softly to Audrey.

The baby stared up at him as though he were the most amazing man in the world.

And he was because he sure stimulated Susan's mind on illogically high levels. She couldn't explain it, and after seven weeks, Susan simply didn't want to. She wanted to know everything she could about him. "Will you tell me more about your sister, Audrey?"

"What do you want to know?"

"What was she like?"

His lips thinned. "I owe you that. We don't talk about her as much as we probably should. Grandpa removed many of her pictures after she died. Said it hurt too much to see her face every day." Even though he lovingly spoke of his sister, a hint of sorrow laced his words.

"How old were you and Nate?"

"When she died? I was in my third year of college. Nate, in his last year of high school." He shifted to face Susan more fully. He let out a long breath as if he were digging deep into a well of sadness. "She'd been sick for so long. We knew it was coming, but we weren't ready."

"When you have a chronically sick family member recover so many times, you figure they will again. When it doesn't happen, it's such a shift." More times than Susan could count, she'd been present in those situations. Heartbreak never quite covered it.

"It's amazing she lived as long as she did. Great kid. Loved anything purple."

Take note. "Did she have a favorite stuffed animal?"

"Yes, a purple dinosaur."

"Of course. Dino?"

He patted his wonderfully toned shoulder. "The very one."

"I never expected you to have a tattoo, much less of a cartoon dinosaur."

"Nate has one, too. We got it for her, the day after…"

For whatever reason, a flash of Bernie's clothing hit Susan's brain. "Oh my gosh. Bernie's shirt. That must have been so weird for you. Like a sign."

"It was." He kissed the top of Audrey's head.

The corner of the baby's mouth twitched into a smile.

Susan didn't often believe in signs or divine intervention, but there were days when she struggled with the idea of something far too personal happening randomly for all the right reasons. "Did she have a favorite song? What else did she love? Games? Shows?"

Susan kept track of every answer, not only to better understand the sister behind the name, but if she came across anything Audrey would have loved, Susan could get it for the baby's room.

Audrey continued to look around, still wide awake.

"I noticed your Dinosaur National Monument hoodie that first day." He took a long pull from his coffee mug, and the perfect layering of cinnamon, butter, and coffee filled the kitchen.

"Got it when I was there."

"What made you stop?"

"I'd never been. I had time, thought I'd spend the day before heading to Yellowstone." *Before I got the phone call verifying I could never have a baby.* "Then I came here."

"Our grandparents took us three there many times. We had to break up the visits because Audrey could only walk for a limited time. She'd get winded. We brought a wheelchair, but she refused to use it."

"Kids want to feel like they belong with their peers. Don't want to be seen as any *different.*" She hadn't meant for her voice to fade with that last word.

So many of her classmates whispered how *different* she was after the car accident. Many wouldn't even make eye contact as if she were some bad luck charm that would cause the deaths of their own parents.

"Susan?"

If I'd only known how messed up my insides were at the time, we could have gotten me straightened out. Maybe.

"Susan?"

She blinked a few times, realizing she allowed sad memories to pull her backward. "What? Sorry."

"Where did you go just now?" He cocked his head, his hair in a perfect bedhead style.

"Nowhere." She nibbled her toast, hoping it would alleviate the knot in her stomach that always formed when she gave in to sad memories.

He raised an eyebrow before taking a healthy drink of his coffee. "You sure?"

He's way too observant. "Yep."

Audrey sighed and slowly blinked as the morning sun brightened the kitchen and the sounds of kids playing outside hit Susan's ears.

As much as the ease of their conversation comforted her, a full explanation of her history simply wouldn't make it past her voice box. "It's only a bad memory, Reynolds. Not worth discussing since it changes nothing." *Absolutely nothing.*

He gave her an understanding nod. "Whenever you're ready to tell me that sad backstory, I'll be here."

Once again, Dr. June surprised her with his compassion. "Thank you. I'll keep that in mind. Tell me more about your sweet Audrey." Usually, Susan counted the minutes during the getting-to-know-you part of any relationship, but with Reynolds, it flowed as easily as breathing. "What else do you remember about her?"

"When she passed, nothing was quite the same."

Susan scanned the kitchen. "Things rarely are after events like that. Peter, Edmund, Lucy, and I certainly had our fair share of change."

"I'm guessing you mean the car accident."

Working with her siblings, he probably heard plenty of

stories. Plus, Lucy held visible scars from her near-fatal wounds. "Something like that."

"It was something. Head-on collision. Drunk driver. Killed your father instantly. Caused your mom lifelong issues. Lucy almost died."

"Sums up that bit of history." Maybe fatigue lowered her guard, but the sadness of that day punched her right in the gut. Before she realized it, Susan pressed her fist against her breastbone while tears flowed freely down her face.

"Is that all of it?"

"What do you mean?" Susan quickly dried her face and let the hair clip out of her hair. She ran her fingers through it and attempted to pin it up again, but one of the springs popped loose. "Figures. It's broken."

"I mean, is that *all* of the story?"

"Yes." *All that's worth sharing.*

His forehead creased as if he didn't quite believe her.

Audrey's sneeze broke the concern.

He dabbed her face with a napkin. Then played a short game of peekaboo. "My mom, Celine, had a head for numbers. Forensic accountant. Had high-end clients. My dad, Clifton, was a middle school teacher. Taught history."

As interesting as his story was, she worried he'd want tit-for-tat after this. "They sound like an accomplished couple."

"They were and they were desperately in love with each other. Like Hollywood level into each other."

"What happened?"

"Dad was more of the classic stay-at-home parent since Mom had long hours but made very good money. He took us to school, made sure we did our homework, and housework."

"A gender role switch. Did it work?"

"It worked decently for a long time. Right after Audrey got her cystic fibrosis diagnosis, Mom earned this huge promotion. Then everything changed." He kissed the top of the sleeping baby's head. "She made so much, my father quit teaching and became her personal assistant. They spent all their time together."

"That must have helped with taking better care of—" The slow shake of his head halted her comment.

"Mom hired a nanny when she and my father traveled for her job. It was a lot because they may have loved *becoming* parents, but when our cuteness wore off, day-to-day parenting was not their priority. Plus, they wanted someone else to watch Audrey."

"Why's that?" The weeks of crappy sleep patterns eased up her spine, sitting heavy on her shoulders. She fought laying her head on the table and closing her eyes.

"Because Audrey got sick. A lot. There were several different nurses hired over the years. The final woman wasn't prepared to deal with it. She quit. I stepped in until someone else was supposed to replace her, but Mom never hired anyone else because I was doing *such a good job.*"

The numerous times she took over her mother's care flooded Susan's brain. She couldn't imagine the pressure of caring for a younger sibling with a life-threatening illness. "That had to be exhausting for you to care for Nate *and* Audrey."

"It was. I tried to make it work, but over several weeks—"

"Weeks? Oh, Reynolds. That's too much for you to be responsible for." She rested her forearms on the table. "What about school? Your life?"

Because I sure missed out on plenty making sure everyone else was covered.

His mouth thinned as sunbeams danced with the stained-glass dinosaur in the kitchen window, sending their rich colors on the edge of the kitchen table. "I called my grandparents. They picked us up. Nate and I each graduated high school from here. Audrey ... died."

"Did your parents ever come around?" As much as her father dying broke her heart, it certainly wasn't by choice.

"Nope. When my grandparents called, they threatened to turn my mom and dad into CPS. Mom promised to send a monthly stipend and sign over custody because she wasn't giving up her job and Dad wasn't going to stop being with Mom."

"My mom pretty much lived for my dad. When he died, she gave up parenting." Her fists clenched in her lap. The anger of her mother falling deeper into depression was still a tender topic, as it left Susan to pick up everyone else's pieces and sacrifice her own life. "No matter how much her children needed her, she wouldn't even try."

"Part of the custody agreement was my mom kept us on her insurance and paid for any co-pays or bills. That way my grandparents could focus on taking care of Audrey without the burden of payments."

"At least that's something. When did you talk to your

parents last?" Susan opened and closed her fists before placing her hands on the table.

"I haven't talked to them since Nate graduated high school." Reynolds took a long drink of his coffee.

"High school? You haven't seen your parents for over, what, fifteen years?"

"And I don't need to. They made it clear how important we were when they abandoned us. When they decided parenting was too hard because they had a special needs child." His usual lighthearted tone now contained a sharp edge.

A charged quiet settled in the room as the last scents of coffee and cinnamon drifted away.

"Thank you for telling me all that, Reynolds. It means a lot that you shared it with me."

He gave her a sleepy smile, his busy night finally catching up with him. "It's a sad backstory, Susan, but that doesn't mean it's not worth telling."

Damn him for making sense. "Why's that?"

"Because it explains who we are. How we've made the choices to end up here. Like you, for instance." He shifted his weight and Audrey continued to sleep.

Her body went stiff. "What about me?"

"It dawned on me that your three siblings went to medical school, and you went to nursing school. Why is that?"

"What do you mean?" *Oh, please don't go down this road.*

"You're disciplined enough. More than intelligent enough to go to med school."

"You're saying I'm too smart to be a nurse?"

"No way. Nurses are amazingly smart, but you didn't even consider it?"

Ugh, why does he know me so well? "I went to nursing school because I'm the smartest and most practical of all my siblings."

His slow smile built to an all-out grin. "I can believe that, but there's more to that story, isn't there?"

"Nope." *So much more.*

"Susan?"

"I applied. I didn't get in." She lied and the look on his face told her he knew that.

He put his hand up in surrender. "That's okay. You're not in the mood."

Oh, I'm in the mood. Holding her coffee mug, Susan took in the chiseled line of his jaw, the wave of his hair, the width of his shoulders.

Shoulders she could lean on at the end of a long day of work or when Audrey hadn't slept or for … other things.

The overwhelming urge to throw him down on his kitchen table and climb on for an amazing ride lunged into the front of Susan's mind.

Never had she wished so hard for a baby to be asleep and safely tucked in her crib.

What the hell, Susan? She'd never been this sexually stimulated by anyone. It was almost unnerving but thrilled every nerve in her body. One look at a shirtless Dr. June and Susan booked a one-way train ticket to Debaucheryville.

She needed to get some sleep before she did something stupid.

Like, kiss him again.

And she really wanted to kiss him again.

Everywhere. *I can only imagine how good he'd taste.*

A mischievous glimmer in his eyes indicated he might have a few interesting thoughts of his own. "What are you thinking?"

She rubbed the knots in her neck, hoping to come off as exhausted. "Nothing. Just tired."

"I doubt that." He arched his eyebrow.

His attention notched up her heart rate. "What do you mean?"

"After watching your incredible brain work, I doubt there is ever a minute of your day that *nothing's* on your mind."

"You seem pretty confident about that statement, sir." This guy understood her better than all of her former fiancés combined. She swallowed hard at the possibility of them working out in the long run. *So much could go wrong between now and adoption day.*

"What I like about you is you're *always* thinking about something."

I constantly think about you naked. She sucked in the air, hoping those words didn't slip out. When he didn't change his expression, she relaxed. "I think *always* is a bit much."

"What would you prefer?"

"Honestly, I'd like to sound more spontaneous versus predictable. Tired of being predictable." She kicked her feet on a neighboring chair and crossed her legs at the ankles.

"Right after we met, you kissed me. There's nothing predictable about that."

He went there. "My apologies if it made you uneasy." Her eyes betrayed her as they lingered on his mouth. The memory of how those lips felt against hers for that one impetuous, delicious moment played on repeat.

How he smiled at her after she pulled away.

How she still didn't regret it.

"Susan. I'm sure, between the two of us, we can figure out a better word."

"Yes, I'm sure we can."

Chapter Fourteen

"GOOD NEWS! SHE'S finally ... asleep." Reynolds's heart fluttered in his chest when he found an exhausted Susan passed out in the kitchen chair. Her legs were still properly crossed, her head resting on the table as she slept with a serene calm on her face.

He took a moment to etch her image in his mind so if this all went south.

In her hand, the small, broken hair clip she fought with earlier. Her hair cascaded in thick, chestnut-colored waves down her back and over her shoulders.

His hands itched to run through it. To feel the silk of her hair between his fingers. The softness of it as she rested her head on his chest after ... *what exactly?*

Every day, the idea of him and Susan becoming far more than platonic co-parents after this was all said and done gained traction.

For weeks, he focused on being the best father, the best spouse-friend, and the best man he could be. It kept his thoughts on point and his lust in check.

The closest they'd come to physical contact were mostly chaste kisses, fist bumps, and falling asleep next to each other, fully clothed, on the couch and in each other's beds as Audrey slept close by. Seeing Susan in such a peaceful moment, knocked the wind out of him once again and turned his thoughts, naughty.

A silent curse before he pulled his tired mind above his beltline, but his sweats didn't help hide his reaction. "Don't screw this up, Rey."

Susan sparked his interest the moment Lucy showed him a photo of her sister. There would never be a more gorgeous woman in his life, but it wasn't her perfectly smooth skin or her long, presently bare legs that pulled him in like a siren's song.

Her grace and fierceness piqued his interest far more. How she gave everything she had, and yet, when he asked her to tell him more about their lives after the car accident she shut down.

Reynolds recognized her deep wounds. The time had to be more than exhausting, especially when she carried the majority of the responsibility to keep her family from being torn apart. Yet, when it came to how it all affected *her* she quit sharing.

And that bothered him, because whatever lingered kept her from opening up.

Something that could easily be his worst fears.

Her uncertainty about being a mother.

Yet, Susan's only hesitation had been her worrying that she wouldn't be enough for him. For Audrey.

That she was broken.

Not once had she expressed doubts about taking care of a

baby like his mother did.

He dismissed his worries. Comparing Susan to his mother was like comparing Emily Blunt as the bitchy assistant in *The Devil Wears Prada* versus Emily Blunt as that ultimate soldier in *Edge of Tomorrow*.

Two polar opposites. Very different women.

One shallow. The other, fierce.

Guess I have a thing for Emily Blunt.

Eyes closed, Susan snored for a few breaths, then settled back into soft breathing as the coffeemaker turned off.

As much as he'd love to stand here and stare at her, she'd fall out of that chair when she hit REM. "Susan?"

"Hello, husband," she mumbled without opening her eyes.

Again, he tried to wake her more, but she responded with a sweet mewing sound.

The sound imprinted on his brain, and he hoped to hear her make that noise again for all the right reasons.

"Susan?" Gently, he scooped her up and waited for her to open her eyes. Nothing. *She's exhausted.*

"Taking you to your room now, Susan." On the way through the living room, her berry-scented hair hit his nose, and his mouth watered. He wondered if she used a body soap to match that shampoo. That only verified the fact he should never wear these particular sweats out in public with Susan smelling like this.

With a quick peek, he checked on Audrey, who slept in her bed. "Be right back," he whispered. "Gonna put Mommy to bed."

Odin sat regally in the doorway, his normal scowl gone, but keeping a watchful eye over the newest resident. A job he took quite seriously because whatever room Audrey was in, the curmudgeon feline stayed close by.

Reynolds planned to lay Susan down, cover her up, and leave, but when he stepped into her room, that possibility went right out the window.

Strewn with notebooks, binders, paperwork, and textbooks, Susan's entire bed was covered. "She got it all organized."

He didn't dare move a page.

After finally getting Audrey to sleep in her own room, moving her to the crib in his could rile her up again. "Sofa chair for me, then."

On the way to his bed, he quietly kicked a few escaped bits of clothing toward his clothes hamper. "Susan, your bed is covered with your work. I'm laying you down in mine."

"Your bed?" She nodded. "Finally."

What. Does. She. Mean?

He ignored her response and kicked his scrubs into the clothes hamper. Steps away from tucking her in and she nuzzled his neck and inhaled. "You smell good."

His mouth suddenly went dry. "I had a shower."

Her hand slipped between his unbuttoned shirt and slid up to his bare shoulder. "I bet you taste even better."

He froze, unsure how awake she was. Waves of lust washed over him as he struggled to keep a tight-fisted grip on practicality. "Susan?"

After a deep inhale, she sleepily opened her eyes, her fingers threaded through his hair. "You are the sexiest, most wonderful man I've ever met."

She kissed him. Not a sweet, lingering kiss as they'd shared a handful of times. Not the kisses on the cheeks they'd given each other for the past seven weeks.

No, this was hungry. Wanting. Like he was the answer to a craving she denied herself for too long.

Her touch turned off his brain and sent his thinking straight into his pants, which did little to hide that fact. A few steps forward and his knees ran into his mattress. "Susan."

"Hmmm?" Her thumb traced along his lower lip.

"What are we doing here?"

Wide awake, she slowly slid from his arms, keeping her body flush to his. "Having you across the hall, sitting next to me, it's been really hard keeping my hands to myself. I don't want to anymore. Husband."

When he heard about the responsible, practical Susan, he never processed how intensely sensual she could be. "I see."

Since she walked into his life, many thoughts of her originated below his waistband.

His hands tentatively rested on her hips. "What are you talking about here? Does this fall under our kissing adjustment?"

She shrugged. "I mean, we didn't specify where to kiss."

Holy shit. "How handsy do you want to get?"

The soft touch of her finger running along the edge of his chin sent a shudder of desire up his spine.

For too long, he wished to be a breath away from her.

Closer. Seemed like every day, every moment since they first met, she occupied his every thought.

Desire swam in her green eyes as her breathing quickened. "Fair question. We are married. Seems like anything is fair game."

"Anything?" *Shit, why did I ask that?* His mouth watered at the idea of kissing her, touching her, tasting her.

With nimble fingers, she unbuttoned his shirt, kissing his skin after she exposed each inch. "Let's complicate things."

"Okay, but how far do you want this to go?"

Her fingers paused, but then continued, pushing the shirt from his body. "What are you comfortable with?"

"N-n-not sure. What are you comfortable with?"

"I'm comfortable with all of it."

For a brief moment, he believed it could be. "Sex?"

"Yes." Her voice cracked with a bit of uncertainty. "Or maybe we slow down a bit. Some mutual exploring?"

"Exploring. Well, that's not sex so not *as* complicated, right?" Desire made the lie so easy to believe.

"Correct." She pressed against him, her hand wandering lower. "Being this close to you I can't stop thinking about you and me together. Naked."

"I've thought about that, too. A lot." *Constantly.*

"Glad I'm not the only one." In one smooth move, she shed her nightshirt and tossed it over her shoulder.

She now stood before him topless and wanting.

As he pulled her closer, his restraint evaporated. "You're not the only one."

The sweet scents of her hair, and her skin, overwhelmed

him. His hand moved up her body, cupping her breast. "You naked in my bed is one of my top three favorite dreams."

A low moan escaped her as she slowly stroked the length of him over his sweats. "I can feel that. What are the other two?"

"You on the kitchen table. You against the wall."

"I'd like to do naughty things to you in that secret library." Her breathing quickened as his thumbs moved up the sides of her body, grazing her nipples.

"That could happen."

She gasped at his touch. "Touch me."

Every brain cell stopped working. He forced his practical brain through his lips. "What does this exploring involve? Because I don't think I have any condoms. That feels so good."

"We don't need condoms for exploring, right?" She arched into his hands.

"For pregnancy prevention, no." He kissed the valley between her neck and shoulder, relishing the softness of her skin. "I'm snipped."

After his marriage, he never wanted there to be a chance of him fathering a child, but when she didn't stop after he confessed about his vasectomy, he wondered why.

Then she grabbed his ass, and he didn't care.

"I trust you've been tested." Her hands slid up his hips and gripped his back.

"Yes. All good." As vivid as his fantasies were of them, nothing prepared him for the real thing. His senses electrified, he willed himself to stay this side of a caveman.

"Then ... I think ... we should get to know each other a bit more."

The instant her lips touched his, Reynolds wrapped his arms around her waist, inhaling her sweet scent. He brushed his lips against hers. His tongue slid along the seam to coax her mouth open. When it did, he heard her give a slight moan as her fingers threaded through his hair.

How did we get here? Two months ago, I was cursing the foster care system, and now, I'm married with a baby, and my sexy wife is climbing me like a tree. Life is weird.

"What do you want to do, Rey?" She slid down his body, resting on the edge of his bed. Her eyes leveled with his waistband, and she licked her lips. "Because I know what I want to do. To you."

He crawled forward as she lay back. Hovering over her, he appreciated her seductive stare. Running his thumb along her lower lip, he took her in. "I want to make you fall apart."

A hard flush of pink to her cheeks. "Be my guest."

"*Merci.*" His finger traced along her collarbone to the tender pulse point of her neck and he placed a gentle kiss there. Then allowed his fingers to explore her naked breasts before flicking her nipple with his tongue.

The sweet smell of her skin, the silk of her touch pulled him in. Any reservations about keeping things uncomplicated, dissolved.

Gently, he worshipped her body, listened to her gasps as he teased with his tongue. Then Reynolds moved to her unattended side and took her into his mouth.

Susan rested her hand on the back of his head. "Don't

stop."

As if I could. Continuing to lick her nipple, he rolled the other between his thumb and forefinger, feeling it harden and swell. "You are so beautiful, Susan."

"You're not so bad yourself."

"Do you want me to explore you more?" *Please say yes.* If she didn't, he'd take the coldest shower known to mankind.

"Yes, more, but—" She reached down and cupped him. "You need to be explored as well."

"Do I?" *I would love that, but I'd last about two seconds.*

"You're so hard. Thick. Big." Her praises only stroked his ego as her fingers danced along the waistband of his pants before sliding underneath and pushing them down. "And I bet you're delicious."

The thought of her lips around him almost made a very messy situation. He needed to slow things down, but it was the equivalent of trying to stop a fast-moving train on a dime. Instead, he slipped off the bed, kneeled by it, and pulled her toward him. "You first. Lie back."

"Such a gentleman. I'm gonna love being married to you." She leaned back on her elbows as he positioned between her knees. His hands slid up her thighs until they reached the waistband of her shorts. A couple of small pink belly scars momentarily caught his attention, but his lizard brain dismissed the observation. "Anything on under these?"

"Nope." A confident answer.

"Good." He started at her knee, placing kisses up her inner thigh while his thumb traced a similar line up the opposite leg.

Nuzzling the bend where her thigh met her pelvis, he inhaled the sweet scent of her and his mouth watered. "Tell me if this is too much." *Please don't let it be too much.*

"I will. Talk dirty to me."

"Really?" *She's amazing.*

"Really." A wicked smile spread across her face as she watched him. She grabbed a pillow to prop herself up slightly so she could play with her breasts as he explored her.

Reynolds might not have been with many women, but he always appreciated a lover who knew what got her off and had no trouble showing him. "You're so fucking sexy, showing, telling me what you want."

"We learned about each other today," she purred. "What else do you want to know?"

"What else do you want me to do?" So many sexy scenarios tumbled through his brain.

"I like oral, giving and receiving."

"Noted." His fingers inched toward her intimacy, and as controlled as she tried to be, her anticipation hitched her voice.

"I like … um … fingers. I like … creative positions. Impromptu moments. Sometimes restraints or role-play."

"What did I do to deserve you?" As he fanned his fingers over her inner thighs, his thumbs ran up her seam. When Lucy mentioned Susan having a healthy sex life, he really underestimated what she meant. And he couldn't be more thrilled. "Tell me more."

For a moment, her lust shifted to longing. As if his words meant more to her than she could properly explain.

Sitting up, she tenderly kissed him, like she savored the moment for her future memories. "I … like you. A lot."

When she pulled back, he immediately noticed her tears and he panicked. "You okay?"

"I'm wonderful."

Was she going to say she loved me? He shook it off because that was insane. "I like you, too."

Susan smiled and brushed her lips to his. "Now, give me more wonderful, Dr. Reynolds."

Her quick dismissal of her emotions concerned him, but when she lay back, lust swam in her eyes once again.

"More wonderful it is." His thumb slid over her shorts and immediately found her clit. "Do you like that?"

"Yes." The fire in her eyes flickered as she gave him an excited whimper while her fingertips grazed her peaked nipples.

With slow strokes, he teased her over her shorts. His mouth watered to taste her, but would it be too much? "Can I keep exploring?"

"I'll hate you if you stop." The desire on her face told him she wanted him on the most carnal level.

With his thumb still working its magic, his finger moved under the fabric and touched the warmth of her excitement. "There you are."

"I am! Oh … that's … good. More." Susan arched her back when he ran his finger along her, then pushed the material aside. He'd imagined having her sweet taste on his tongue so many times, and now, she was more gorgeous than he could have ever imagined. "Susan, I need to taste you."

"Taste away." The moment his lips met her wanting skin, she gasped, "Oh gosh ... that's ... amazing." She fisted the sheets while his tongue danced, savoring her wetness.

"More?"

"More!"

Resting his hand on her lower belly, he lifted her mons, revealing that perfect bundle of nerves. Instantly, he licked her clit for the first time.

Susan exhaled. "Oh gosh! That's ... that's..."

Reynolds didn't wait for her to elaborate. He put his mouth on her and sucked, savoring the feel, the flavor of her. It was more than he could have imagined, especially when she panted his praises. "Oh ... feels so good ... Reynolds ... so good."

A soft thump and a flash of movement out of the corner of his eye caught a second of his attention. She'd tossed the pillow behind her before arching her hips toward his greedy mouth. "Don't stop eating me."

"Yes, ma'am." Starting at the top of her lips, he dragged the flat of his tongue up her before returning to caress her clit with his tongue and sliding two fingers inside. "Like that?"

A wanting whimper as she watched him feast. "Yes, keep going. Please. Keep going."

His tongue teased, dancing around her bundle of perfection as his fingers moved inside her to a torturously slow tempo. "Still good?"

"Yes. So good. Tell me what you're doing." Her eyes never wavered from his.

"You like that?"

"I like hearing what you want to do to me. How you want to do it to me."

Glad to know she's got a freak flag. As tightly wound as she could be, he worried about this part of their relationship. Of course, he didn't think he'd have to worry about it today, but why question it now?

"You taste so good. I might have to explore you again." As he intimately tongued her, she rolled her nipples between her fingers. "And again."

"And I might have to find out how delicious you are." Her eyes darted down, and she licked her lips.

That alone almost had him climaxing like some randy teen looking at his first pair of boobs. "I bet you're good at it."

"One way to find out." She began to sit up, but he stopped her by kissing her and slowly lowering her to the bed again.

"Wait. Wait. I'm not done with you." Working his way down, he took his time with each needy breast. His fingers slid down her body to find her wetness.

Her hips moved in time with his strokes. "Reynolds, please. I need your tongue on me."

"Absolutely." Licked her sweet honey. Sucked her clit. Knowing she was close, he pushed his sweatpants off his hips and fisted himself as he feasted on her.

Her fingers threaded through his hair as he sucked on her clit. "Oh. Yes! Yes!"

She dug her nails into his shoulders, rocking with his increasing tempo.

His hand pumped as his mouth intimately kissed her, and her words of approval increased their speed.

"Reynolds, I'm … I'm…" She tightened around his fingers, her hips moving faster as he nibbled her with a technique he'd perfected.

"Yes, Reynolds. Yes!" Her muscles gripped his fingers like a vise and bathed them with her orgasm. Her hips thrust and her thighs squeezed around his wrist.

As soon as her grip relaxed, he sat back and boldly stroked himself.

With pink still in her cheeks, she sat up and kissed him without pause, sweeping her tongue into his mouth. She sucked on his bottom lip as her free hand cupped his balls.

He gasped at her eager attention. "Susan. Don't stop."

"Love watching you. So sexy," she coaxed as their hands sped him straight toward his own release.

Leaning in, she whispered as her fingers worked their magic, "Come for me, Reynolds. I want to see you fall apart."

And he did.

Chapter Fifteen

A FTER THEIR UNEXPECTED, but orgasmic explorations, they each visited their bathrooms to clean up.

As the water ran down his body and the endorphins faded, reality set in. *Oh shit.*

The concern circulated in his mind as fatigue got the better of him as he toweled off.

Shit. Shit. Shit!

Was this going to be awkward now? Had they destroyed all the groundwork of the past seven weeks?

Shit. What have I done?

As fantastic as they worked together both in and out of the bedroom, Reynolds needed to keep his head straight. He couldn't ruin it because his dick needed attention. Specifically, her attention. "Breathe, Reynolds. It was consensual. Mutual. And you're married."

With his practical mind solidly in place, he exited his bathroom, fully expecting to find Susan somewhere other than naked in his bed. "Susan?"

She pulled back the covers. "Join me?"

A one-time slip up he could excuse, but this? She was habit-forming. If he were a lesser man, he'd take full advantage of this moment. Take her to bed, pull her close. Relish her scent. Her taste. The feel of her around him.

"Reynolds? Did you want to do some more exploring?" Her siren call invisibly pulled him toward her, but he stopped just short of crawling under the covers. Instead, he sat on the edge of the bed and cupped her face before tenderly kissing her. "I'm going to sleep on the futon in Audrey's room."

"Wait. What?"

"You need sleep."

"Yes, but… You okay?" Concern replaced her fiery-eyed lust.

"I'm great."

She pulled out of his touch. "But…"

"I loved what we did because you're the sexiest woman I've ever been with."

"You can stop right there."

"Wait. Hear me out."

"It's okay. You don't have to explain anything." The strain of sadness in her words almost cut him to the quick as she searched for her shirt that had landed somewhere by his bookshelf. She had it on faster than he could stop her.

He caught her by the arm before she left. "Susan."

She rolled out of his grasp. "What?"

He hated this. He hated they fell into this situation so ass-backward. They couldn't simply date, mess around, or learn about each other, but they didn't have that option and never would. "Susan, I want to crawl in that bed with you. Hear you scream my name again."

"And?" Despite her indifference, her pupils dilated.

He mentally preened at how viscerally she reacted to him. What they just did was beyond his best sex fantasies, but Reynolds wanted more. "I need this, us, to work in every way."

Her brow furrowed. "I want it to work, too. What do you think I'm doing? I'm here to stay. Why are you pushing me away?"

"That's not what I mean to do. I promise."

"Then what do you want? Because I know for sure you want me. That's obvious. And I want you. We want to be a family with Audrey. The three of us. This isn't hard."

As much as he cared about her, the idea of not being a father hurt down to his soul. Long ago, he dreamed of having a large family, big gatherings, a house filled with too many kids to count, but genetics simply didn't work that way. He accepted that, which put him on this path to be a father of one. Now, the perfect woman wanted to parent with him, and when his thoughts didn't originate below the belt, more questions popped up than answers. "When you were picturing a family, how many kids did you imagine having?"

Her forehead furrowed. "Why?"

"Just answer the question, Susan. How many?"

Locking her arms across her chest, she clenched her jaw. "Honestly? A bunch."

For whatever reason, her honest answer calmed him. He approached, resting his hands on her shoulders. "We can't have a bunch."

"I get that, and I accept that." She took a step back as if she planned to bolt for the exit.

"You told me you were fine not having a biological child."

"And I told you not to ask me about it again." Tears ran down her face and he tried to understand her.

"Susan. Please tell me."

"Tell you what?"

"Why are you really okay not having a biological child?"

Her bottom lip quivered as her voice cracked. "Why can't I simply be fine with it? You got a vasectomy to keep from having bio kids. We each made a choice."

"Because my mother loved the idea of being a parent, but when it wasn't what she hoped it would be, she bailed."

"I'm not going anywhere." She stepped out of his reach, which only frustrated him.

What isn't she telling me? "This is probably my *only* chance to be a father. After everything I've been through, if this falls through, I won't try again. My heart can't take it."

His confession appeared to soften her angst, but then he screwed it up. "I *need* this to work for me to be a dad. To be her dad because I know I'd be amazing. And if I have to choose between her and anyone else..." *Shit.* He did it again. Focused on fatherhood more.

"Ah, I see. This is *truly* only for the baby." Disappointment hung thick on her every word. "I get that you want to be a father, but I wouldn't have entered this lightly if *I* didn't want to be a mother. To parent with *you*."

"Yes, of course. I didn't expect any less. But you're giving up the chance—"

"Reynolds!" She adamantly shook her head, her cheeks pink. "Please stop telling me I'm giving up anything."

"But, Susan—"

"No. Stop right there! You've been at this longer. Had a situation that brought you on this path far before we even knew each other existed." Even as fire flickered in her eyes, sorrow hid behind her anger. "I want to be a mother. I want to be here. I want this to work, but you're right. I overstepped when I initiated our exploring expedition. I should have considered how much is at stake here and slowed us down."

He hated this part of dating or whatever the hell they were doing. The uncertainty, the guessing, the imbalance of emotional practicality versus physical attraction. Holding his hand out to her, he said, "Susan, sit with me."

When tears fell, she only seemed to be more annoyed. She angrily wiped them away as she sat on the bed. "You don't have to explain it, Reynolds. I get it."

"You get what exactly?" It took everything he had not to pull her into his arms and comfort her in every way he knew how.

The fierceness in her response now morphed into insecurity as she pulled her knees to her chest. "It's stupid."

"Tell me anyway." He learned that response from his Audrey because *no matter how much you insist something isn't stupid to you, it could still feel very stupid to them.*

Her elegant fingers swept through her hair, allowing it to slowly layer across her shoulders. "I understand about not screwing this up, but part of me thinks if I were sexier—"

"I'm gonna stop *you* right there." Frustration got the better of him, sending him to stand. "You're making me nuts, Susan."

"The feeling is mutual. Being this close to you all the time, not doing anything, even hugging or any sort of physical affection, it's not going to work. People need contact. They need touch. And care. Even if it's simply respectful gestures and great hugs. And kissing."

"You're right. I will do better." *And pull the majority of my thoughts above my beltline.*

"There's no denying we've got major chemistry after all that amazing ... exploring."

"Even before. Explosive levels of chemistry." If he had his way, he'd spend every day making her fall apart in the best ways.

All you had to was pull your brain out of your pants.

Keep your hands to yourself.

Not wear sweats.

"I enjoyed the hell out of being near you, but that's not the only thing making me crazy. The uncertainty of the adoption. What if it doesn't happen? Where does that leave us?"

She wrapped her arms around herself. "Is that another way of saying I'm not who you want if I'm not a mother? Am I not ... enough?"

"What? No!"

The hurt in her voice told him someone said those very words to her. Words meant to cut her down. Wound her.

The mere idea of it boiled Reynolds's blood. "Susan, you're more than enough. You're ... you're..."

"What?" she snapped as though she'd reached the end of her self-assurance rope. "I'm what exactly?"

He pulled her into his arms. "You're everything I've ever wanted."

She began to push him away, but he gently held her close. "I don't know what *everything* means. Seems like a lot of pressure."

He hated himself for inciting her insecurities, but he wanted *all* of what they could be together. "You're the most gorgeous, intelligent, fantastic, driven woman I've ever met."

Tilting her head up, she looked him straight in the eyes, as if she were deciding if he was being honest or throwing bullshit. "But I'm not sexy enough—"

"Susan! Do you have any idea how hard it is for me to keep my hands to myself when I'm around you every day?"

"The way you said that, I'd guess about as much as I have trouble keeping my hands off you." She snorted as if the joke were far funnier in her head.

Tucking his pride away, he pointed to his pants. "There's a reason I can't wear sweats or scrubs around you."

Her eyes darted to his crotch, and she bit her lip, the longing back. "They're like the sweatpants of truth, then?"

Dammit, why does she have to throw a superhero pun at me right now? As if I couldn't want the woman more.

After a quick kiss on her forehead, he put space between them. "I've had so many dreams about you in my bed. And on the kitchen table. And in that library."

"Especially in that library. Maybe in the loft?" The corner of her mouth twitched, then spread to a coy smile. "So much room up there."

"In the shower." He leaned forward, but then held firm.

A nervous laugh escaped her while she slid down to her side and curled up with one of his pillows, like some beautiful seductress who tempted him far too easily. "Shower's fun."

"I don't know who hurt you before, but everything they said to you was bullshit." Kneeling next to the bed, he cupped her face. "Please hear me. I need it to work between us."

"You mean co-parenting effectively? I get it. I'll keep my hands to myself."

"No!" *The woman could be too practical for her own good.* "I want us to be a family."

"I thought we were."

"A *real* family. Not platonic co-parenting. Not married only on paper. Not staring at a calendar family of upcoming events."

"You mean *after* the adoption. More than … more than sex?"

"Yes. Sex. Way more than sex." His heart thudded in his throat at his confession. "And way more sex."

Her eyes went wide with understanding. "Oh, you're talking about—about … umm…"

"All of it."

"All. Of. It." The lust that swam in Susan's eyes only moments ago suddenly evaporated.

And fear replaced it.

What just happened? "Susan, are you okay? You look like a scared deer."

"No, no. I'm fine. Ab-ab-solutely. I hear you. You want all of it, meaning you want all of me." She wrung her hands.

"That's usually how it goes."

"Not usually."

He sat at the end of the bed. "Talk to me."

"It's just the sad backstory of it all, Reynolds. Nothing worth mentioning."

"Someday you have to tell me all of it."

"What for? It doesn't change anything."

"Because I want to know who to thank."

Her forehead furrowed. "What do you mean?"

"Who was too fucking stupid to appreciate everything about you. I need to thank those poor, selfish bastards for allowing me to have you in my life. In Audrey's life."

A small fuss from the other room.

"Speaking of Audrey." She rubbed her temples and began to stand. "I'll get her."

"I've got her. You get some sleep. You've got a new job coming up and I'm off for a few days." He gently kissed her cheek, but before he pulled away, he whispered, "I'm gonna be real clear about this. It's taking everything I have to not take you up on your offer to crawl back into that bed again. But I want more."

"Got it. You want the entire happily-ever-after, rom-com story."

"Every word of it."

Chapter Sixteen

"**H**OW ARE YOU doing?" Lori glanced back and forth between Reynolds and Susan as they sat at the kitchen table. She drank out of the mug his grandmother made her long ago. "You're at the halfway point. Twelve weeks down. Twelve to go."

"Day by day." Reynolds rubbed the sleep out of his eyes. His noon-to-midnight shift ended at three this morning. He managed only four hours of sleep before Lori arrived.

He hoped to get some rest before softball practice this afternoon.

Lucy moved him to pitching and he'd been doing extra upper-body workouts to get ready. The workouts also helped him expel the nervous energy from staying relatively platonic with Susan for the past five weeks.

They hadn't let things get as heated, but they also hadn't revisited their wanting-it-all conversation. *You're such a dumbass. You could be working off so much extra energy every day, but you had to go scare her.*

"We're figuring it out. Our siblings have been lifesavers." Susan held Audrey, who greedily sucked down a bottle. "She really loves this new formula."

Lori crossed her legs and settled in. "How's the new job?"

"It's good. Not as many patients as we hoped by now, but it's the summer. More due dates in the fall."

"Right. Winter holidays give us a baby boom in the fall. How many babies have you delivered since you've arrived?"

"A few a week."

"I heard Gabby delivered her and Kyle's baby last week."

"She did." The local manager of Main Street Diner had lived in Marietta for less than a few years, but she immediately gained the attention of local firefighter Kyle Cavazos, who also posed for the fundraising calendar.

Lori clapped her hands together. "Enough small talk. You're halfway there."

Susan feigned shock as Audrey finished off the last ounce of her breakfast. "Seems like we started all this yesterday. Goodness, that was fast, little girl."

"It's racing by and I'm cautiously optimistic."

Worry pushed Reynolds to drain his coffee mug in record time. "Seems if someone from either of their families wanted her, they would have stepped up by now."

Lori winced. "Not necessarily. Sometimes family members wait until the termination of parental rights. Then they step in."

"That's messed up." Susan gently patted Audrey's back.

"It is, but some relatives don't want to deal with the parents' form of crazy. They wait until the adult has no rights. No stake in the game. *Then* they step in."

Reynolds considered adding some whiskey to his next cup of coffee. "But you don't see this happening here, do you?"

"It's not impossible, but it's unlikely as all first-degree relatives stated they aren't interested in raising a baby."

"First degree?"

"Sorry. Brothers, sisters, parents, grandparents."

"I see." A thick silence filled the room as the growl of a motorcycle gunned its engine. Kids played in Bramble Park across the street. The very park they took Audrey to every day.

"Let's say the father does come back. What then?" Susan asked the question that Reynolds simply couldn't, but the worry in her eyes didn't go unnoticed.

Lori pursed her lips. "It can go a few different ways. He comes back, doesn't want to have anything to do with her, signs the papers. Walks away. He could want her back."

"He's a college kid, right? How is he going to raise a baby? This should be a no-brainer."

"He would need to show he can take care of Audrey, and have support. His genetics will trump everything, so it sets the bar very low."

Audrey let out a large belch that surprised all of them.

"Goodness!" Susan mocked her surprise as she continued to pat Audrey's back. "What can we do to sway things in our favor?"

Lori let out a long breath, and Reynolds already knew the answer. "Nothing."

"What do you mean nothing? That can't be right. What about the nighttime feeds, diaper changes, being with her constantly since she came out?"

"Don't shoot the messenger, but as a foster-prospective adoptive parent, that's your job. You don't get extra points for doing your job." Lori closed her eyes for a few moments as if she were gearing herself up to give them more bad news.

Susan glared, but the anger wasn't meant for Lori. "It's not a job. It's parenting, and he gets a higher rank because he tossed a few seeds in the ring?"

"Genetics will rank the highest when the court is making its decision as the foster care goals are always to reunite the children with their family."

"We're her family."

"Not genetically. If the father was a member of any Native American tribe, the Indian Child Welfare Act would have kicked in, but that's not the case here."

"He takes off then he wanders back in, he gets dibs, and we're left with what? Nothing?" The threat of Audrey leaving tortured him daily, but it wasn't the only thing that concerned him.

Since their heavy exploration session a month ago, Susan and he managed to keep their passions in check. He constantly thought about her amazing body all the damned time, but he wanted more than great sex. He also wanted her to talk to him more about her life and what she'd been through. The difficulties she faced and triumphed over.

And why she doesn't want to have a biological baby. As much as he hated coming back to that, he needed to understand her reasons. What if she decided five or ten years down the road adoption didn't fill that mothering need? Or she left with someone she could get pregnant with?

After he told her about his neglectful parents, he hoped she'd follow suit with baring her soul, but she closed down tighter than a steel drum.

The steady sound of Lori tapping her finger on the rim of her coffee mug pulled him out of his thoughts.

"One thing I don't think they stress enough in foster care and adoption training is how to find a common thread with the bio parents." Lori took a long drink.

"What do you mean?" After a few more good belches from Audrey, Susan laid the baby in her bouncy chair on the floor.

Odin wandered into the kitchen and took watch at the edge of the chair, an air of indifference on his furry face.

Audrey immediately noticed him and excitedly babbled.

"There are situations where the parents feel pressured to keep the child. By their families, their friends, their church, society, community."

"That's a great reason to keep a baby. Because someone told you to." Susan locked her arms across her chest.

Dread sat like a rock in Reynolds's gut. As much as he hated this conversation, they couldn't ignore it. "Are you saying the parents can be convinced to relinquish?"

Lori moved her mug away from her. "That's absolutely not what I'm saying. Not convinced. I never want any bio parent to feel manipulated into relinquishing custody. Ever. Still, there are times when a bond or common thread between the bio family and the prospective adoptive parents is found. An understanding. A sign. Whatever you want to call it."

"Both wanting a child but only one set of parents is able to take care of her isn't enough of a common thread?" Susan's voice hardened, her mama-bear side peeking out.

That only made him want her more. "You're suggesting we figure out some sort of overlap between us and the bio father?"

"There are layers of emotions here. There's no rhyme or reason for why people make the decisions they do, but yes. Should he come back, that's exactly what I'm saying." Lori nodded before taking the last swig of her coffee.

"Get him to understand why he needs to relinquish for the good of *himself*." Even with his exhausted brain, Reynolds understood the monumental task at hand, and he hated it.

Why can't people just do the responsible thing?

With a long exhale, Lori braced her hands on her thighs. "Be very careful, friend. This conversation needs to happen organically. You can't force it."

"How hard can it be to convince a college kid with no income or a way of supporting himself, and left in the first damned place, to sign the papers?"

"Don't fool yourself. Every adoption is different and anything that feels forced can easily push people in the other direction. But before we worry, the father has to show up. So far, he's evaded any contact." Lori tapped her watch. "I've got to go. Want to check on a few more families before the crazy of July Fourth weekend begins."

She gave Audrey several cheek kisses. "Bye, cutie. I'll see you next time."

Audrey responded by drooling on her hand and kicking her feet in a feeble attempt to get closer to that one-eyed cat that hardly left her side.

As she walked Lori to the door, Susan sucked on her bottom lip, an endearing twitch when she needed to figure out a problem. "But we're three months in and there's not been a peep. It's promising."

"If he hasn't come forward by now, it's less likely. I can't promise he won't."

"I understand. Bernie's doing okay?"

"Yes. She's been staying with her best friend, Ben, and his parents. They are taking good care of her." Lori pulled out her keys and her sunglasses.

"She's safe, then?" That gave Reynolds some relief. The girl deserved to be around people who gave a shit about her.

"She's heading back to school in the fall."

"That's good news." Susan's thin smile mimicked his own worry. "Your honesty helps, Lori, and I'm so glad Bernie is finding her feet. As for the rest of it, I really don't want to hear if Audrey would leave."

"Hang in there, friends. Right now, the odds are in your favor." The social worker smiled.

"Thank you." Susan yawned.

Reynolds rested his hands on Susan's shoulders. He meant for it to be an encouraging gesture, but all it did was antagonize the fact they'd respected each other's intimate physical boundaries. And it sucked. "You're the best."

Lori placed her hand on the doorknob but paused. "Hey, guys. I appreciate all the dedication and by-the-book parenting. You're a social worker's dream, but I have to ask. Have you two had any time alone?"

Susan shrugged off his touch. "What? No. Of course not."

The pitch of her protest triggered Reynolds to snort a laugh. "Sorry. It's been crazy here."

Lori's eyes darted between the two of them, and a hint of amusement threatened to curl the corner of her mouth. "No, I mean, alone time as either a night out for the two of you or even each of you having time to yourselves."

Susan nodded in understanding. "I thought you meant…"

"Hey, whatever. As long as it's consensual and you're both happy, I'm good. You are married after all. You're allowed date nights together."

Gathering his wits about him, Reynolds sighed. "Either one or both of us has always been with Audrey. Even when people offer to help, they come here."

"No babysitter? Had a night out? Or had her spend the night with one of your siblings?"

"We can do that?" The lift in Susan's voice indicated the idea of alone time very much interested her.

Lori continued, "Absolutely. All of them passed background checks. They aren't going to abscond her."

"That helps so much, Lori." Susan put her arms out to initiate a hug. "I thought we had to do this all on our own, not let her out of our sight until the adoption was final."

Reynolds's constant state of fatigue didn't hold such a grip on him as he knew they had a bit of leeway. "That's good news."

"You're not robots. You're human. Everyone needs a break now and then. It's healthy to get some space and pampering with a spa afternoon or a nice dinner out. Or whatnot." With a quick wink and a kiss on his cheek, Lori opened the door.

The afternoon smelled of summer. A perfect day to be outside and maybe sleep on a blanket at the park across the street. Or in the porch swing.

"Give yourselves a date night. It's important because every couple needs time alone. Time to simply connect. Even platonically." Lori's eyebrow raise indicating she didn't believe they'd kept things simple.

Alone. As stoic as he'd been, being alone with Susan could easily test the limits of his restraint. *Especially when she snuggles up to me like right now.*

Her arm slid around his waist as they walked out to the front porch to see Lori off. "Thanks again, Lori. Day by day, right?"

She quickly descended the steps. "Almost to your happily ever after, friends. Keep the faith."

Chapter Seventeen

S USAN SLOWLY STIRRED her untouched coffee for the tenth time. "I'm seriously freaking out here."

"It's about damned time." That all-knowing smirk of her brother's, spread across his face.

"Stop it, Peter. Reynolds wants a happily-ever-after kind of family. What am I supposed to do with that?"

After Lori's goodbyes and encouraging them to have a night out, maybe alone time, Reynolds excused himself for a much-needed nap.

For an hour, Susan attempted to calm five-weeks of pent-up nerves by staying busy, but decided a walk outside would do the trick. She strapped Audrey to her chest and powerwalked down the street and ended up at Lucy's house.

When Susan arrived, Peter and Edmund were loading up the equipment. As much as Susan didn't want her brothers involved, her concerns poured out anyway.

"Like a real marriage, happily-ever-after kind of forever family?" Peter's face scrunched up like it did when something confused the shit out of him. "And you're freaking out? Most people would be thrilled to hear this."

"You think I don't know that, Peter?" Susan abandoned

her coffee to search Lucy's cabinets. "Do you have any brandy? Or tequila? Or arsenic?"

Edmund played peekaboo with Audrey. "I guess that answers my question about if you two are having sex yet."

"We aren't having sex." Not the traditional kind. But damn she wanted to.

Five weeks ago, his gallant confession about his attraction to her practically incinerated all her panties, if she'd been wearing any. Made her want him even more. Until then, she didn't think her craving for him could get more intense. At this rate, she'd run out of batteries before the end of the summer.

"Okay, explain to me again, why aren't you having sex?" Lucy cocked her head.

Turning to face her three wide-eyed siblings, she immediately regretted admitting her situation. "I told all of you. This is a practical…"

"Logical. Responsible," they answered in unison.

"What's logical or practical about sex?" Edmund laughed as he made a face at Audrey. "It's passionate and unhinged at times. Nothing rational about it. That's why it's fun. Irrational. Crazy. And sometimes outside."

"Outside? That's specific."

"Why do you think I own property outside of town?"

"Are you serious?" Susan laughed despite her nuclear stress levels.

Audrey kicked her feet at her uncle's enthusiastic commentary as Lucy sat back in her chair and crossed her arms, her mouth pursed in thought.

"Do you have any alcohol?" Susan hoped to numb her panic before it became all-consuming.

After three failed engagements, Susan accepted the white-picket-fence fairy-tale ending wouldn't happen for her, but then Reynolds showed up and complicated everything.

Now she feared losing it all, and that idea hurt worse than breaking all three engagements combined.

Lucy pointed to the far cabinet. "You do everything with a purpose. We should trust that. Right, guys?"

Peter laced up his sneakers, his jaw set in annoyance. "Susan, I'm worried about you."

"Why?" But she honestly wasn't interested in his answer.

"You and Reynolds did this all backward."

"Don't I know it."

"I mean, you have Audrey and she's wonderful." He waved to his niece, and she babbled something important.

"But?"

"You always wanted a big family."

Oh, I do not like where he's going with this. "And?"

His lips thinned, and he exhaled as if he didn't want to say it. "Is only having her going to be enough?"

"Yes."

"Why do you have to stir the pot, Pete?" Edmund rolled his eyes.

Throwing his hands up in frustration, Peter continued. "It's a fair question. Susan, I love that you're happy. I love seeing you three together, but is that enough? Don't you want a baby of your own?"

"Audrey is my own." *At least right now she is.*

"You know what I mean, Susan. I respect *his* choice to adopt, considering his genetics—"

Susan's insides clenched. "Wait. How do you know about his genetics?"

"He brought it up. We talked about it at work the other night when it was slow."

"I could strangle you right now." Susan found a small bottle of Kahlua. She unscrewed the top and debated on whether to add it to her coffee, drink it from the bottle, or inject it straight into her veins. She chose the coffee to see where it led from there.

"You respect his genetics, but not my decision, my choice not to get pregnant?" *I should have just injected it into my carotid.*

"You're my sister. It's different." Peter zipped up his gym bag with enough force that it pinched his finger. "Dammit."

Lucy didn't miss a beat. "Band-Aids. Third drawer left of the sink."

Susan fumed at her brother's response. "Please explain yourself, because there always seems to be an entirely different set of rules for me than there is for the three of you."

"Whoa, whoa, whoa!" Edmund put up his hands. "Don't get mad at me. I think Audrey's great. I like Reynolds. Nate takes some getting used to, but Jade has a piece-of-shit brother. In comparison, Nate's not bad."

"That's putting it mildly." Lucy raised her eyebrows at the mention of Jade's brother, Junior, who presently served time for grand theft auto and manslaughter.

After he stole a high-end BMW a few Labor Days ago, he

decided to test its top speed but ended up plowing into the back of a car parked by the side of the road.

He instantly killed a well-loved local, Harry Monroe. Then Junior hid the car on Jade's property until she discovered it and turned him in.

"I am so glad he's locked up, Edmund." Susan checked the bottle for how much was in it and if it would be enough to help her forget this conversation. "When I heard about the hell he gave you and Jade before they arrested him, I was worried sick."

"Don't worry now. He's not getting out in this lifetime." Edmund started a game of patty-cake with Audrey consisting of him doing pretty much all the work and her drooling on herself.

She squealed in delight.

Even with the joyous baby noises, Peter scowled like he sucked a super-tart lemon. "Susan, I love what you're doing for this girl's baby."

"Her name is Audrey and she's mine. Ours." *After I empty this bottle of Kahlua, I'm going to smash it over his head.*

"Fine. Whatever you want to call it."

"It's called foster/adoption. Or designated custody. If you're going to shit all over my life choices, have the respect to shit all over the correct terminology." Her fury shook down to her fingertips and Peter's thick arrogance only antagonized it.

He put his hands up in surrender. "Hear me out. I'm concerned that if this doesn't pan out, you're going to be heartbroken. I don't want that for you. Again."

For a moment, a sliver of sanity took hold. "Neither do I."

Lucy braced her hands on her thighs. "Switching gears, I'm more concerned that the father hasn't signed off than I am about this happily ever after possibility. Is there no one who can find this guy? Make sure he relinquishes?"

"Lori came by this morning. She's doing the best she can. Believe me, Lucy, I stare at the calendar all the time. I'm afraid to plan anything past the first week of October because I don't want to raise our hopes." She added a few drops of Kahlua to her coffee. Then added a few more.

Peter slapped a Band-Aid on his wounded finger. "We all deserve to find someone special. I do hope this works out for all of you."

His dry compassion derailed her frustration. Even with all the chaos they navigated, when it came down to it, they all looked out for each other. Wanted each other to be happy.

"But, Susan—"

"Please stop. How I find my happy is none of your business. It's my choice to be with someone who does not want a biological child."

"What about you?"

"What about me?"

"If it does work and you adopt her, wonderful. I will love her, but you're stuck in this *practical* situation. What happens in five or ten years when you wish you had another baby? Or find else someone you don't want to be so practical with—"

Her stomach twisted. When Reynolds told her he never planned to have a bio child, she tucked away her infertility situation, never planning to tell him or anyone, because it wouldn't change anything.

But the more Peter pushed, the closer to the edge of confession Susan inched. "I'm not *stuck* in any situation, Peter."

"Not having sex with the man you're raising a child with is a practical long-term situation, then?"

"We *will* have sex. We're on our timeline." Her hands shook so much, she didn't trust herself to pick up her mug without spilling it.

"As tightly wound as you are, I think it might be *time* to have sex with your husband."

"I think it's nice you've waited this long, but yeah. Y'all need to get nuts." Edmund placed his gym bag by the front door with the softball equipment.

"Thank you for your compliment and encouragement, Edmund." *And yeah. The first chance I get to taste him, I'm gonna make his knees buckle.*

Thinking about their one slip up had her panting at the idea of it happening again. And again. She added more Kahlua to her untouched coffee.

Lucy's phone beeped and she sent a quick text. "I hope the best thing possible happens."

Her two younger siblings' input helped alleviate some of the tension in the room, until she glanced over, and her body immediately stiffened. "What?"

Peter's lips thinned like they did when he struggled to hold in a strong retort, but certainly wouldn't. "It's reasonable to wait until you're ready, considering the circumstances, but when you find someone else who you can have a baby with—"

All she saw was red. "If you don't want to support me, that's fine, Peter. Despite the fact, I've supported you about a thousand times over. No questions asked. Even when you discovered you had kids you never knew about."

"Come on. This is different. So far out of your normal."

"Of course, it's different *for me*. It's because I'm not the same normal as all of you. As everyone else. Right?" No truer words had been spoken.

"That's not what I said."

"It kind of sounds like you did." Edmund shrugged.

"Whose side are you on?"

Audrey kicked her feet several times before interesting noises began emanating from her.

"That can't be good." Lucy leaned away.

"I'm on the side of whoever doesn't have to take care of whatever is heading for that diaper today." Edmund scooted his chair back more than an arm's length.

Peter scooped up a wayward softball and dumped it into the equipment bag. "We still need to talk about this."

"No, we don't." Taking a long drink of her cold, spiked coffee, Susan cringed.

With a hard jerk, Peter zipped the bag closed, this time, avoiding injuring himself. "For someone who's always thinking ahead, you're not being very *practical or logical or responsible* about this."

That's. It! Susan slammed the pantry door so hard, it

popped right back open. "Right, because I always have to be the practical one. The one who *never* gets to cut loose or go off the rails or do something for no other reason than she simply wants to. Everyone else needs me to be a constant so everyone else gets to do whatever they want."

"What the hell is going on with you? Ever since you got here, you've acted weird."

"I don't have to explain anything to you, Peter! You're not my father." Angry tears ran down her face. She hated that an accident so long ago kept taking things away from their family. That one cruel act hurt so many for so long.

"Give it a rest, guys." Lucy stood between them, something she never needed to do before. She pointed to her brothers. "You two are going to miss your batting practice times. Thomas and Reynolds will meet you there. I need a strong stand against the ICU tomorrow."

Red-faced, Peter left without another word, and Edmund tapped Audrey's foot as he prepared to leave. "Bye, cutie. Remember, I'm your favorite uncle."

The baby cooed, then farted.

"Good luck with that." Edmund made a quick exit.

Susan's entire body trembled with anger.

How dare he decide anything for my life!

Now he's concerned?

Where was he when I needed help?

When we needed help?

"Sit." Lucy pointed to a chair.

More tears pricked at the backs of her eyelids, but Susan couldn't lose it here. As the truth of her secret bubbled to the surface, for the first time in her life, Susan didn't want to confide in her siblings.

She wanted to confess the entire awful truth to only one person. And he wasn't here.

If she gained the courage to confess it all, she risked losing everything. She simply couldn't stand another soul-crushing failure, but she had to tell him. Soon.

"Susan?" Lucy's gentle voice pulled Susan away from mainlining her disgusting coffee.

With her heart pounding in her throat, Susan rubbed her hands on her thighs. "Sorry, I yelled like that."

"Don't be. You're long overdue for an outburst, and Peter's sticking his nose where he shouldn't." Lucy poured out the contents of the mug.

The words sat on the tip of her tongue, but Susan did what she'd done since the day their lives shifted sideways. She deflected to make it easier for everyone else. "I'm sure you're confused about all this."

"That's putting it mildly. I mean, out of the four of us, you were the least likely to make a decision this … this—"

"Irrational?" Susan hissed as she locked her tears up.

"I was going to say impetuous, but yes, irrational might be a better fit."

As hard as Lucy's honesty hit, Susan admitted this decision was irrational. Impetuous. And possibly irresponsible, but Susan made a promise to Reynolds and sweet Audrey.

An opportunity like this would be next to zero and the man *deserved* to be a father. "Reynolds and I, we have a plan."

"Of course you do. When have you never had a plan?" Her phone buzzed and she quickly answered a text.

In fact, co-parenting with a smart, compassionate, sexy-as-hell man who kept invading her dreams and shower time was damned near close to a perfect plan as Susan would ever hope to find. "We'll officially adopt her and, at that point, reevaluate."

"Reevaluate what? Having sex with each other?" Despite her holding her mug in front of her mouth, Lucy's smile could be seen to her irises.

Why Susan ever tried to put up a front when it came to her sister, she had no clue. "I've always done the right thing, the logical, practical, responsible thing."

Lucy nodded. "Far more than should ever have been expected of you."

"It's what was needed at the time."

"No. You gave up your entire childhood. Every teenage milestone, a normal social life, everything to make sure Edmund, Mom, Peter, and I were taken care of."

"Lucy, I didn't—"

"Let me finish." Lucy did not attempt to hide her emotions. "Mom dumped way more on you than she should have. You gave up too much to parent all of us. To support us. I don't think Peter understands the extent of it because he was at college a couple of years after the accident."

"He did get a part-time job to help, but once he turned eighteen, some of our benefits went away."

"You stayed up late every month to fill out all the paperwork so we could keep what benefits we had."

"You knew about that?"

"Yes. I know you talked to our teachers each week, that you quietly signed us up for free meals at school." Lucy swallowed hard. "That you gave up the chance to go to medical school."

Lucy's statement hit Susan harder than if her sister punched her in the stomach. "How did you know about that?"

Audrey yawned, tightened her belly, and passed gas multiple times. Susan cringed at the disaster that was soon to come.

Like the disaster of not confessing everything?

Of keeping all these secrets?

Of fighting with your brother over twenty-year-old trauma?

Lucy tapped her sister's hand. "You left an acceptance letter out on the counter one time. There had to be more."

She could deny it, but Lucy would call her out. "Yes, there were several more."

"What was your MCAT score?"

Pressing her fingers to her forehead, Susan whispered, "Thirty-five."

"You scored higher than all of us and you didn't go? Why?"

"I only applied to see if I had what it took to get in. And as much as I wanted to go, nursing secured a high-paying, *local* job much faster."

Lucy rubbed her stomach as if the conversation hurt. "The only reason none of us fell off the deep end was because of your extreme discipline and constant sacrifices."

"It's what needed to be done—"

"Stop. You did way more than what was needed." Taking her sister's hand, Lucy continued, "I don't know what you're doing right now, but what I do know is when you look at him, your eyes light up like the Fourth of July. I've *never* seen you so happy. Not with anyone."

"He's certainly something." *He's everything.*

"And the way he looks at you. His gaze could melt icebergs. He's seriously hooked."

Heat flushed across her body, and she giggled. "He's pretty hot."

"If this illogical or impractical situation makes you so over-the-moon stupidly happy then I—*we* will support you, one hundred percent. You've earned a bit of untapped pandemonium." Lucy pulled Susan into her arms and hugged her tight.

Her sister's kindhearted encouragement punched a hole in Susan's armor. Tears of pain and sadness freely flowed. "When did you get so grown up?"

"It happens to all of us eventually." Giving her sister a sweet smile, Lucy added, "Maybe, one day, you'll feel comfortable enough to tell me why you needed to cancel your weddings. Walk away from him, any of them, so quickly."

"Perhaps." The muscles in Susan's neck untangled with Lucy's unpressured request.

Outside the kitchen window, a pine tree's branches of rich green needles momentarily hid a cute black, brown, and white bird. It sang for a few seconds before flying away.

"I am worried about you."

And I thought we were doing so well. "Don't start."

"There's more to you being here than you're confessing, and it's eating you up inside."

Shaking her head, Susan refused to have this conversation. Not here. Not now. If she said it out loud, it cemented in. Made it all true. "It doesn't matter what it is. Talking about it won't change anything."

"I disagree."

Jumping to her feet, Susan put some space between them. "Fine. Disagree. But I'm not going to talk to you, any of you, about it."

Lucy shrugged as if Susan's curt response hadn't bothered her. "Then talk to *him.*"

"Why would I do that? So he can look at me differently? Reject me? Break my heart?" She held back a sob until it hurt. "Lucy, I've tried love three times and it's failed terribly. Crushed me."

Broke me. After all the words of endearment and love everlasting, the venomous words about something she couldn't control, couldn't change, cut her deep.

"You've had a rough run of it, but it won't always fail." Lucy clasped her hands in front of her. "To be fair, I don't think any of those situations, those guys were your true love."

"True love? You sound like Fiona from *Shrek.*"

"I love Fiona. She has amazing hair."

Audrey babbled and sucked her on her fingers.

Fatigue soaked into her every pore. "Lucy, I don't even

know what true love is or if I'll ever find it. I do like what I have with Reynolds right now. If that's all I get, then it's enough." *Of course, after this adoption is final, if I don't get my hands on him, heads are gonna roll.*

As she always did, Lucy answered with kind honesty. "The feelings for those other three fiancés are nowhere close to what you have for Reynolds. I can see it in your eyes. This time, it's so different."

"I'm always different." *Predictable different. Scary different. Almost perfect different. Absolutely not perfect different. Ruined different.*

"No. You're always amazing."

Resting her hand on her belly failed to settle her stomach. "Lucy, it hurts so much when it goes wrong."

Audrey rubbed her eyes and her stomach gurgled.

"But you're willing to adopt with someone you barely know? I mean, don't get me wrong, everything I've learned about Reynolds is great." Her phone buzzed. "Come on, guys. Keep it straight. Edmund at first. Reynolds pitches."

Susan smirked at her sister's competitiveness. "He's wonderful and sexy and damned near perfect, but I can't mess this up. There's a child to think about. It would be completely irresponsible of me to allow anything to threaten this baby's chances. Or his opportunity of becoming a father." *Or my opportunity to become a mother.*

"I agree, but what if—"

"Lucy, please don't *what if* this. I can't..." *I don't think I can repair my heart again.* Suddenly, oxygen wouldn't effectively enter her lungs.

"Susan, breathe." Lucy grabbed her sister's hands, sandwiching them between her own.

"I can't—" Leaning away, Susan fought not to lose her shit, but Lucy's grip stayed firm.

"Hear me out. Please."

Susan didn't want Lucy's upbeat rebuttal because it would make complete and unarguable sense. "Fine."

"What if you allowed all of this to happen just as it should? Without trying to control an ounce of it?"

An incredulous laugh escaped her. "Do you have a brain tumor? Have you met me?"

Putting her hand up in surrender, Lucy cautiously answered. "Listen. To. Me. I'm not telling you to go have sex with Reynolds right now, although, if you did, I would totally understand it."

"Stop it. You're making me insane." *And rationalizing my irrational lust.*

"But—but wait. What if you decided to let your heart lead this time? For the first time?"

"I've loved people before."

"That's not what I said. Let your heart *lead*. Not your brain, where you rationalize your feelings for someone and call it love."

Susan's pulse quickened. The sweet suggestion simultaneously thrilled and terrified her. "Lucy, you're asking way too much of me."

"Yes, but Susan, you've tried for so long to control every single moment of your life. To make sure all of us had a chance. Now it's your turn." Lucy wrapped her arms around her sister. "Let your heart take the wheel and let us carry the heavy stuff."

"What if it's a disaster?"

"It won't be."

"What if you're wrong?"

"I'm not."

"What if—" Susan choked back a sob and buried her face in her sister's auburn hair. "What if I fall in love with him?"

"I think you already have. Stop fighting it. Stop searching for reasons to deny you love him." Lucy's calm permeated into Susan's soul, offering her a moment of much-needed peace. "Trust him. Love him. Let him love you both and allow the good stuff to happen to your sweet little family."

"None of it makes sense."

Lucy laughed. "Love never makes sense. I fell in love with Thomas when I stitched up his face. We were up for the same job, and I barely knew him. It didn't matter. Cupid hit me anyway."

Nodding against her sister's shoulder, Susan desperately wanted to be guided by the passion of love rather than by the hard edge of logic. To give up her heartbreak and bad memories. To walk away from everything that screwed her over.

Still, her sister always made things sound really good. And possible. "Why do you make it all sound so perfect, Lucy?"

"Because, Susan … it can be."

Chapter Eighteen

HOURS AT THE batting cage and team practice loosened every muscle in his overstressed and sex-starved body. On his way to his car, Reynolds couldn't wait to get home, take a shower, eat, and fall asleep to fantasize about Susan.

Maybe soon they could agree to more than quick hugs, fist bumps, and cheek kisses.

He waved to Lucy and Thomas as they drove out of the lot, but then Peter called out, stopping him before he reached his car. "Hey, Reynolds! Can I talk to you for a second?"

That simple question led to a half-hour conversation, sending Reynolds home in a much different mood than he was when he finished his last pitch.

Guilt hung heavy in his heart along with a lot of questions for one afternoon. Questions he'd ignored for too long.

"How was practice?" With her bare feet kicked up on the armrest of the couch, Susan laid a book on her lap.

Audrey played in her bouncy chair, the rattles near her feet.

Nanny cat Odin sat next to his ward, a look of indifference on his face even though the feline had yet to let the baby out of his sight since she came home.

Then Audrey kicked just right, sending the rattles into a spin. Her eyes widened and her breathing increased, as if to say, *Did you see that?*

Unimpressed, Odin yawned, showing off his now three teeth before flopping down, turning on his back, and extending a paw to rest on Audrey's chair.

Reynolds laughed at Audrey's exuberance. "Exhausting, but productive. Lucy's happy with the team."

"She's all about beating the ICU tomorrow." Susan closed the book and swung her lean legs over, feet to the floor. Her newly painted red toenails were a complement to her perfect feet. "You've got to be starving. There's food in the refrigerator if you're hungry. Glad to warm something up for you."

How naturally she said it all. Like him walking in the front door was a routine they'd done for years instead of weeks.

"Always taking care of everyone else, aren't you?" Her brother's words circled in his brain on the drive home. He explained to Reynolds how Susan always put the needs of others before her own.

Like forfeiting a biological child so I could become a father. That last one made him question everything between them.

Concern creased her brow. "Peter said something to you."

The open windows allowed the evening breeze to wander in, bringing the crisp smell of summer to the house.

Audrey looked up at him, smiled, and tightened her

stomach before cringing.

Reynolds wondered what that meant. "He did."

She rolled her eyes. "What did he say?"

"I need to take a shower first."

"Well, I can't help you with that." Her foot tapped a steady beat on the hardwood while a few kids rode by on their bikes.

"Bummer."

"Tease."

Audrey's diaper made disgustingly interesting noises.

"She okay?"

Rubbing the bridge of her nose, Susan exhaled as if she were resigned to the inevitable. "She's been doing that most of the afternoon. I anticipate a Mount Vesuvius–level event any second now."

"I'll be right back to help."

Right then, Audrey's pants rivaled the brass section of a Sousa march. The baby's eyes widened as if she had no idea where the noises came from.

Reynolds made no effort to restrain his amusement. "That was frightening."

"I think it's this new formula."

"I wouldn't give her more right now. I'll make it quick."

Susan teased, "Liar. You're running for the boats."

"You caught me." He waited until he rounded the corner before stripping off his shirt and showering in record time.

Still, he wasn't fast enough, because by the time he returned, he found a minimally clothed Susan in the shower, hosing off a poop-covered Audrey.

The stench in the room slammed into his face as he approached. "Good God. How are you breathing right now?"

Without losing a beat, Susan answered, "Intermittently."

He chuckled at her quick wit, something he'd come to appreciate. And love.

The baby's soiled clothes and bouncy seat cover rested on a towel in the sink. An odor-neutralizing candle burned on the counter. "We might need a few more of those."

Without an ounce of stress, Susan worked. "She exploded within a minute after you left."

"I didn't know that much stuff could come out of a baby at one time." He flipped on the exhaust fan and prayed for that smell to get out of his nostrils before Labor Day.

"It's amazing what babies can do." The fluidity of Susan's movements was a sight to behold. How she soaped and rinsed the infant from top to toes without grimacing once about the literal shit she had to deal with. "She's got it everywhere. Even under her arms. Around her neck. Behind her ears."

Audrey smiled and chewed on her hand.

He chuckled. "She's like a live-action Jackson Pollack painting. How can I help?"

"Hold her up, let me get some oatmeal wash on her. Afterward, you can burn that."

"That can be arranged." He knelt by the shower door, holding his daughter by the waist. "What in the world did you do?"

Audrey babbled, completely unimpressed that she might have invented a new form of chemical warfare.

Susan grabbed the shower wand. "Get you soaped up, then rinsed off."

Their double team effort produced a squeaky clean and poop-free baby. Once again, Audrey smelled as fresh as clean sheets and oatmeal while she told them all about it.

"Can you dry and dress her while I fumigate the tub and shower?" Susan poured a bit of cleanser in before using a long-handled scrub brush.

The lemon-scented disinfectant momentarily over-whelmed the smell of the destroyed items in the sink.

"Glad to." He swaddled Audrey, but before leaving, Peter's valid points ticker-taped through Reynolds's brain. As intrusive as Peter's concerns were, the same concerns crossed Reynolds's mind more than once.

Weeks ago, she avoided giving him a straight answer about having a bio baby. Now he needed to understand why Susan willingly gave that up.

The last thing he wanted was a woman who said she wanted to be a mom on paper, but then bail when the opportunity to live her dream crossed her path.

Like his mother did.

Lingering by the door instead of taking Audrey to her room, Reynolds cleared his throat.

Susan sprayed down the bath and her legs before she noticed him. "I'll be there in a minute."

"Thanks for doing all that." She turned off the water and dried her hands. The front of her clothes was completely soaked, but she wrapped a towel around her. "I'll take a shower after we get her situated."

The room smelled 1,000 percent better than when he walked in, but Susan always made everything around her better. Shinier. Healthier. Incredible.

But he wouldn't let her make things better for the sake of it, his dreams at the sacrifice of her own. They were too far along in this process to avoid the conversation anymore. "Peter and I talked—"

Her jovial mood went sour. "Let me guess. He's convinced I'm obligated to stay with you for our *practical* arrangement. I won't find someone I want to have sex with and make a baby. Does that sum it up?"

"Pretty much, yeah."

"I wish my brother would just respect my choices like I've respected his." Susan handed Audrey a plastic duck before motioning them to walk out. "If you're wondering, yes, I want to have sex with you. I've made that abundantly clear."

"You have, but he has a point." He followed with a towel-wrapped Audrey in his arms.

"He has no point. Peter doesn't know jack shit about what or who I want, because he's convinced he's right."

"What and who do you want, Susan?"

"I want you! I want you in every room of this house in the naughtiest ways possible. I want to taste you so badly that I think about it constantly. I want to *husband* you so hard, your knees give out." Her cheeks flushed. "I never meant to admit that out loud, but now you know."

"Holy shit. That was intense." Her honest statement rendered him speechless. He didn't know what to do. What he did know was he hoped Audrey fell asleep as soon as possible so they could discuss this further, because he wanted to understand what her version of *husbanding* him to the point of knee-buckling meant.

"Reynolds, believe me when I say I'm happy with our arrangement. I am. Trust me, I would never agree to any of this if I didn't believe it to be a good thing. I certainly wouldn't have married you, even only on paper, if it wasn't the right thing for me. For us."

Although he wasn't completely assured that was her only reason, he was convinced that Audrey just peed on him. "Seriously, kid?"

Her blue bright eyes indicated she was not at all serious.

Susan yanked the drawer so hard that she almost pulled it out of the dresser. "You have to decide who you trust more in this situation. Me or him."

Reynolds placed Audrey on the changing table and double-checked his shirt. "Yep, nice, warm, and wet. Great."

Dabbing his clothes with a clean burp cloth, he answered, "I trust you, Susan, but I worry that as fast as this all happened, it could cloud practical choices about any future babies." He quickly applied a diaper before Audrey made a mess of the changing table.

"What do you mean?"

Not have biological children was a logical decision for him, but there were plenty of days he wished he never had to make it. That genetics were more forgiving, but he didn't regret where he stood now. "I don't see me adopting again. This process is exhausting. Maybe after a person adopts once, the state gives them more consideration for future placements, but as far as I can see it, this is it for me."

"I haven't even been at it as long as you. I can only imagine how long this journey has been." Holding a clean onesie in her hand, Susan began to reach for Audrey.

"Why do you want to give up the chance to have your baby? Don't you want one?"

"If this goes through, Audrey would be my baby. Our baby." Her hands trembled while trying to unsnap the onesie.

"Susan, please."

"What? It's not the same? Is that what you're saying?" She threw the clothes at him and backed away. "Why can't adoption be enough? Why do I have to get pregnant to be a *real* mother? Why does only birthing a child make me a *true* woman? A complete woman? When a man says he wants to be any kind of dad, the entire world swoons."

"I never said anything like that."

"But you're thinking it. If you weren't, you wouldn't keep asking me about it. Questioning my decision."

That, he couldn't deny. "I've upset you, but please hear what I'm saying. My mom loved being a parent on paper. She got swept up in it, but when it wasn't fun anymore, she didn't follow through. She didn't even bother to stick around. She ran after what she wanted, and my father followed her like a puppy. They left me to take care of Nate and Audrey."

"And my mom checked out the moment my father died. We've talked about this. We're choosing not to be our parents and I would *never* leave you."

The intensity of her response confusingly comforted him. "We are deciding something different, but why won't you answer my question?"

"Why can't I be allowed to enjoy this opportunity to adopt her and that be it? Why can't that be enough?"

With them being halfway through the waiting period, he couldn't ignore difficult conversations anymore. Their future depended on transparency. "Susan, I want to, but you're not giving me much to understand. I told you exactly *why* I chose adoption."

"And I told you about my friend Chloe. How I've wanted to adopt for years."

"Yes, it was a reason you want to adopt, but it doesn't explain the other."

When she made a sound like words lodged in her throat, Reynolds knew he struck a nerve. "You say you're good with all of it but won't tell me why."

"But I—"

"There's more than what you're telling me. I can see it in your eyes. I'm sorry if it's difficult to discuss, but we have to work through this before October."

"Why can't you simply trust me, Reynolds?"

"Why can't you simply trust me? What can be so complicated that you think it's not worth saying?" he snapped.

If he'd slapped her, she would have looked less wounded.

Then it dawned on him.

This wasn't only pain. This was grief. *Broken.* "Susan, I—"

Without another word, she backed out of the room and disappeared behind her door.

Chapter Nineteen

F OR THE NEXT hour, Susan sat in the shower and sobbed. Then she dried off and silently cried into her pillow.

The day Reynolds confessed he never planned to have a biological baby relief flooded her veins. She'd never have to explain her infertility, but reality came calling like it always did.

Like when it took her father.

Like when she realized she had to cancel each of her engagements.

Like when she discovered she couldn't get pregnant.

Her wounded heart beat hard against her ribs. Deep-seated sorrow held her down, almost convincing her to confess nothing because it wouldn't change anything.

She shook off her denial. *You have to tell him, or this will never be resolved. He will never fully trust you. Why would he?*

Lucy was right. If Susan didn't want to tell any of them what happened, she needed to tell Reynolds.

Give him the option of asking her to stay or go.

She put it off long enough, and she berated herself for not coming clean sooner.

She waited until he returned to his room.

When the rhythmic creak of the rocker they put together last month slowed and then stopped, Susan dried her eyes and exhaled her worry.

Time to suck it up and deal.

Like I always do.

She washed her face and put on a dry shirt before standing in front of his closed door. With her heart in her throat, she softly knocked.

When he opened it, he wore only his sweatpants of truth. He stepped back, giving her plenty of room to enter. "Come in."

Fear superglued her in place. The cruel truth sliced up her throat. "I can't."

"Yes, you can." Subtle annoyance underlined his words.

Staring at his feet, she let out a long exhale, building up to her confession. "I can't … have a baby."

He shifted his weight as she waited for anger.

Annoyance.

Disappointment.

Rejection.

It wouldn't be anything new. Her former lovers found fault with her. Wanted her to be a pretty package but molded to their liking inside.

Someone who put them before her family.

Someone who'd move away and leave her younger siblings to deal with a chronically depressed and disabled mother.

Someone who could have a baby.

As much as it hurt to expose her soul, if she wanted him

to stop picking that thread, to explain why she wanted to be an adoptive mother so damned much, she had to trust he wouldn't crush her like the men before. "I've disappointed you—"

"Stop talking, Susan."

"Okay." When he embraced her, she crumbled in his arms. His deliciously smelling body wash offered comfort and unmercifully stroked across her nose.

He scooped her up and she clung to him as if a strong wind would carry her away.

When the coolness of his sheets touched her skin, it registered he carried her to his bed. Gently, he laid her down and crawled in behind her, pulling the covers over them both.

"Talk to me."

With her bottom lip quivering, she focused on the stack of comics and books about superhero movie art on one of his shelves. "I should have told you before it got this far."

"Who said you can't have a baby?" With a tender touch, he ran his fingers lightly over her hair. The caring gesture momentarily calmed her fears, but it didn't neutralize the pain.

"About a year ago, I had an ectopic pregnancy."

"Holy shit, Susan. That's serious. Lucy didn't tell us…"

Her hand squeezed his arm. "Please let me finish or I'll lose my nerve."

He wrapped his ripped arms around her, and she held his hand to her belly. "I didn't tell my siblings anything about it at first because my fiancé was there with me and there wasn't time. When they went in to remove it, they found that I ... um..."

"Breathe, Susan. Take your time."

"You need to understand why I'm not giving up anything about a bio baby. You told me to trust you, so here it is." She exhaled hard. "They discovered that my insides were a mess."

"What do you mean, a mess?"

If I don't stop crying, his pillow will be soaked by the time I'm done. "First, the ectopic ruptured my fallopian tube."

"Holy shit!"

She shushed him as Audrey stirred in her bed before settling back down.

He lowered his voice and kissed her shoulder. "You could have died."

Everything about Reynolds had been different. Why she expected his reaction to be anything but concern, she didn't know. She hated that her first instinct was to expect disappointment, but so many had let her down. "Second, my surgeon told me there was a lot of soft tissue damage that didn't repair in the best ways. Lots of scar tissue. Adhesions. One of my tubes was completely gone. Probably ripped up and dissolved long ago so it was incredible I got pregnant at all."

He propped himself up on his elbow, looking down at her. "How did all that happen?"

The words stuck to her tongue like peanut butter. She forced them out. "The car accident."

"From twenty years ago? I don't understand."

She rolled to her back, but stared at the ceiling, still fearful of looking him in the eyes. "I sat in the middle back seat. It was only a lap belt. They were standard at the time. The head-on impact threw us all over the place. Amazing only my father died, really."

"It's amazing anyone in the front seat survived." When her forehead furrowed, he followed it with, "A few months ago, it was a slow shift in the ER. Edmund started talking about the accident and pulled up some articles."

Her hand rested on her belly and his followed. "I remember being beat up, being incredibly sore."

"You had to be. They clocked the guy going a good ten to twenty over the speed limit when he hit your family."

The day was always a series of details, moments she pieced together. "I remember the weather. Fighting with Edmund about having to sit between him and Peter. Again. The restaurant Mom picked out. Song on the radio. The breaking of glass and…"

When her voice hitched, he pulled her closer. With him flush to her, the weight of the memories didn't seem quite so smothering. "Nothing, until I'm staring at an overhead light in a trauma room. A nurse asked me if I could feel my feet as she ran a pen across my sole. No idea where my family was. If anyone else was alive. Or even if I was. What happened? How I got there. How long it had been."

"What else do you remember?"

"Hurting. So much. Bruised. They cleared me of any internal bleeding, but I hurt for weeks. Nothing that would have been picked up with an X-ray. CT scan cleared me of any acute belly bleeding."

His embrace encouraged her to continue. "Things didn't heal in a way that would help me conceive later in life. Adhesions formed. Caused problems that couldn't be typically picked up by any sort of pelvic exam or an ultrasound. They only found it because of the ectopic."

"That's intense. Are you okay?"

She turned to face him and tucked her hair behind her shoulders. "That's the first thing you think of? If I'm okay?"

His forehead creased in confusion. "What else would I ask?"

"You'd be surprised."

"Tell me."

"Why? It's just—"

"Sad backstory." He ran his finger along her jaw. "You can't use that excuse anymore. If we're going to co-parent, going to be ... married, you've got to be honest with me. Tell me all of it. Even if it's awful. Even if it changes nothing.'

Taking him in, she didn't see everything she feared.

No judgment or disappointment.

All that swam in those hazel eyes of his was understanding.

And love. *Oh, don't get ahead of yourself.* "My sad backstory is this. I've had three fiancés. I've called off three engagements. The first because he always wanted to be first, above anyone else in my life."

"First? What was he, four?" He caught her tear with his thumb before it hit the pillow.

She admired the lines of muscle in his arm. The perfect triangle of his deltoid where that cute purple dinosaur lived. "Something like that, but I wouldn't rank him above my family. Not then. I broke that off."

"The second?"

Audrey fussed a bit, then settled back down.

"He wanted me to leave Florida. Go with him to his new practice on the West Coast. Demanded that Edmund and Lucy take care of my mother."

"How old were they?"

"She was entering her junior year of high school. Edmund was in his first year of college. I couldn't do it. They'd come to rely on me, and I was the only one who could get our mother out of bed. They had no idea how to juggle her care, her paperwork. Her depression. I worked to pay the bills. I wouldn't simply walk away from them. All that and he cheated on me."

"Two jerks down. And the third?"

She closed her eyes, refusing to witness Reynolds's reaction of pity. "He also wanted me to leave Florida. Mom passed before we started dating and everyone was on their own. Seemed like my time had come, but the emergency surgery happened. When we discovered that I couldn't get pregnant, he changed."

"Changed how?" Reynolds growled a noise she found simultaneously endearing and sexy.

"He told me to do whatever was necessary to fix my *issues* because I was broken. He wanted a baby because if I couldn't, then why were we together?"

"Fucking asshole. Who says that? Who says that bullshit after the person you love has a life-threatening—"

She kissed him without restraint. Hot tears ran down her face as the weight of sadness lifted off her tired soul. "Thank you for hearing me."

"You didn't get the surgery, did you?"

"I strongly considered it." She cupped his face. "The day before I met you, I talked to a specialist friend of mine. She does GYN reconstruction. She said with my tubes gone and my uterus not sitting well, I would never get pregnant much less carry a baby to term."

"The day before?"

"That's why I was there at 0-dark thirty, driving in the pitch black, in the snow, like a moron because I couldn't sleep. Too upset about everything."

"I was there because I couldn't sleep either. Drove in to meet a birth mother who never showed. Angry at the system. Started driving and stopped because the roads were so treacherous."

"And then we met and birthed a baby."

He cupped her chin. "Guess that was a pretty good meet-cute."

"It was." Her heart thudded in her ears as she anticipated his touch. *Maybe rom-coms are more realistic than I thought.*

Tentatively, he brushed his lips to hers before running his tongue along the seam of her mouth. "Susan."

"Touch me." Her heart beat in quick time as she soaked in every ounce of him.

"Yes." He pulled her flush.

The fragrance of oranges and spices filled the air around

them. She ran her fingers through his thick hair, relishing the softness of it against her skin. The way she dreamed about and only gotten a nibble of before.

Her body short-circuited as his tongue danced along the opening of her mouth before sliding partway in.

The length of him pressed against her and she was done waiting. She sat up and held her arms over her head. "Reynolds."

He began to remove her shirt when Audrey wailed, and her stomach sang.

They both froze for a moment before they each laughed.

Hope and lust swam in his eyes, despite the impending disaster that would certainly take place across the room sooner than any of them wanted it to.

With another soft kiss, he chuckled. "We need some alone time."

"We really do."

When he got out of bed to grab a T-shirt, she almost pouted at him covering up. *So close to getting my hands on that chiseled body.*

For the first time, Susan didn't overthink what this moment meant.

For the first time, she opened her heart and allowed someone in. Someone who'd earned her trust.

Now, all they had to do was make it to the finish line for Audrey and they'd get their—

"How much shit can come out of a baby?" Reynolds cringed. "How did she make all this happen so fast?"

Susan popped out of bed. "I'll start the shower."

"And I'll get the hazmat suits."

Chapter Twenty

"I'M GONNA HANG out with Nate and some of the first responders for a little bit. That okay?" He walked with her, holding Audrey as Susan pushed the stroller.

"Please, go spend time with your guys." Since they had the game at the recreational fields near the high school, all of them walked. Something she could rarely do back in Florida.

"You're the best." With the greatest care, he handed Audrey over before kissing Susan on the cheek. "Hope that formula is out of her system."

"Is that why you're not coming back right now?" She laughed.

"Busted."

"Coward." Since her massive meltdown and soulful confession yesterday, their frustrated tension had become nonexistent.

Now, Susan's body unmercifully ached for him. She didn't know how much longer she could keep her hands to herself. Hopefully, soon, she wouldn't have to.

Before he left with Nate, Reynolds jogged back and kissed her on the cheek, whispering, "Maybe we can find some alone time when I get *home*."

The way he stressed *home. Was that code for I'm gonna sex you up?*

She said a silent thank-you to the bikini waxer she visited after she got her toes done a couple of days ago.

"We'll be *home*." Her eyes betrayed her as she watched him walk away. The mixture of sweat and his signature scent hit her straight on, and she willed herself not to turn feral.

The broadness of his shoulders.

The movement of his walk.

The tightness of his ass.

"Still waiting for October, huh?" Peyton wandered up, holding a large drink and bag of popcorn from the ballpark. She wore a cute set of patriotic denim shorts, a V-neck Monsters University T-shirt, matching socks, and her well-worn running shoes.

There were times when Susan regretted telling her boss the details of the adoption arrangement. "Probably not."

"Good for you, because that's one good-looking man."

"Agreed." Susan kissed the top of Audrey's *The Wiggles*, and Dorothy the Dinosaur bonnet as the baby's wide eyes seemed to soak in everything around her.

The summer weather proved to be mild by Florida standards, but hot enough to feel drained when out in it too long.

Peyton tossed her trash in the bin. "After the magic you do at the clinic, good to know you're human."

"More than human, my friend."

A huge football-player-sized kid waved to Reynolds from across the parking lot. He sat in a pickup driven by a woman who looked like she considered cigarettes an essential food group. "Dr. Rey! How's it going?"

He waved back. "Good, Ford. And you?"

"Saw you pitch. That was awesome." He motioned in Susan's direction. "You got game."

A sheepish grin spread across his face. "Thanks, kid."

Ford held up his beefy hand as the driver shifted gears, a not-so-subtle sign she planned to drive away from this conversation soon.

"Cast is off. Feels good." He opened and closed his fists. "Be ready for football season."

"Strong work. Have a good July Fourth. Good luck with your classes. Hope I don't see you anytime soon!"

The kid laughed as they drove out of the lot. "But you probably will."

"You know where to find me."

If she weren't already ovaries-deep interested in the man, that casual interaction would have caught her attention. Reynolds possessed a charm that put people at ease when he spoke to them. Essential for an ER doctor and sexy as hell. "I swear, I'm gonna lose my mind soon."

"Some would say you already have." Lucy held up the diaper bag. "You left this in the stands."

Susan rolled her eyes. "Thank you."

"I, for sure, would have. Come here, cutie." Peyton held Audrey as Susan massaged the kinks in her neck.

"That was an amazing game. Good call to ask Reynolds to pitch." Susan always appreciated how well her sister brought a team together. Whether in the ER or any sporting event, she had the innate ability to understand each person's strengths and highlight them to the fullest.

"He was outstanding." Peyton rocked side to side with a yawning Audrey.

He was incredible. "Now you get bragging rights until next year." Susan laughed as Jade and Edmund yelled "We're number one!" from across the parking lot.

They waved before loading up their softball equipment in the back of her classic pickup. She dropped the tailgate and Susan noticed a couple of sleeping bags, an air pump, what looked like an air mattress, and a picnic basket. "Where are they going?"

Lucy smirked. "They're going out to his property to get naked weird."

"Completely throw-down naked outside weird?"

"The very same." Peyton patted Audrey's back. "He bought some land and he and Jade go out there all the time, make a pallet in the back of her truck, and go after it."

"That kind of sounds like fun," Susan admitted even though she would happily take a normal closed bedroom situation with Reynolds right now.

"Oh, it is." Lucy waggled her eyebrows.

Susan threw her head back and laughed. "Now I see why all of you like it here so much."

Out of the corner of her eye, Susan noticed Peter and his group of Shelly, her kids, and his kids. He gave her a respectful nod, and Susan accepted the silent olive branch.

Even though their fight drove her to confess something that ate at her gut for far too long, Peter overstepped.

He needed to learn to stay in his lane and to listen. Accept how much he didn't understand about what happened after their father died. With the new job, Audrey, and Reynolds, Susan didn't have the energy to explain it all.

"Dr. Rey did a great job." After handing Audrey over to Lucy, Peyton adjusted her ball cap as she wiped the sweat from her forehead. "Good grief, it's hot out here. Aren't you hot?"

"It's warm, but nothing like a Florida July Fourth." Susan played with Audrey's feet and the baby giggled.

"You okay?" Lucy cocked her head. "You look flushed."

Waving them off, Peyton patted her stomach. "I've not felt great this last week. Think I'm overdoing it. Not eating well. I had flu and COVID tests this morning. Both were negative, so that's not what's going on."

"It would be weird to have either of those in the summer." Lucy narrowed her gaze. "I haven't seen any cases come through the ER in the past few months."

"I've been so tired. I'm passing out as soon as I get home. I'm either starving or nauseous. Maybe I have a sinus infection? I've had those before."

A perfect summer breeze blew by, momentarily lowering the temperature around them.

Susan and Lucy shared a look like, *I think I might know what's going on.*

"You've been working a lot of hours, Peyton. Can you go home and get some sleep right now?" Susan watched Audrey talk to the tree that shaded them.

"I will. First, I need to walk over to the clinic." She

pointed toward the hospital. "Make sure we're staffed for the next few days."

"I can drive you." Lucy tilted her head toward her car. "I had to bring a lot of the softball equipment."

"Nah, it's only about six, ten blocks. I'd rather walk. Get my steps in." She tapped her watch and yawned, but when Officer Rob Shaw pulled into the parking lot, Peyton's entire demeanor changed.

"Hey, ladies." Even with his sunglasses on, it was obvious his attention was meant for only one of them. "Who won?"

"ER, baby!" Lucy high-fived Susan.

"Congratulations."

"What's on your agenda tonight, Rob?" Peyton twirled a lock of her hair between her fingers.

The only time a very put-together Peyton Grey twirled her hair like a middle schooler with a crush coincided when Officer Shaw appeared in the immediate vicinity. *Interesting.*

He gave a casual shrug. "Probably too many calls about kids and fireworks. You ladies have any big plans?"

"Going home. Kicking my feet up." Peyton pulled her keys out of her pocket.

Lucy started to answer, but Rob didn't wait. "Well, if you run into any trouble, Peyton, you know where to find me."

"I sure do."

"Need a ride to your car?"

Lucy and Susan realized they'd suddenly become invisible.

Peyton pointed behind him. "I've got to go check something at work so I'm walking. But you can keep me company if you're not busy."

"Glad to do it." He nodded to Susan and Lucy. "Ladies."

They waved as Peyton got her police escort up the street and around the corner.

"That's an interesting series of events." Lucy's comment triggered Susan to laugh.

"Well, her favorite month *is* August."

"Nothing says hottest month of the year like a shirtless police officer holding a pair of handcuffs, who stares at you with bedroom eyes ready to—" Lucy put her hands over Audrey's ears. "Sorry, little one. That's adult speak."

Audrey excitedly told them something about the tree.

Or it could be about the sky.

Or the piece of trash that the wind intermittently blew around the parking lot.

"What a total coincidence that she loves the month he posed in. How crazy is that?" Lucy nudged Susan with her elbow. "Speaking of crazy, what would you say if we offered to take care of Audrey tonight?"

"What?" The idea of a small break certainly held appeal.

"I doubt you and Reynolds have each had a break of any kind. Juggling jobs, making sure things are in line for the adoption. Him getting ready for this game."

"It's been more difficult than I thought it would be, but we're surviving."

"Three months down. That's good," Lucy agreed.

"It is, but I stress when Lori calls or comes by. She said it's looking more probable, but she can't guarantee anything until the judge says we're good."

"No word from the bio dad yet?"

"Not a peep. Lori explained that if we get to six months and no dad can be found, then they cite abandonment. Sever his rights."

Lucy wiped a line of sweat off her forehead, her hair matted to her scalp from wearing her ballcap all afternoon. "What about Bernie?"

Although Lucy's fair questions made sense, they twisted Susan's stomach tight. "Lori said Bernie is doing well. Going back to school in the fall."

"That's wonderful. Good for her."

Rolling her head from side to side, Susan stiffly smiled. "I can't make it all happen any faster than it will. I'll focus on what I can do. A good shower and a stiff drink after this little one goes to bed."

Audrey yawned, which led into a long, babbling dialogue.

"Then let us take her and you can do all those things now." Lucy snuggled with her niece before planting a series of quick kisses on the baby's face. "Go home. Get some sleep, Susan."

"Are you sure? I mean, she exploded last night." Susan relished the idea of taking a long shower after being outside all day. She could deep condition her hair, blow it dry, get a face mask in.

She even wore leggings because she didn't have time to properly shave her legs this morning. The possibility of smooth legs matching the smooth skin of her bikini wax kicked her heartbeat up a few notches. The simple pleasures were endless.

"Exploding or not. We would love to keep her." Lucy waved Thomas over after he shook Peter's hand.

"Do you have a crib?"

Thomas jogged up. "I ordered a pack-and-play for this very occasion."

"Geez, you two think of everything."

"Go on. You're wasting time." Lucy shooed her away.

"Are you sure you have everything?" For the first time, Susan felt unsure about leaving Audrey. She was in completely capable hands with Lucy and Thomas, but the idea of being without her stirred her fears.

"Susan. You're what, ten houses away? If we need anything, one of us will come get it. Now go!" Lucy turned Susan around and shoved her in the direction of her street.

With one more quick kiss for Audrey, Susan quick-timed it back home.

Pushing worry aside, she entered the house, only to find Reynolds's gym bag and shoes just inside the door. But he wasn't home. "Probably next door."

When was the last time she was alone with nothing to do and no one to take care of?

Instead of wasting time thinking of all the possibilities, she headed straight for her room and stripped down, relishing the freedom of simply being naked without concern of anyone needing her. She spent the next hour pampering herself, starting with an empowering song playlist then gave herself a facial and hair mask, followed by a long shower, a full leg shaving, and a good washdown with her favorite raspberry and vanilla body wash.

She ended her pampering hour by completely blow-drying out her hair. Since the baby, she'd done none of those things with no sense of urgency. How glorious!

She threw on her shower wrap, still singing one of her favorite songs, and headed for the kitchen. The moment she turned the corner, she came face-to-face with Reynolds.

Freshly showered and smelling like oranges and cinnamon. And he wore only his dark blue sweats.

Oh no. Her mouth watered as her lizard brain immediately took over. It took everything she had not to walk over, rip down those pants, and make his knees buckle. "Reynolds?"

"That's a great song."

"Thank you." Chagrin pinked her cheeks, but she wasn't sure if it was due to him hearing her singing voice or the fact she wore only a towel wrap. "I thought you were at Nate's."

"I was, but then he got a phone call from the hospital and headed out. I came home. Cleaned up. I knocked on your door but heard the shower running. Thought you were cleaning her up."

"That was very considerate of you, but it was only me. Next time, feel free and join me." When his face flushed, Susan wondered what would happen if she let this towel wrap fall to the floor.

"Did … did you want to get dinner or order a pizza? Can I make you anything?"

"What are you offering?"

He opened the refrigerator but didn't look inside, his eyes solidly on her. "Thinking of something fancy. Grilled three-cheese sandwich? Then watching a non-family-friendly movie."

Disappointment settled in when he turned toward the stove and quickly pulled out a pan. She hoped they'd at least get handsy, but the evening wasn't lost just yet. "That sounds perfect. Do we have anything to drink to celebrate the victory today?"

"Far right, top shelf."

"Got it."

"You need any help?" With his back to her, he pulled out a griddle, cheeses, bread, and butter.

"Nope." The ornate bottle sat right where he instructed. "Found it."

"It's my grandfather's whiskey."

"Sounds promising." *And potent.*

"Problems?"

"Nope." She handed him the bottle.

He grabbed two cartoon-themed mugs and placed them on the table. "How much?"

"A splash. Not much for whiskey, but I'll try it."

With a flick of his wrist, he gave her a quick pour and then gave himself a slightly longer one. "This was my grandfather's favorite."

The aromas of vanilla and sweet something drifted around her nose as she brought the mug to her mouth. "What are we drinking to?"

"To being halfway there."

"Celebrating the halfway mark it is." *And for me keeping my hands to myself. For the most part.*

With the exception of that one slip up, they'd found a rhythm that helped them keep them both in check.

Not that she wanted to, but she had to. Even after her massive confession yesterday, she couldn't be sure if that put them on equal emotional investment regarding the adoption.

Still, she didn't regret it.

Why risk anything now?

"Happy July Fourth, Susan." As the sun still brightened the evening sky, they tapped their mugs.

Susan took a sip as Reynolds tossed back his drink as if he'd swallowed liquid fire plenty of times. "Feel the burn."

His eyes closed and a serene smile spread across his face as his body tensed. She'd seen that smile once before.

When she touched him.

And she so wanted to see him make that face again.

Tonight. *Like right now.*

So much so, Susan almost dropped her mug, but quickly recovered and tossed hers back. The vanilla, cherry, and heated flavors layered on her tongue and burned her throat. "That'll clear your sinuses."

"It can. More?"

"Sure." Although she wasn't sure if she'd drink it. She placed her cup on the table.

"Lori called just a bit ago." He gave himself a pour but didn't drink it.

"Does she ever stop working?"

"Guess not. Said she's already contacted both sets of bio

271

grandparents. None of them are eligible, even if they wanted to adopt." He corked the bottle but left it on the counter.

"That's good. Sad." Susan wondered what kind of questions Audrey would have for them when she got older. Why her bio family didn't want her, or why they couldn't have her?

"The only hurdle now is the father signing off."

"And he walked away in the first place, so he's probably itching to sign the papers." She leaned against the table.

"Probably." Despite his confident wording, a hint of concern threaded through his voice.

Susan appreciated that Reynolds worried as she did.

He placed four pieces of buttered bread on the griddle. It sizzled on contact. "Audrey passed out after being outside all day?"

"She's at Lucy's."

With a flick of his wrist, he turned off the burner and moved the pan away from the heat. "We're alone?"

The jovial mood Reynolds held since she walked in here suddenly shifted. He swallowed hard, his eyes firmly set on her mouth.

"We are." Her heart thudded in her throat at the lust in his eyes. *What is happening right now?*

"Until when?"

"Until tomorrow morning." With her feet firmly planted, she wouldn't make a move. Not this time.

Under his hungry stare, she wavered between dropping her wrap and going to her room, locking the door, and imagining he was one of her battery-operated friends.

"Reynolds?"

"Yeah?" The dishtowel in his hands lowered to cover the front of his pants.

Oh? The sweatpants of truth. Her heart ticked up a notch. "You okay?"

"About to be."

Chapter Twenty-One

REYNOLDS DIDN'T REMEMBER moving, but when that sweet scent of berries hit his nose, it quickly registered she was in his arms.

"I've been thinking about you all day." His tongue greedily swept between her lips. She tasted of whiskey and sexy promises.

Wrapping her arms around his neck, she moaned his name. Her voice was dripping with want.

His hands slid down her body until his fingertips touched the hem of that wrap. The wrap he imagined ripping off her with his teeth like some feral creature. "Do you have anything on under this?"

"Nope."

"Good." As soon as he lifted her, she wrapped her legs around him. With slow steps, he moved them to a flatter surface. Gently, he placed her on the table.

"Here?" She raised an eyebrow.

"Seems as good of a place as any. I mean, I am hungry."

"It must be true, then." She pointed to his sweats that were fighting against his erection. "I don't want to deny a good man what he desires."

He loved how confident she spoke when sex was on her mind. "You are a sexy freak, you know that?"

"Thank you. With everything else in my life being so restrictive, I had to let loose somewhere."

"Lucky me."

"You have no idea." Without breaking eye contact, she unbuttoned her wrap and began to open it, but she paused. A flicker of worry in her eyes.

He hated that she doubted her beauty, her sexual power, the strength of her body.

Even if it took a thousand years, he would make sure she never doubted herself again. He placed his hands on hers and helped her undress. "You're perfect."

She stroked him over his sweats. "Once again, the pants don't lie."

"Neither do I." He kissed her as his hands ran up her back and down her sides.

His thumbs grazed the outsides of her breasts as his tongue swept into her mouth. With his heart pounding against his ribs, he savored the soft feel of her lips against his own.

Her fingers played with the waistband of his pants and quickly found their way under the soft material. The moment her hand wrapped around his cock it almost sent him over. "Susan."

"I've craved touching you again." Lust soaked her every word. "To kiss every thick inch of you. To have you in my mouth. And deep inside me."

"You keep saying dirty things like that and I might never

let you leave." As he sucked her bottom lip, she moaned his name and gently moved her hand up and down his length.

"I can say dirtier if you want. Tie you up with the golden Lasso of Truth." Her words caressed his ear.

"Do you have one of those?" Her superhero sexy talk only made him want her more, and until this moment, he didn't think that was even possible.

"I do."

He groaned.

"I also have *the* golden bikini."

"The golden bikini?" Every Star Wars nerd's fantasy come true.

"Yep." Susan raised an eyebrow in that seductive way that always got him hard as a rock. Her thumb slid along his sensitive head, and she smiled against their kiss. "What do you want?"

Cupping her face, he soaked her in. "Marry me."

"Again?" She giggled.

"Again. And again."

Her elegant fingers wrapped around him as she set a slow, torturous tempo. "And again."

Being so close to her each day, Reynolds held on by a thread before now. "Susan, how far do you want this to go?"

With her free hand, she moved his sweats off his hips, and they fell to the floor. "I want all of you."

The cool air danced across his naked ass, giving him a moment of clarity.

A voice of doubt whispered that he should tell her to stop. Bring some logic to this illogical situation, but he couldn't. Logic had no place here. Not today. Not when they were this close to getting everything they wanted.

Not when they *both* had such heavy stakes in the game.

When she licked her lips and her eyes darted down, he knew it was now or never to turn back. "Can I?"

He didn't want to turn back. "I don't know if I'll last very long."

A coy smile across her perfect lips. "I'll take my chances. Sit down."

The moment he sat in the chair, she kissed the tip of his nose and down his chest. Her tongue danced across his belly, and she rubbed her breasts against his thighs.

His hand slid down her spine, taking in the curve of her hips, the roundness of her ass. "Perfect. Just ... holy crap."

She gave the head a seductive, long lick before kissing it. "You good?"

"I'm fucking great."

"Wonderful. Tell me if it's too much."

Watching her take him into her mouth, inch by inch, then pull back slightly, had him gripping the chair. It would never be too much. Reynolds wondered if the next fifty-plus years would satisfy his want for her.

With expert sucks, she continued to torture him. A skill she appeared to enjoy as she gave him a mischievous grin during pauses.

I'm a dead man. "That feels so good."

She reached for her mug and tossed back the drink inside. As seductive as she attempted to be, the strength of the whiskey surprised her. "Oh, that's intense."

"So are you." His hands rested on her breasts, his thumbs taunting her pert nipples.

She momentarily arched into his touch before pulling him closer to the edge of the chair. It gave him more access to her as she leaned forward and kissed him. "Keep touching me."

"I love that you know what you want."

"I want you. All of you." The moment she slid him inside her mouth again, the heat of the whiskey almost shot him off the chair. Her tongue caressed his cock as she gave it the attention he dreamed about for too long.

"Holy shit ... Susan."

"That's it. Tell me what you want."

As she increased her pace, her hands moved up his thighs, his body, and back. Every nerve of his begged for release.

"That's ... damn..." His hips began to rock, meeting her movements.

She pulled him out, pumping him at the base. "What do you want me to do? I want to hear you say it."

"Make me come."

"Gladly."

"And I want you to put you on that table, eat you until you scream my name."

She moaned against him and increased her pace. The vibration of her words intensified her touch.

Reynolds couldn't have dreamed how responsive she would be to him, to his words, to his touch. She was his every fantasy come true, and when she took him deeper, it was too much.

He pushed her off him and grabbed her hand, bringing her to her feet. "I'm about to be done sooner than I want to be. I need to touch you. Taste you."

"Let's go to bed."

He tossed back the booze from his cup and wiggled his eyebrows at her. "Let's see how you like it."

"Now who's the freak?"

Walking them across the house, they barely made it to the hallway when he pressed her back against the wall.

He brushed his lips from the base of her neck to her collarbone, inhaling that sexy body wash she used. "What do you want, Susan?"

"You," she breathed.

"Where?"

"Everywhere. Any way you want."

"Any way I want?" Where had she been all his life? Reynolds cupped her breasts, before flicking her nipple with his tongue. "You want this?"

She arched into his hands. "Yes, more."

He didn't need to be asked twice. He sucked her as his hands wandered her body, caressing her curves like a slowly winding road. One hand slid down her hip, over her stomach, and along the seam of her.

"The whiskey. Tingles. So good," she gasped before gripping his shoulders.

His mouth met hers as his fingers played between her folds, his thumb finding her sensitive spot and caressing it with the greatest of care and attention.

Her hips moved to meet his touch. "Yes, Reynolds. I want you inside me."

"I think we need a flatter surface than this."

"Your bed or mine?" He didn't care which, just as long as they got there and soon.

"Yours."

"Good." He grabbed her hand and walked her into his room, backing her up to his bed.

She reached down and stroked the length of him before sitting on the bedside and taking him into her mouth again.

"Susan! That's! Yes!" His knees threatened to buckle and it dawned on him how expertly she husbanded him.

She purred and increased the pace alternating between slow, lingering, and quick sucks.

This was playing out better than his dreams and Reynolds relished how her hands caressed him as her tongue worked its magic.

When she pulled him from her lips, he knelt in front of her. "My turn."

The fragrances of raspberry and vanilla drifted around her, and he hungered for her taste. "Susan."

"I wanna feel that whiskey."

"You smell so good. Bet you taste even better."

"If that's what it took for us to get here, I should've used this body wash long ago."

He marveled at the 'goddess before him. Her hair fell loosely about her face. Her perfect bare breasts, waiting for his touch.

Never had a woman's presence so consumed him but

here he was, willingly racing to the siren's call and not giving a damn if he drowned.

Reynolds greedily kissed her, savoring the feel of her lips on his. The taste of the whiskey on her tongue. Then he worked down her body, taking his time with her breasts. Sucking each perfect nipple as he played with the other.

She writhed under him; her fingers threaded through his hair as she encouraged him on. "Feels so good."

"I'm not done."

"And I'm not stopping you."

His thumb slid down her body to her sex.

Her face flushed the perfect pink in anticipation of his intimate attention. "Please."

A trail of tender kisses down her belly led him to his destination as his hands fanned against her inner thighs. A wicked smile spread across his face as he kissed the inside of her knee and inched his way to her intimacy.

Her breathing increased as she watched him slide his tongue between her lips and find her clit.

"Reynolds." Her head fell backward.

His tongue teased her intimate flesh while his fingers traced her outer folds.

She moved with the tempo he set. "Yes, that feels so good. Please, don't stop."

As if I would even consider it. "Love tasting you. Teasing you."

"More."

"As you wish." He taunted her bundle of nerves while sliding a finger inside.

"You are amazing ... oh ... yes." She ran her fingers through his hair as he feasted on her sensitive flesh. Sucking her. Licking her. Worshipping her like the goddess she was.

She writhed against his face. His tongue danced in a feverish tempo to drive her to the edge and then back again.

"I'm so close. Please. Please."

"What do you want?" He kissed the inside of her thigh as his mouth curled into a seductive smirk. "Tell me."

Because he loved hearing her say it. He loved everything about her. He loved her.

With her hair in total disarray and her cheeks a healthy shade of pink, she gasped. "Make me come."

Hearing her cries of delight only made him harder. By the time he got inside her, it wouldn't take long, but he sure as hell enjoyed every second of what they'd done so far.

"Please. More. Harder," she begged. Her eyes were on him, impatience on her face.

"Only because you asked so nicely, but next time, I'm going to make you wait." His tongue teased and taunted her before he intimately kissed her. "Like that?"

"Yes."

"What about this?" He added a bit more suction as his fingers moved in and out of her.

"So close. Please keep going."

"What about?" When he added a second finger and swirled his tongue around her core, her fingers dug into his shoulders and her back arched.

"Reynolds ... I ... Oh my ... Yes! Yes! Yes!"

The ripple of her climax gripped his fingers, his tongue

teasing every ounce of bliss from her. He'd never tire of this, of her. Of them.

Her hair cascaded about her face like a woman who'd been properly pleasured. "I want you in me."

She pushed herself up the bed, extending her arms.

"So bossy." Reynolds crawled up the bed like some predator finally catching his prey.

And the prey liked it. "We got complicated tonight."

"And it's not over yet."

He kissed up her belly, licked each nipple just to hear her approving sighs.

Susan's nimble fingers threaded through his hair as he slowly slid home.

She clenched around him, her fingers pressing into his back as if she were afraid he'd bolt. "I've waited so long for this. For you."

The last waves of her climax rippled across him. "Susan. Fuck me. You feel so good."

She wrapped one leg around him, pulling their hips closer and herself wider. "I plan to."

"Don't take this the wrong way, but you are a lot more adventurous than I expected." And he loved how she continued to surprise him.

"Thank you. By the way, you are so much better than battery-operated machinery." Her honesty always humbled him.

He moved his hips with purposeful seduction, trying to last longer, but failing. "I'd like to think I rank a lot higher than a vibrator."

"You are certainly a better kisser." She rocked her body to meet his. "So much better."

His body tightened as he closed in on his release.

Her warm wetness caressed him with every thrust.

She wrapped her other leg around him and grabbed his ass, pulling him deep inside her. "So good. Feels so good. Keep going. Don't stop."

"Kiss me." Their mouths met in a frantic kiss as he increased his tempo, pushing himself over the edge and finally finding the perfect rhythm that sent him over.

Chapter Twenty-Two

"DID YOU EVER babysit growing up?"

"Why?" With a gentle touch, Susan dabbed the infant dry before laying her on the changing table.

A subtle scent of lavender and oatmeal filled the cool September air that drifted in from the open window. Far better from the noxious mess they discovered not thirty minutes ago.

"Because you're an excellent diaper changer." He pulled Audrey's crib sheet off and cringed as he neatly folded the worst parts in the middle and wrapped the outside to cover the potential toxic spill. A skill he'd perfected over the past several weeks as they figured out what formula didn't cause Audrey such unstable diaper situations.

The corner of her mouth curled up. "Are you complimenting me on something you hate doing, hoping I'll do it more often?"

"I would never!" Reynolds feigned shock right before he disappeared down the hallway. "I'm gonna go burn this."

"Good idea." No sooner had he left the room, than Audrey kicked her feet and peed. "Seriously, kid? At least you're on the changing mat. Regretting not taking that formula out of your diaper bag when Aunt Jade and Uncle Edmund took care of you yesterday."

She cleaned Audrey up in quick time, the chore more like a habit now. Done with little fanfare and almost no thought. After she laid her heart out weeks ago and they'd become officially complicated, Susan and Reynolds found an easy rhythm in every aspect of their lives.

That included hazardous situations like this one.

Audrey happily kicked her feet and babbled while Susan nodded. "You're right. Your daddy is amazing. And curse him for being sexy while helping with diaper emergencies."

Reynolds's exuberance wasn't limited to his parenting duties. The man radiated confidence and happiness while his seductive ways kept Susan more than jubilant.

So much so that Peyton recently asked her if it was already October.

Each day they got closer to the deadline, Susan let the grip of control loosen and believed they would make it. All three of them would be this wonderful family.

Maybe one day make it four of them since Reynolds recently suggested after Audrey was officially theirs, they consider adopting another child.

Although she appreciated his positivity, doubt quietly crept in, but she refused to let it take hold. She'd never be able to gather all the pieces of her shattered heart if she even approached the thought of this collapsing.

Breathe, Susan. With expert skill, she dressed Audrey in a Wonder Woman–themed onesie. She kissed the baby on the forehead, marveling at the child's ability to change the entire mood of the house. "You done exploding?"

Audrey cooed and sucked on her fist.

"You're hungry. How about we try a bit of sweet potatoes and apples today?"

"So, did you? Babysit?" He leaned against the doorway. The crisp scent of his soap drifted around her, sending libidinous butterflies flittering in her panties.

"For someone other than my siblings? No, there was never time." Susan dropped the dirty linens in the hamper as her sexy Adonis stood in the doorway.

"Why not?"

She held up her hands and pointed to Audrey. "Watch her, please. I need to clean up."

"Gladly. Come on, sweet girl." The steady beat of his footsteps behind her indicated he waited for Susan to tell him more.

As she entered the bathroom, a quick look at her reflection left much to be desired as she'd yet to clean up after her very busy shift of prenatal visits and delivering two babies.

Mascara smeared under her eyes, her hair needed a good brushing, and she for certain wanted a shower. "Peter and I shared parenting duties for the first few years. We worked our schedules so one of us was always home with Edmund, Lucy, and Mom in the afternoons, evenings, and weekends. Helped with homework, chores, grocery shopping, that sort of thing."

"Your mom couldn't help at all?" Resting the baby against his shoulder, Reynolds rubbed her back.

Susan closed her eyes and exhaled her annoyance at his

honest question. With them steamrolling toward the finish line, she promised to be more forthcoming about her sad backstory, even if it hurt like hell to talk about. "Mom struggled to get out of bed most days."

"She that banged up after the accident?" His gentle prodding helped peel back a layer of pain Susan never addressed.

And she hated it, as burpees-are-great-for-building-your-core-and-upper-body-but-they-suck-to-do hated it.

Reynolds settled on the edge of Susan's bed; Audrey waved her arms as she sat in his lap. Odin flopped down in the doorway.

The baby's bright-eyed wonder indicated she would fight her afternoon nap again before she passed out for a few hours.

And maybe give them a few hours of alone time.

With her hands clean of toxic waste, Susan dried off. She turned, leaning against the counter. "My grandmother, Mom's mom, she was all about the fifties housewife thing so that made our mother the same."

She smirked remembering the fights and pushback. "Mom tried hard to sway Lucy and me in that direction. Our grandparents insisted we attend boarding or finishing school or wherever uber-rich people send their daughters to brainwash them. Dad stepped in, and refused to send us away. Caused a rift between my mom and her parents so we never saw them again. Mom clung to my father like he was her only lifeline."

Susan appreciated his thoughtful ear as she shared more

of her life with him than she ever had with anyone outside her family.

"Sounds like your mom was lost."

"More than lost. The moment our mother heard our father died, she quit." *She quit on all of us.*

"What do you mean she quit?"

Audrey stretched and yawned.

"She quit being a mom. An adult. She cried all the time because our father was gone. Because she was alive. Because her injuries were so severe, it hurt to move, but it hurt to do nothing. She chose the path of least resistance. Lay there, waiting for death to take her."

He gave her a knowing nod. "That had to be rough for her."

"It was, and I hurt for her, but *we* needed her." Sitting next to him, Susan stared straight at a blank space on the wall. "We all knew she lived for my dad, but when he was gone, I realized she *lived* for him. Everything was about him. Every decision. Every meal. What she wore. Every breath was about making him happy."

"Was your dad a difficult person?" Reynolds wrapped an arm around her waist, encouraging her to move closer.

"Not at all. In fact, he was very laid-back. I rarely heard him yell. They never argued, at least not in front of us. They didn't always agree but seemed to find middle ground." She drummed her fingers on the comforter. "Looking back, it was so clear how much of herself she gave up to be his wife."

"What do you mean?"

How good it felt to release this frustration. She'd been

carrying it around for so long. "My mom was raised by a woman who was all about the man being the head of the household. That women are there to make their husbands' lives better. Easier. Less complicated."

"Yes, such a healthy outlook on the world." He placed Audrey on his shoulder as she settled in, her eyes slowly blinking.

"When my dad died, she decided she had nothing to live for. That her world ended."

"Her kids weren't enough?" The sharp edge of his response told her his question was rhetorical as he understood what happened when parents checked out.

"No. It wasn't enough. I had to keep it together. Make sure everyone got what they needed. I had to—"

"Give everything up to save your family."

"Yes." *He gets me.* "Charlie did put some happiness in her last few years."

"We gotta get that guy out here."

She rested her head on his shoulder as Odin meowed from the doorway. "Thank you."

"For what?" He kissed the top of her head as Audrey's drowsiness disappeared with Odin's complaints. She wriggled to turn, excitedly squealing at Nanny Cat.

As soon as Audrey's approval caught his attention, the cat sauntered like he walked the red carpet at a Hollywood premiere.

"For listening. Hearing me." For twenty years, deep-seated anger took up residence as permanent knots in her shoulders. It kept her from enjoying the world around her and simply accepting the things out of her control, like matters of the heart.

For the first time, Susan allowed her heart to take the wheel. And it felt wonderful.

To think, all she had to do was move across the country, during a snowstorm, and deliver a baby in a convenience store with a man who took up permanent residence in her lizard brain.

Now, two weeks until the deadline, things looked positively promising, and all of this rom-com-level happiness was due to the man sitting next to her.

She leaned in and kissed the now-sleeping baby in his arms. "She just passed right out, didn't she?"

"Babies are all or nothing."

Audrey's soft snore brought a smile to Susan's face. "Wanna put her down and join me in the shower?"

He leaned in and whispered, his words hot on her ear. "Be sure to get that raspberry vanilla soap because I'm gonna clean you up before we get really dirty."

"How dirty?" A thrill danced up her spine.

"Filthy." He playfully growled before placing Audrey in his room.

Susan turned on the water, and as she waited for it to heat up, she stripped and stepped in. The steam fogged up the glass as she turned the intensity of the shower to massage the knots out of her shoulders.

But after a few minutes, Reynolds hadn't joined her, which was very unlike him, especially when sex was the point. She cracked the shower door. "Reynolds? You coming?"

Nothing.

Without washing her hair or body, she grabbed her wrap, dried off, and opened her bathroom door to find him sitting on the side of her bed. "Reynolds?"

His shoulders were rigid, like he stood at attention. "Lori called."

That sent her heart into a rapid rhythm. "And?"

"He's back."

"Who's back?" Although the sadness in his voice told her everything.

"The bio father."

"And?"

Reynolds exhaled a long breath. "He wants to meet Audrey."

Chapter Twenty-Three

"HE THINKS HE wants the baby."

Reynolds's heart slammed against his ribs. "He *thinks* he wants her? Well, I *think* I want to take an Alaskan cruise when I'm sixty, but that doesn't mean I should."

Lori sucked her bottom lip as she paced the kitchen in mismatched tennis shoes. A sure sign she dressed in haste to meet them this morning. "From what I understand, family members told him he has to own up to his mistakes."

"Mistake? She's not a mistake." Susan placed Audrey in her highchair.

Odin flopped down underneath.

"His words, not mine." Lori rubbed her temples. "Look, this isn't a done deal, okay? This is him stepping in to play."

"But we're so close, Lori. Two weeks." Reynolds's gut churned like he drank too much of his grandfather's whiskey on an empty stomach.

"I know. I know. It sucks!"

"What happens if he does want her? How does this play with the time we've had her?" Susan asked, but Reynolds already knew the answer.

Letting out a long breath, Lori shook her head. "It

doesn't."

"I don't understand this system at all," Susan snapped. "We've taken care of her pretty much her entire five-and-a-half-month life. The nighttime feeds, the exploding diapers, the routine doctor visits. The excellent parenting? Bernie designating us as custodians and potential parents? That doesn't count for anything?"

"We've talked about this. The court sees it as your job as her designated custodians. You get no special consideration for doing what you're supposed to do."

"And this kid just shows up and what?"

"Not sure. I can tell you he has no idea what he wants." Drumming her fingers on the table, Lori paused.

When Susan pulled out some baby food, Audrey squealed so loudly that Odin left the room.

This can't be it. This can't be the end of our story. Reynolds thought he'd blow a vessel in his head. "Lori, please help us. Help her."

She rested a hand on his arm. "I'll do everything I can to do what's best for Audrey, but the courts want to reunite the bio family when they can."

"Even bio family who refused to step up? Before she was born, he abandoned her mother. She was homeless, living with a felon to survive. The only reason Bernie or Audrey are alive is they ended up at that store and not dumped in a snowdrift by that scumbag."

"What do we do?" Susan sniffled as Audrey opened her mouth wide for the first bite.

Lori exhaled. "Tomorrow—"

"Tomorrow?" Reynolds eyed the cabinet that held Grandpa's precious whiskey.

"Tomorrow, the father is supposed to come talk to us at CPS. He wants to see her. I will arrange a time." Lori braced her hands against the table's edge. "One of you or both of you will bring her to the CPS offices. I'll take her to a playroom, and we'll supervise a one-to-two-hour visit. You'll take her home, and we'll take it from there."

"He can't just take her home that day, right?" Susan's words trembled as they came out in harsh whispers.

"No, there's a process. Might take a week or so. We want to run background checks on anyone who will be around the baby or be designated to care for the child. See where he plans to live. How he plans to support her. We're not going to send her into an unsafe environment."

"What else?" Susan held a spoonful of mashed sweet potatoes midway to Audrey's mouth as she waited for Lori to answer.

Audrey leaned forward, her mouth open wide like a baby bird. When Susan didn't follow through, Audrey babbled as if to say, *Hurry it up.*

"Right. Here, sweetie." Susan scooped up more food after Audrey sort of stripped the spoon of the orange mush.

These stupid beautiful moments will be nothing but a memory if she leaves.

"We'll let him know what social services are available. If he's the sole parent, he'll qualify for some help. Many times, parents this age want to have co-guardianship with another adult like a grandma, aunt, or grandpa. We'll need to run checks on them and see if they qualify for any help."

"What do you mean by help?"

"Childcare. Food stamps. WIC. Insurance."

"Been there. It's a lot of paperwork to navigate." Susan grimaced like she tasted something bitter.

Reynolds wanted to scream, punch a hole in the wall, and get so stinking drunk he forgot this conversation. But that wouldn't change the reality of it.

She might be leaving.

And that probably meant Susan would, too.

His heart simply couldn't take it. He grabbed his coat and his keys.

"Where are you going?"

He threw his arms up in frustration. "I don't even know."

Lori pulled out a chair. "Rey. Come on. Sit down."

Reluctantly, he plopped down as Susan fed a very hungry baby. Tears rolled down his face, and he did not attempt to hide them. "She can't go."

Patting his hand, Lori coaxed, "I don't know if she'll go, but I have to do this by the book. You don't want anything being questioned in six months or six years. This is for Audrey and what's best for her."

For the next hour, Lori talked them down, giving them multiple scenarios that could work in their favor. Even with her comforting words, Reynolds couldn't see anything but red.

After Lori left, they spent the evening playing with Audrey before she passed out.

That left Susan and Reynolds sitting silently on the couch. A deep sorrow filled the room. A room, as of yesterday, that held nothing but happy memories.

How did it all go bad so quickly? How unfair this process was. The false sense of hope as the finish line approaches, only to have their legs pulled out from underneath them. "Susan."

Tears streamed down her face as she sat stiff-backed, her hands resting in her lap. "Reynolds. I can't."

"You can't what?"

"I can't do this again." Her head gave him a small shake, making her ponytail swing behind her.

"I don't even want to think about it right now, Susan."

"We have to. We have no choice."

He couldn't give up yet. All the pieces to this complicated, six-month puzzle weren't in place yet. *It can't end when we almost had it put together.* "I'm not ready to give up yet, Susan."

"It's not a matter of giving up, Reynolds. It's more of what the court will decide."

"I'm not ready to give up on us, either."

She turned to face him, her eyes wide with pain. "What?"

Taking her hand, he sandwiched it between his, like he'd done in Lori's office almost six months ago when he asked Susan to co-parent. "Us. I'm not ready to lose both of you."

Her bottom lip quivered, and she pulled her knees to her chest. "I'm so tired of fighting."

"What do you mean?" He moved closer, but she recoiled and it broke his heart.

"I'm so tired of fighting for the basic things that so many others get without thought. Love. Marriage. A family. The whole, stupid fucking fairy tale!" Tears flowed freely down her face. "What did I do to get such a tumultuous ride, huh?"

"I wish I had an answer for you. For us."

She buried her face in her hands. "Why couldn't it be simple?"

"Because we like complicated." His attempt to find humor even annoyed him.

"Don't, Reynolds. This hurts enough."

He reached for her, but she stood, placing space between them. "Susan, please don't push me away. We already complicated things, multiple times and in multiple ways. We knew the risk when we took this step."

"We're two weeks away and it all falls apart?"

"It doesn't all have to fall apart." Reynolds moved closer but didn't try to touch her as he motioned between them. "*We* don't have to."

She blinked away her tears. "You want to stay married if Audrey leaves?"

"She's leaving?"

Chapter Twenty-Four

NATE'S VOICE HIT them before he stepped in the doorway, his eyes wide with worry.

Reynolds hopped to his feet. "Nate. I didn't hear you come in."

"Obviously. Lori looked upset. I came over." Nate's worry was a bandage of compassion on a gash of pain.

"The bio father's back." Reynolds shoved his hands in his pockets. "Lori just told us."

"Shit. What happens next?" He softly pounded his fist on the doorframe.

"We have to take her over to CPS for visitation."

"Why?" Nate's eyebrows furrowed.

A sweet smile spread across Susan's face at hearing her brother-in-law so invested. "Glad to see you on board, Nate."

His support will help get Reynolds through this. Because she didn't think she had it in her to help anyone else mend the wounds of heartache again. She barely had enough strength to help herself to stand.

"To meet her…" The word *father* almost slipped out, but this irresponsible kid wasn't her father. Reynolds was.

Susan exhaled. "The bio dad."

"Time for Grandpa's whiskey." Nate beelined for the kitchen.

Reynolds turned to Susan. "You want to join us?"

The oppressive belief of hope sat on her chest. She needed out of here. "No, I need to clear my head. Go for a walk."

She didn't wait for him to respond but put on her shoes and headed down the street.

Reds, oranges, and yellows danced in the trees as the crisp chill of September swirled around her. The sun beat down on her tear-stained face as late-afternoon joggers made great use of the sidewalks.

The faint sound of the bell from the elementary school at the end of the block caught her attention. "That's where Audrey would have gone to school."

The dream of terrible art projects and class events was gone in an instant. Susan couldn't keep her sadness from taking over, but she didn't want to lose it here on the sidewalk, especially with someone running up behind her.

"Susan?" Peter's hand rested on her shoulder.

With the weight of sorrow tightening those knots, Susan turned and buried her face in her brother's chest. "She might be leaving."

"Come on." He smelled of sweat as his breathing slowed. Peter laid his arm across her shoulders and walked her down the block to his house.

She plopped down in the first chair as he left for a moment, only to return with a couple of full shot glasses. Clear liquid could be anything from vodka to tequila to cleaning liquid. She didn't care as long as it numbed the pain.

He sat across from her, his forearms on his knees, and waited.

A quick flick of her wrist tossed back the liquid that immediately burned her throat. "I'm sorry I yelled at you. That's tequila."

"I'm sorry I didn't understand why you were so upset."

"What?" Had Reynolds told them?

He put his hands up in surrender, a heavy sadness in his eyes. "I should have trusted your decisions, because I trusted you to make so many others when we were kids."

"Lucy said something, didn't she?"

"Yep. More like she chewed my ass. Shelly did, too."

"You're overdue a good ass-chewing." Susan downed the second shot without asking if he wanted it.

His lips thinned. "Lucy explained a lot to me and Edmund. Things I—we didn't know."

"Like what?" The tequila surged through her veins, loosening the knots in her neck that would certainly never fully go away.

"How many medical schools did you apply to?"

The pain in his words caught her attention. It wasn't the confident or even arrogant tone he took when he wanted to make a point, but sad and even remorseful.

"A dozen."

"Why didn't you tell me?"

She slumped in the chair, wondering how much to confess. "What for?"

He ran his fingers through his hair in frustration. How

her brother wasn't bald after these last several months, Susan had no idea. "What for? You got a thirty-five on your MCAT. You gave up something you wanted so the rest of us could…"

"Peter, stop. It would've required moving Edmund and Lucy out of their schools. Took Mom away from her doctors, her specialists. It was hard enough finding anyone who'd treat her. Getting her out of bed most days was a chore."

"I wish you'd said something." Gone was the demanding tone, replaced by an almost apologetic cadence.

"What good would it have done? You had your studies. You lived three hours away. You barely got home during the holidays because of how much studying you needed to do." Bringing up their struggle always sent her on a one-way ticket to Frustrationtown, but the multiple talks with Reynolds did more than get her sweet rewards.

They helped her let go of the loss of her family. Her childhood. "I wasn't leaving that for Lucy and Edmund to take care of. It was too much."

Peter looked like he'd been electrocuted.

"Besides, we couldn't afford to lose my income."

Peter waved his hands in front of his face as if he heard her wrong. "What do you mean, lose your income? I thought we had money saved from the fundraising. Did you pay the bills?"

"After you turned eighteen, that social security check was gone. I had to make up the difference."

"No, wait. That can't be right. I thought we had enough

in the account to cover it all. Our grandparents left us money."

"No, they didn't."

"Wait. What?"

The heaviness of the burden she carried for so long began to lift with each confession. "Mom had a falling out with them not long before the accident. They didn't leave her anything."

Peter shook his head. "Unbelievable. Mom told me ... never mind."

"I signed us up for free meals at school. I waited tables. On the weekends when you were able to be home, I worked doubles."

"Oh shit. I thought you worked that much because you were mad I left."

"Not at all. Did you ever wonder why we had so much food from that place?" Susan continued, the dam of pain, broken free.

"Because you worked there?"

"No, because the owner was an old friend of Dad's. He asked how we were doing and when he understood how dire it was, he insisted I take all the untouched mistakes home. That any unsold prepared food at the end of the night, I could have. I even went by on my days off." Many times, she reviewed those sad memories, but now, they didn't keep hold of her as fiercely as they had in the past.

"You gave up so much and here I am, telling you don't know what you're doing." He scoffed. "Now who's the asshole?"

"Peter, you've always been the asshole." She laughed, finding a bit of joy in her sadness.

"What are you going to do about Audrey?"

She tucked her hands under her legs. "There's not much we can do but wait and find out what the bio dad wants."

"What about Reynolds?"

That sent her heart rate up and her bottom lip quivering. "What about him?"

"Will you stay together in your *practical* relationship?" Try as he might, Peter couldn't keep a bit of snark out of the word *practical*.

Susan bounced her leg at a nervous tempo. "It's no longer practical."

"Then what would you call it?"

"Complicated."

"A regular relationship, then?" A sympathetic smile spread across his face. "Whatever you decide, whatever the two of you decide, I'll support you."

"Thank you."

"Gotta be honest, sis. I never thought I'd see the day when you went off the deep end. Did something outrageous." He went to the kitchen and returned with the bottle of tequila, pouring them each another shot.

She grabbed a tissue from the box on the coffee table. "Yeah, I bet. To be honest, I don't want to give any of it up, either."

"Why would you? You love the guy."

"What? I don't ... I like him. *A lot.* But..." Shit. She loved him. She loved him so much, that the idea of them not working out hurt down to her marrow.

"Susan?" Peter's forehead furrowed.

She grabbed the shot glass, tossed the drink back, and nodded as the fire slid down her throat. "I love him."

"Yeah, you do."

Chapter Twenty-Five

ON THE DRIVE to Bozeman, the only sounds in the car were Audrey talking to her reflection in the baby mirror and the hum of the tires on the road.

Since Lori's call two days ago and their disagreement yesterday, they said little to each other. Each of them probably worried about upsetting the other.

Her emotions were a tangled mess, like a ball of Christmas lights that no one could unwind without breaking a few bulbs.

When they pulled into the CPS parking lot, it hurt to breathe.

Reynolds parked near the front. They sat for a few moments as the engine cooled.

Multiple people entered and left. Some with children in tow, others wearing clothes that looked like they pulled them from a pile of dirty laundry. Some were impeccably dressed.

"I'm sorry I pulled you into this." Sorrow dripped from every word. "I shouldn't have asked you to give so much."

"Please don't apologize. I understood the risks. I just didn't think … I hoped it would work. That we would work." She sucked on her bottom lip, still looking out the passenger's side window. Afraid for him to see her pain and his disappointment.

"Doesn't mean I'm not sorry for hurting you." Amazing how crippling grief can consume even the most alpha of men.

"You didn't hurt me." She wanted to hold his hand, touch him, but she couldn't bring herself to reach for him. Pain mixed with anger at how wickedly the universe played its cards.

How misery was so easily distributed.

"There's Lori." He swallowed hard and Susan wiped her face with her sweater sleeve.

They signed in and were escorted to a waiting area before Lori took Audrey.

The parents who looked like they wore dumpster-level clothes sat in the corner. Susan recognized the style from one of the TikTok videos she discovered a few nights ago when Audrey couldn't sleep. Despite the initial appearance, those were anything but low-level couture.

Susan and Reynolds chose to sit next to each other, their broken hearts keeping their conversation nonexistent as they watched an old gameshow rerun.

Most people worked on their computers, tablets, or their phones. A few read books, but most spent a lot of their time nervously watching the doorway.

For what it was worth, Susan appreciated they weren't alone regarding possible parenthood, but it wouldn't soften the blow if the father wanted her back.

After an hour, Lori returned and handed Audrey to Susan before she motioned for them to follow her to a conference room.

Her solemn smile told Susan everything she feared would happen when they started this five months, two weeks, and three days ago.

"Well?" Reynolds asked before Lori closed the door.

"He wants her."

A punch in the stomach would have hurt less as Susan sunk into a chair, still managing to hold on to the sweet bundle in her arms. "Why?"

As calm, cool, and confident as Lori had always been, she grimaced as if she wanted to vomit all over the floor. "He said his grandmother insisted he had to raise her."

"Come on, Lori!" Reynolds's voice rebounded against the walls. "He wants her because his grandmother told him to? That's stupid."

"That's what he said."

"We have nothing to turn things in our favor?"

"He's the biological father, Reynolds. I can't change that fact. If he wants her, he's going to get her, unless the court finds him or his grandmother a danger to Audrey or he's wanted by the police already. Even then, it will take months to process and sever his rights. If there's any question, she would stay in your care in the meantime."

The weight of grief crushed Susan's soul, and it would only get worse when she held this child for the last time.

Reynolds stomped around the room like an angry bear. "What about the common thread?"

"I tried to figure one out, but right now, I don't see

one." Lori grabbed a tissue from the box on the table. "Like every case, there's a group of us who discuss what would be in the best interest of the baby."

"That means what?" Reynolds's words were sharp as daggers.

"We review what's happened so far and how we find the best possible outcome."

Soaking in every moment, Susan held Audrey close, inhaling her perfect baby smell. Memorizing the shape of her face.

Audrey reached up and tried to poke Susan in the eye with her tiny, busy fingers.

Keep it together. Keep it together. Losing it would solve nothing. "What happens now?"

"The father's talking to some other people in my department." She tilted her head.

Reynolds's eyes lit up. "He's still here? Let me talk to him."

Lori leaned against the door as he grabbed the doorknob. "No, Reynolds. We're not there yet. I promise that if I can arrange a meeting between you and the bio father, I will. But he has no obligation to talk to you."

The tension in the air sat thick with fear.

She's leaving. We're over. Susan could barely think the four brutal words and she sure as hell wasn't going to say them out loud.

"Lori, I can't do this again," Reynolds whispered as his shoulders slumped.

She pulled him into a fierce hug. "I'm so sorry, Reynolds. I truly thought you two had this one. I really did."

Susan stood. "Reynolds. Come on. We're wasting time."

He turned to her, his hair wild from angsty fingers. "What do you mean?"

"Let's go home and enjoy what we have left."

Chapter Twenty-Six

"**Y**OU'RE A PIECE of shit, you know that, Ford?"

Upon entering the convenience store where his life changed forever, Reynolds almost turned a one-eighty when the argument hit his ears.

The past twenty-four hours pushed him to his max. After he, Susan, and Audrey left CPS, they drove home and did their best to spend happy moments together.

Once Audrey fell asleep, Susan crawled into bed with him. As upset as he was about the entire situation, he fully welcomed her passionate, almost desperate lovemaking session.

They woke this morning to Lori texting them to be at her office by eleven where she informed them that Audrey would leave tomorrow.

Susan drove back to Marietta to make it in time for her afternoon patients and to give their families time to say goodbye to Audrey.

Reynolds, who drove over separately, simply wanted to drive around to clear his head. But first, he needed coffee.

"Why am I shit, Ben? It's not my fault." A familiar male voice hit Reynolds's ears right as he came around the corner from the back door.

"Hey, Ben." Reynolds made a beeline for the coffee machines.

"Perfect timing, Dr. Reynolds," Ben stated.

Not today. "Glad to be helpful."

Without taking his eyes off the mega-sized to-go coffee container, Reynolds moved forward. "What's on your mind?"

"This is the baby's dad. Not that you've earned that title." The clerk's voice was full of snark and fury.

Reynolds froze. "What do you mean the baby's dad?"

"Ford, Bernie, and I went to school together."

"I know that guy." The low chuckle of his repeat patient hit his ears.

Holy shit! Ford is the birth father?

Should he text Lori about this? Should he leave before saying anything stupid?

"Dr. Reynolds! Dr. Reynolds!"

"Let me get my coffee first, Ben." Reynolds willed his hands still enough to fill an extra-large coffee cup three-quarters and add enough cream to put a lactose-intolerant person down for the count.

"Calm down, dude," Ford mocked.

"You calm down, you piece of shit," Ben growled.

A quick text to Lori before Reynolds turned around. "What's on your mind, Ben?"

Holding his hands out like he was presenting a specimen at a lecture, Ben announced, "*He* is the father of Bernie's baby."

Reynolds always wondered why the universe had so much fun fucking with him. Standing there, his frequent-flyer ER patient who made too many stupid choices.

Now he was about to make another one that would hurt a lot of people. Reynolds didn't know if he should be happy or worried. "Ford."

"Hey, doc. What are you doing here?"

"Getting coffee. Trying not have a nervous breakdown."

Ford grimaced as if he didn't get the sarcasm. "That sucks. My grandma says coffee makes people nutty."

"Drink enough of it, I guess it could."

"Did you hear me, Dr. Reynolds? This idiot is the father." Ben's voice was more insistent than a few moments ago.

"How do I know *you're* not the father!" Ford stabbed a thick finger at Ben.

Despite being half Ford's size, Ben didn't back down. "Two reasons. One, you took a paternity test. Second, I've never had sex with Bernie."

The way the kid gritted his teeth through the last part of that rebuttal sounded like it hurt to admit.

Reynolds glanced at his phone. *Come on, Lori. Call me back.*

Ford scoffed. "Really? I thought you were friends."

Ben came around the counter. Even standing at his full height, he only came up to his friend's chest.

Still, Ben reminded Reynolds of a pissed-off Chihuahua, telling a much bigger dog to find another yard to shit in. "Friends don't always sleep together, you idiot."

"Bernie and I were friends."

"Some great fucking friend you are." Ben's finger stabbed Ford in the chest. "She got pregnant and you dumped her when she told you. If that's what you call friendship, you suck."

That's fair.

"What was I supposed to do? Stay here and do what? End up like my brother? Dude's got five kids and he's not even thirty." Ford moved out of Ben's finger-poking range and rubbed his breastbone. "Or work at a convenience store for the rest of my life."

"You were not supposed to abandon her! That's what you were *not* supposed to do! Not leave her homeless! You were supposed to help her out!" If Ben didn't wear his emotions on his sleeve, his increasingly higher-pitched responses would certainly key someone in to his mental state right now.

Ford shook his head. "Homeless? She wasn't homeless. She stayed with her parents."

"They kicked her out as soon as she told them, but you wouldn't know that would you? Because you left. Stopped talking to her, you dumb shit."

No response from Lori yet. What frustrated Reynolds more was even if he recorded this, it would make no difference in family court. Ford was her biological father. It didn't matter what he thought happened in his absence.

The lights flickered for a few moments as the coffee machines all geared up for another round of brewing.

Reynolds simply watched the entire scenario unfold. Like

earlier today in Lori's office, there wasn't a fucking thing he could do about it to get the outcome he wanted.

The family he almost had.

His heart shattered again.

Ford's forehead scrunched up as he processed. "That sucks for her, but you gotta understand, I have a scholarship and *can't* have a kid."

"But you do."

"I didn't want a kid."

And yet, you are taking her anyway.

"Then maybe you should have worn protection, ya idiot." Ben grabbed a box of a popular brand of condoms and threw them at his friend's face.

Damn, he didn't demand for anyone to pay for that. He must be really pissed.

The comment appeared to have deflated Ford. Impressive as he stood at least six-five and probably had to turn sideways to get his shoulders through most doorways. "Bernie is a smart girl. I just figured she took care of things."

"She did take care of things. Even when she had to live with a convicted felon, she took care of herself and the pregnancy. Then, because you weren't around and weren't going to be around and your parents slammed the door in her face—"

"Wait. What? Oh, Grandma's not gonna like this." He nervously chewed one of his fingernails. "Shit, you think that's what they meant about me making a dumb mistake? Why they're moving and didn't tell me their new address?"

"Yeah! Yeah, I do," Ben scoffed.

"I thought they were talking about me getting that fishing lure stuck in my hand. Or breaking my knuckles." Ford tapped his thick finger on his chin for a few more seconds. "Is that why they changed my phone number? She wouldn't know where I was?"

As if this situation weren't insane enough.

"Bernie took care of finding the baby, your baby, a good home with good people. But you wouldn't know any of that because you're a selfish bastard who can't think about anyone but himself."

Oh, Ben almost had a great speech there and then he had to insult the guy. Reynolds took a few steps forward. "Why don't we bring this down a notch?"

Without pause, Ben pointed to Reynolds. "That guy helped deliver your daughter."

The *your daughter* punched Reynolds so hard in the chest that he almost forgot he was holding coffee. When the cup slid a few inches from between his fingers, he quickly recovered before it splashed to the floor. *Please, don't take her back.*

Then Reynolds heard himself say those words and hated his selfishness.

Ford finally turned in Reynolds's direction and tucked his thumbs in his belt loops. "Wait, you did that?"

"Did what exactly?" Reynolds sipped a bit of his coffee without spilling any on his shirt.

"Delivered the baby."

Notice he didn't say my *baby.* "I did some of it. Susan is the one who delivered her."

"Who's Susan?" Ford leaned against the counter and crossed his thick arms as though he were waiting for an answer he liked or understood.

"She's my ... um ... my..." Words stuck on the back of his tongue like glue.

They were legally married, but what were they exactly? Colleagues? Lovers? Parents? Friends? All of the above? "Susan's a midwife. She coached Bernie through her labor here in this store."

"Without drugs? That's intense. I hear pushing a baby out hurts like a bitch."

Ben held his hand up. "Bernie almost broke my fingers."

"You were there, too?" Ford almost looked hurt.

"Yes, she came here, and that piece of shit guy robbed the store, and she went into labor. Then Dr. Reynolds and Susan the midwife caught her. Here look." Ben held up his phone and tapped the screen.

For the next several minutes, the two stared at whatever was on Ben's phone and Reynolds wondered if there was anything in the store stronger than beer.

"That's insane." Ford's complexion paled. "Oh! And she popped right out."

"What are you watching?" Reynolds wanted to step closer but kept his distance.

"Bernie took a video of the baby's birth. She sent it to me." Ben pointed. "That's Susan."

Ford's eyes glassed over. "You two are good together. What's that crap all over the baby?"

"It's called vernix." Reynolds glanced at the snack machine that rotated one hot dog. He wondered how long it had been there. "After that, Bernie gave us joint custody of Audrey."

"Who's Audrey?"

With a deep exhale, Reynolds managed to answer without his voice cracking. "The baby." *But not my baby.*

"That's a nice name. Don't know if I'll keep it, though." Ford shrugged but wiped away the tear that managed to escape.

"You shouldn't." Ben clenched his jaw as he tucked his phone back in the cradle behind the counter.

"You think I should change it?"

"No! I think you should relinquish custody, you big dumb—"

"Okay, okay. We get you're pissed, Ben." If Reynolds didn't rein in this kid, he'd never get through to the bio dad.

Not that he blamed Ben one stinking bit for saying everything Reynolds thought. "To answer your earlier question, Ford, Susan and I have taken care of Audrey since she came home from the hospital."

"Wow. Thanks."

"Right. You're welcome."

"She potty-trained yet?"

Reynolds shook his head at the kid's ignorance. "She's five months old."

Ford's slack-jawed stare implied that his brain might have short-circuited. "Soooooo..."

"She's gonna be wearing diapers for at least another year, probably two."

"That sucks. I hate changing diapers." Stuffing his hands in his well-worn jeans pockets, he moved closer to Reynolds, but kept well out of arm's reach. "The social worker told me about all that. You being a single dad and then meeting that lady. Is that the one I saw you kiss after that game on July Fourth?"

"Yes." *The same day Susan and I took it to the next level.* "We got married."

"No shit! Congratulations." Ben gave a few counts of applause.

Ford scoffed. "You got married? Why?"

Initially, he planned to say because it looked better regarding the adoption, but at this point, he honestly answered, "I love her."

"Who?"

"Susan. And Audrey. We're a family ... right now."

"A family. Wow. That's a lot. Your wife is hot."

"Yes, she is."

"I can see why you married her. She's got a great ass."

You have no idea, kid. "Enough about Susan's ass."

Ben motioned toward Reynolds. "If you sign those papers, dipshit, he and Susan can get on with their lives and take care of the baby. *Their* baby. You can do whatever the hell it is you're going to do, you selfish bastard."

Calm down! "Ben, you've said your piece."

For a long moment, Ford stared straight into Reynolds as though his gaze were made of laser beams.

All Reynolds could do was hold his breath and wait.

Ford shifted. "You want to adopt her?"

"Yes." *Desperately.*

"Why?"

"Why what?"

"Why'd you pick adoption? Just have your own kid." The air of arrogance regarding paternity dripped off the kid's commentary.

Reynolds had heard similar statements from people who simply didn't get it. "It's not that simple."

"Why not?"

"Because it's not possible," Reynolds exhaled.

"You gay?"

Ben threw his hands up in frustration. "That's not a reason people can't have children, dude."

Tilting his head to the side, Ford narrowed his gaze. "You're a dude, right?"

"Always have been." Despite the stupidly tense situation, Reynolds chuckled.

Ben buried his face in his hands. "How in the hell did you get a scholarship anyway?"

Ford flexed his arms. "Because I can stop the defense dead in his tracks."

"You can barely spell your name."

"Whatever, dude. Doesn't matter. I'm tough as shit."

Ben sneered as he leaned against the front counter, and something in his body language changed. "Tough enough not to break your hand on a brick wall? So tough that you're taken out with a beer bottle or a BBQ grill or a fishing lure?"

Ben knew about the ER visits. *Interesting.*

"Hey, that fishing lure hurt like shit, and my eyebrows

did grow back. But those things aren't gonna keep me from playing."

"Maybe not, but what are you going to do when some lineman hits you from the side, blows your knee out? Or you do something stupid again like car surfing? End up in the ER with a broken leg like Tommy? There goes your scholarship. How the hell are you going to support a baby then? Tell me that, you dumbass." Ben's thick glasses magnified the intensity of his stare.

For a moment, Ford's arrogance waned. "It won't happen."

"Just like you wouldn't get Bernie pregnant?" Ben's ability to easily insert doubt in his friend's confidence made Reynolds wonder if the bespectacled teen planned a future in litigation.

Ford shifted his weight before he changed his focus. "What's your story, doc? And it better be good."

It almost sounded like Ford wanted to cover all the questions he'd be asked by his demanding grandma before deciding what to do.

"Or what, Ford? You gonna strap her to your back and take her to football practice?" Ben beat his fist on the counter. "Take her to class? Study between diaper changes?"

"My grandma said I had to raise her."

"Your parents had a chance to raise her and they slammed the door in Bernie's face."

Ford's beefy jaw clenched. "You're a liar. They said she never talked to them."

"*They* lied because I was there." Ben wiped his nose with

the back of his hand. "She asked me to go with her, but I stayed in the car. They didn't even let her inside."

Ford turned away and braced his hands against the frozen treats cooler near the front of the store. "I can't believe this. They said they didn't know."

Reynolds wished this situation was unique, but it wasn't. Family dynamics could be chaotic at best and destructive on multiple levels.

"And what's your grandma gonna do to help with this?"

"Nothing."

"That's right. Fucking nothing." Ben took a bag of candy and chucked it at his friend as he turned around. It hit Ford square in the chest and fell to the floor like a tin can being tossed at a tank.

This is solving nothing. Reynolds glanced at his watch. *I'm losing time with Audrey. And Susan.* If there was any time left for them as a family. Or a couple.

How did it go sideways so quickly?

Not even a week ago, the finish line sat right there. He and Susan even joked about what Audrey's Halloween costume would be, taking her to the Christmas crawl, her first photo with Santa. Celebrating New Year's together.

One selfish decision crushed their dreams.

Considering Ford hadn't grasped the basic responsibility of fathering a child, Reynolds kept his answer simple. "You want to know why I chose adoption. It's not in the cards for me to father a child so a long time ago, I decided to adopt."

With a shrug of acceptance, Ford replied, "I mean, you're a decent guy. Sewed me up a bunch. Helped me when

I broke my hand, but why should I let *you* adopt my kid?"

Now he wants to be possessive?

Where was he when Bernie needed a place to stay?

When she needed help?

Tucking his anger away, Reynolds put his coffee down and approached. Screaming at this kid would accomplish nothing but convince him to take Audrey for all the wrong reasons.

And it would break Susan's heart all over again.

His brain throbbed with the monumental task at hand.

Could he make this kid understand and save his family?

Taking the father in, Reynolds pulled from his foster care parenting training, hoping to find some pearls of wisdom that would sway things in their direction. "I don't know what you want to hear, Ford. Between Susan and me, we make a good living. My house is paid for. I have no debt. Audrey will be in a good school. She already has a lot of family that adores her. She will be safe. She will be with parents who love her. She will lack for nothing. I'll make sure she goes to college or trade school. Whatever she wants to do. What more can I say to convince you to allow us to adopt her?"

"I need to hear something really good because if I don't take her back, my grandma is gonna beat my ass. She's already told me she doesn't believe in adoption."

Ben's fists clenched at his sides. "Your grandma is delusional and selfish."

What is this mindset of not believing *in adoption like it's the Loch Ness Monster?* "She doesn't believe that there are children who have no one, genetically, to care for them?"

His forehead furrowed. "Um…"

Ben rolled his eyes. "He means no one who's biological."

"Oh! Man, I don't know. My grandma doesn't explain anything to me. She just tells me what to do." Crossing his thick arms across his chest, he slumped as if the weight of the world hopped on his back. "I don't even know how she found out about all this anyway."

"I told her." Ben put his hands up. "But I thought she'd tell you to sign the papers."

"You're a piece of shit! Why would you do that?"

"Because you wouldn't answer any of the social worker's emails or calls. Ms. Susan and Dr. Rey needed an answer. It wasn't fair for them to keep waiting for you to follow through."

"But my grandma—"

"That's not a reason to keep a baby, Ford," Reynolds gently interrupted. "You should raise your daughter because *you* want to do it. Not because someone else decided it for you. Especially someone who isn't going to help. I mean, where are you going to live? In the dorms?"

The kid's eyes went wide as if he hadn't even considered it. "Shit."

"How are you going to make this work? Who's going to watch her when you have practice or during games? When you need to study or have a date?"

"Shit. Girls probably won't date me if I have a kid." He sucked on his bottom lip for a few beats. "Look, you're a nice guy and I want to say yes, but unless there's some sign from

God, my grandma's not gonna accept any excuse I give her."

"Your grandma isn't in charge of the baby's life. You are." Reynolds hoped his words were kind but stern.

Ben stomped his boot and ran his fingers through his hair so forcefully that Reynolds worried the kid would scalp himself. "Your grandma doesn't even take care of herself. Why should she be in charge of this decision?"

"My grandma is in charge of everybody's life in my family. She tells *everybody* what to do, and if we don't listen, she makes our lives hell."

She sounds delightful. Bet she's fun at the holidays.

"No, she's mean and hateful and wants everyone as miserable as she is." Ben momentarily turned to Reynolds. "I've met her. She's not a great person most of the time."

"She likes you for some stupid reason," Ford scoffed as the aroma of the nacho cheese warmer drifted around them.

"Maybe it's because I'm nice to her."

"No, that can't be it." Ford scratched his right shoulder.

This was the toxic environment Ford wanted his child to grow up in? Reynolds doubted the teen saw anything wrong with his family because it was all the kid understood.

It was possible Ford might be insulted if Reynolds said anything to the contrary.

The idea of screwing this up ate at Reynolds's gut. He might have already drowned the entire thing by talking to Ford at all.

This was Reynolds's worst nightmare come true.

After today, he would lose two of the most important people in his life. His heart hurt at the thought of it all.

Find the thread. Lori's words echoed in his ears, but as many times as he and Ford met, not once had Reynolds found anything they connected on other than ER visits.

Please. Please, give us some hope. His angst hung so heavy that Reynolds didn't care if he said those words out loud.

"So, doc? What's it gonna be? Dammit, I think I got bit by something." Ford pulled up his sleeve and scratched.

How could he connect with this kid? And then he saw it. "Is that—"

As he turned his shoulder toward Reynolds, Ford's eyebrows pinched together. "Hey, doc. This stupid bug bite gonna mess up my tattoo?"

Reynolds's heart leaped into his throat, blocking his oxygen as Bernie's words on the day Audrey was born in this very spot, slammed into his brain.

Her shirt. His tat. His favorite cartoon.

Audrey. Susan.

The thread.

"Come on, doc. I just got the colors redone."

"Your tat will be fine, Ford. In fact…" Exhaling a long breath, Reynolds pushed up the sleeve of his shirt. "I've got one just like it."

A whisper of hope when Ford's eyes went wide. "Holy shit."

"Fuckin' A." Ben's bright eyes magnified by the thickness of his glasses.

"Is that enough of a sign?" A wide grin spread across Reynolds's face as relief replaced angst in Ford's eyes.

"That'll do it."

Chapter Twenty-Seven

THIRTY-SEVEN MINUTES.

That was how long it took Reynolds to drive home after Ford promised to return CPS and sign the relinquishment papers.

Quite honestly, Reynolds didn't remember a damned thing until he pulled into the driveway and turned off the ignition.

A quick swipe of a fast-food napkin dried his face.

For a moment, it didn't seem real, but as it sank in, the smile on his face stretched from west to east coasts. Reynolds barreled in through the front door and slid to a stop at the doorway of the empty kitchen. "Susan!"

Odin lay next to his very empty food dish and glared as though his daily needs were not being sufficiently met.

"I'll get to you in a minute, cat. Susan?" He checked the bedrooms. No one home.

The news threatened to fall out of his mouth to the first human he found, but the first person who should hear it was the woman who helped him make it all happen.

The woman who laid her broken, raw heart out to help him become a father.

"I'm gonna do everything I can to make sure we are a family." A quick text later and he discovered she was at Main Street Diner. Not bothering to get in his car, he ran the two blocks, the good news sending him like a rocket ship up Court Street on a windy afternoon.

When he turned the corner, Lori screeched into a spot, parking outside the lines. A sure indication she was too excited to care. "Rey! What in the world?"

"Hey, Lori." He hugged the breath from her.

She squeaked and pushed him away. "I was heading over to check on you and I got a call. The kid came back to CPS and relinquished custody?"

"Then he did go back? Kept his word?"

Her eyebrows disappeared under her thick bangs. "Wait. You're not acting surprised. Rey. What did you do?"

"I talked to him." Several people walked out of the diner, and he patiently held the door open as he shifted his weight like a runner needing to sprint.

"I said that might not be a good idea."

"Honestly, Lori, I didn't plan anything. It happened organically. I promise." *A sign. Grandma will be more than pleased since it's her favorite cartoon as well.* "Hold on. I'll explain everything."

"Can't wait to hear it."

When they entered, he easily found Susan. At the far end of the room, she sat at a row of tables with her siblings, their partners, and Nate.

With it being the midafternoon, the staff cleaned tables and restocked supplies. The rich smells of grilled meats and fresh bread slammed into his face, but they didn't distract him from his focus.

Audrey squeezed a banana between her fingers and told everyone at the table about it.

Reynolds wished he had a camera so he could pass this image to his child, to his grandchildren.

Out of the corner of his eye, he noticed Lori with her phone up. "Go do it, Rey."

Holy shit, this is going to happen. As he approached, he willed his elation to calm.

Although the adoption news would certainly help delete the worry of the baby ever leaving, it only partially repaired the wounds between Susan and him.

The uncertainty of everything working out.

The moment she made eye contact with him, Susan's smile thinned. Then her eyebrows furrowed when her gaze darted to Lori. "Reynolds? Is it already time? To send her back?"

A great sadness momentarily swept across the table.

Reynolds took great joy in changing that. "He signed."

"What?"

"He signed." He planned to give it a bigger buildup, but those two words perfectly summed it up. *Here are two more.* "She's ours."

Nate jumped out of his seat. "Really? She's staying?"

"How about that?"

Lori dropped her backpack on the floor next to an empty chair. "The father said he's ready to relinquish, and he's presently talking to my boss to sign everything. The next stop is setting a court date to make the termination of parental rights official. Then a date is set for the adoption to be finalized."

"Are you serious?" Edmund clapped his hands together, then kissed Jade, his fiancée. "I'm gonna be an uncle again!"

Flo, a long-time employee of the diner, yelled from the kitchen, "That's great news! Here, let me bring out a couple of pies for you to share. Celebrate."

Lucy, Thomas, and Shelly each hugged Reynolds as Lori walked around, motioning for Susan to hand over the baby. "Go hug the man."

Peter respectfully shook his brother-in-law's hand. An air of caution still lingered between them, but the only Davidson Reynolds wanted to impress stared at him wide-eyed.

Hesitantly, Susan placed Audrey in Lori's arms before squaring her shoulders and confidently walking into his embrace.

But Reynolds knew her strength was all a façade.

She held her heart by her fingertips and any slight slip would send it crashing into a million pieces. "Reynolds?"

A beep from Lori's phone and she held it up. "He signed!"

He rested his forehead against hers. "She's ours."

Susan choked back a sob. "But I thought he said nothing would change his mind."

"I gave him one."

"You did what?" Susan popped her head back. "I don't want to hear this."

Lori froze. "Oh geez, Reynolds. What did you do?"

He grabbed Susan's hands before she got away from him. "Please. I did nothing illegal. I swear. It was a true common-thread moment."

"Thread moment?" Nate settled back in his chair and Lori handed him Audrey.

Susan motioned for reluctant Peter to scoot over a couple of chairs so she and Reynolds could sit down right as Flo brought out a chocolate silk pie and a huckleberry pie along with a stack of plates.

Fellow waitress, Casey, followed with napkins, forks, a pie server, and a can of whipped cream. "Enjoy!"

Jade and Lucy quickly distributed the plates and forks as Reynolds explained how he accidentally ran into the bio father after leaving Lori's. He told them what the conversation entailed, the family dynamics, and…

"But what was the sign?" Susan patted his forearm like an impatient child waiting for the best part of the story.

Lifting his shirtsleeve, he revealed his Dino the Dinosaur tattoo. "This."

Nate lifted his sleeve while balancing Audrey on his lap. "This?"

"That."

"Are you serious?" Lori rocked a slow-blinking Audrey, who still held mashed bananas between her chubby fingers. "*That's* what he needed to see?"

"I guess so. Ben also showed him the video of Audrey's birth so that might have helped."

Susan gasped. "That's why Bernie recorded everything?"

"Yes. And now because of that purple dinosaur, she's

ours," he answered without taking his eyes off Susan. He couldn't. Her admiration damned near sent his pants two sizes too small.

Lori reached for a fork. "Hell, if I'd known he only needed to see your tattoo, I would have told you to show off your arms sooner, Reynolds."

His thumbs brushed the backs of Susan's hands, relishing the softness of her skin. "He said that Audrey was where she was supposed to be. He trusted Susan and me to do right by her. To take care of her."

Although Reynolds couldn't be sure if things were right between him and Susan, what he did know, by the time Christmas rolled around, they'd officially be parents.

That Audrey was here to stay.

One thing at a time, Reynolds.

With her fork, Lori scooped up a bit of the chocolate silk pie Lucy gave her. "Not an hour after the bio dad insisted he wanted her, he walked right back, saying he changed his mind. My boss just texted that the kid looked relieved."

Suddenly, Susan leaped from her seat and hugged his neck. "Thank you."

Tentatively, he rested his hands on her hips. Relishing everything about her. Her scent. Her touch. Her voice. Her love. "You're welcome, Susan."

"You made our family happen," she breathed before sitting back and drying her face with a napkin.

Lucy slid a piece of chocolate silk pie over and handed Susan a fork.

"A tattoo of a purple dinosaur?" Jade shrugged before

taking an extra bit of whipped cream. "Why is that a big deal?"

"It was our sister's favorite. And apparently, it's the father's—" Reynolds cleared his throat. "The bio dad's and his grandmother's favorite as well."

Between bites of his huckleberry pie, Nate added, "Whatever works, right?"

"Now you're getting it, Nate." Lori laid a blanket over Audrey as she gave in to sleep, her hands still full of mush.

Among all the celebrations, Peter shook his head. "Explain this to me. A tattoo of Dino is what fixes all this?"

Lori's eyebrows cocked. "Peter, before you ask me nine thousand questions, most of the time, we have no idea how adoptions will play out. How emotions will narrate an outcome."

"Explain it to me like I'm five."

"Dude, you're not going to enjoy this?" Edmund placed a piece of pie in front of his brother. "Maybe you need to eat."

"I don't want pie." Peter pushed the plate away, but Edmund slid it back.

"Maybe you need to eat it before I shove it in your face."

"Fine." Peter picked up his fork, and Lori explained the complexity of the foster care system as Audrey suddenly woke and babbled.

The information appeared to appease him, but Peter asked, "So, no backsies?"

"Once the judge finalizes the adoption, no backsies." Lori lifted an eyebrow as if challenging him to ask anything else. "We good?"

"We're great."

Now all Reynolds had to figure out was how to make it great between him and Susan.

Chapter Twenty-Eight

"UNDERSTAND, I'M OVER the moon that we're going to adopt her."

"But?" His eyebrow arched in that sexy way that made her think dirty thoughts.

"We ... we need to back up with us." Even as she said it, her heart hurt as the strong smell of vanilla and bananas hit her nose. Her fingers threaded through her hair and found a gooey glob of food. "So gross."

"Welcome to parenthood." Reynolds chuckled as he wiped down Audrey's greedy fingers.

"Glad to be here." From the moment Reynolds told her the adoption would happen, her angst fought with her elation. No doubt, they were great parents, and they were amazing at getting each other off, but were they a good match in the most important ways?

And how much food was in my hair? She hesitated to check.

He stripped Audrey of her onesie, only to find smashed food all over her belly. "How much banana did Nate give her? Why are we backing up?"

Holding in a laugh, she passed him the wipes box.

"Why? Because I opened my heart up and almost lost everything. You. Me. Audrey. Us."

The corner of his mouth twitched up. "Us. I like hearing you say that."

It would be so easy to push her fears aside, fall into his arms, his bed, and ignore the worry that festered there. "We've never actually been on a real date."

"Is that what you need to calm your worries? A date?"

Damn the man for being so perceptive. "No. Yes. Something. A honeymoon. A shower."

"All those are great suggestions." After a good wipe-down, Reynolds cradled a less banana-y Audrey in his thick arms.

The sweet scene of her husband listening and their daughter talking nonsense shot the blissful reality of family life straight into Susan's veins.

Then doubt cruelly whispered in her ear as it had so many times before. She was so tired of it being a constant companion, yet she guarded her heart for so long, it would take time to accept she had gotten what she'd always wanted.

Without looking at her, he asked, "What are you thinking, my beautiful wife?"

Her insides melted at his complimentary query. "That this has all been emotional whiplash."

"You're right. It's been a lot."

The faint smell of banana drifted around her, making Susan cringe at how much mush she had yet to find. "To answer your question, maybe not a serious date, but yes, I'd like a bit of the romancing. I'd like to be wooed and seduced."

"I can do all that. And I have."

"*Expertly.*"

"Did you hear that, Audrey? Daddy's an expert."

Audrey answered with a series of noises that sounded close to being actual vowels.

Waving him off, she went to her room and stripped off her shirt. A quick glance in the mirror made her grimace. Her hair sat in a lopsided twist while smears of mascara highlighted the bags under her eyes. "We started with married life and a baby. We've barely had any alone time. We never even had a honeymoon."

"But what we have gotten has been stellar."

She rolled her eyes at his successful attempt to be charming. "Reynolds. Please."

Wandering about her room, Reynolds kept his voice calm as he held eye contact with Audrey while he spoke. "What are you saying? That you don't want to be with me? With us?"

The fear of so much going wrong took hold again. She pinched the bridge of her nose to get herself to center. "I want us to be together, to be a family. I simply need a moment for my heart to recover. Get to know you."

"What do you want to know? I'm an open book." He held his free arm out wide. "Ask me anything."

Audrey added her two cents to their conversation as Odin napped in the rocker, the cat making the most of the late-afternoon strip of sunlight.

"It's not that simple."

Lucy's words echoed in her head. *But it can be.*

"Why does it have to be complicated, Susan?" His eyes roamed her body when he finally looked up. "Damn, you're gorgeous."

"Thank you, but now you want simple when we both pushed for complicated?" Her fingertips throbbed, indicating how fiercely she gripped the doorframe to her bathroom.

"You grip that wood any tighter, you're likely to break it." He held his hand out and when she laid hers on top, he pulled her in, tucking their hands to his chest. "Susan. It's okay to be scared."

"I'm not scared." Her words trembled as Audrey babbled. "I'm terrified."

"I'm scared, too, but I'm right here with you."

"When I've almost gotten what I wanted before something always took it away. Now, I got the whole Hallmark rom-com ending and it only stresses me more."

He stroked her hair, his spicy scent calming her angst, but raising her stress levels for the right reasons. "You've had a lot of shit happen to you. I can't promise more shit won't, but what if we enjoyed the here and now? Didn't give too much thought to the maybes?"

"Hello? Have you met me?"

"I have and I've loved every bit of you." His jovial mood shifted to adoration. "Susan, I love you."

"What? That's insane." She began to move away from him, but he kept a gentle hold of her hand as she offered no resistance.

"This entire situation has been insane, but that doesn't

mean it's not what's right for us. And I love you for every practical, logical, and responsible thing you do."

He truly gets me. Emotions lodged in her throat. "Really?"

He leaned toward her until their foreheads touched. "Really. But I love all the sexy stuff a lot, too. A whole fucking lot."

"There's a lot more sexier stuff." An entire wardrobe of items she'd yet to reveal.

"I can't wait to spend the next few decades seeing them on you," he whispered against the tender skin of her ear. "Then taking them off you."

A shiver ran down her spine as the thrill of the next many years played out in her brain.

Snowball fights. Family trips. Adventures. Three stockings hanging on the hearth.

Her gaze scanned him. *Sex.*

So much sex.

It all played so beautifully.

The incoherent words of the baby sank the wishes soul deep while tears freely flowed down her cheeks. "I want to believe it will happen, but—"

He kissed her slowly as if he had all the time in the world to cherish her body.

Then Audrey's diaper made some concerning noises.

"Parenting is so sexy." She smiled against his lips.

Odin woke from a dead sleep, grimaced, and walked out of the room.

"So are you." Reynolds turned Susan around and patted her ass. "I'll take care of her. Get yourself cleaned up. I've got this, my beautiful wife."

An hour later and banana-free, she exited her bathroom wearing her shower wrap when there was a knock on her bedroom door. "Reynolds, I'll be out in a minute."

A few seconds later, another knock.

"Good grief." With a double-check on the snugness of the Velcro, Susan opened the door. "Reynolds, I—"

But it wasn't Reynolds.

Sitting in her foam seat, clean, and cutely dressed in a Captain Marvel dress, Audrey looked up at her and smiled. In her hand, a card was covered in drool.

Squatting down, Susan gently took the card. "What's this?"

Audrey excitedly giggled.

"Really? You don't say. Who sent it?"

The baby's eyebrows lifted as she gabbed about something that was probably quite fascinating.

Like the fact she had thumbs.

"Okay, you're right. I'll just read it." Inside, a handwritten note.

Dear Susan,

I've noticed you living across the hall, and I think you're the most amazing woman I've ever met.

If you're receptive, I would love to take you out to dinner sometime. And one day, Paris.

It's short notice, but if you're free tonight, I know a perfect place for us to have a nice date. Here in town. Not Paris.

Looking forward to seeing you soon.

All my love,
Reynolds

PS—I hope this isn't creepy.

He appeared in the doorway of his room, his shirt and pants perfectly pressed. Him looking far more handsome than anyone should ever be allowed. "If you're free, can I pick you up at six."

"Using the baby to ask me out is cheating, you know." But her quick heartbeat certified she loved it.

And she loved him. She loved him for how much he respected her and believed in her. Loved her. For wanting her despite her obsession for order and her imperfect insides.

Because she was more than enough.

He scooped up their daughter. "That is true, if you're going to date me, you have to understand. She and I, we're a package deal."

Susan leaned against the doorframe. "Is that so?"

Audrey excitedly squealed in agreement. Her cute little feet kicked as her eyes went wide as though she'd discovered her toes.

"Where is this place you intend on taking me?"

"We could go to the Graff for steaks or Main Street for one of Gabby's specialties or Rocco's if you want Italian food."

The corner of her mouth curled up at his attempt to make their first *date* special, but before she answered, the doorbell rang.

"The babysitter's here." He and Audrey disappeared around the corner.

"The babysitter?" Susan ducked back into her room and threw on some clothes, including a bra and panty set she'd wanted to show him for months. *Just in case.*

When she walked out, she found Peter standing by the front door.

Her brother shook Reynolds's hand. "Thanks for doing this."

Peter nodded. "Thanks. She deserves someone who'll do anything to make sure she's happy. After all of this, I know you will."

Her brother's compliment hit Susan straight in the feels. *I'm so glad he sees what a great father Reynolds will be.*

"Damned right I will. I love her," her husband answered without a hint of sarcasm.

"When her previous boyfriends said those very words to me, I was never convinced if they meant it, but you do."

He's talking about me? Peter had never been so transparent. It looked good on him.

"I appreciate that, Peter." Reynolds kissed and then blew a raspberry on Audrey's cheek. "Love you, Princessaurus."

She giggled, happiness emanating from her rosy cheeks.

Let your heart lead this time. Let us carry the heavy stuff.

Lucy's wisdom rang true.

Suddenly, the future didn't look as scary.

A new sense of freedom warmed her soul as the tight grip of worry relaxed its viselike grip. She could either deny herself happiness with endless what-ifs or she could appreciate what she had right now.

Amazing how a happily-ever-after kind of love healed so many wounds. "You're the sitter?"

Her brother tilted his chin up as though he were the proudest uncle in the world. "I hope you don't mind, but we'd like to take her for the night. Shelly, her two, Freddie and Tia, my two, and I plan to spend time with this cutie."

If joy had been an alien, it would have popped straight out of her chest right now. "That's wonderful. Thank you."

Not since before the accident that changed their lives had Susan felt this kind of calm understanding with her brother. The final piece of the puzzle back in place.

Now she could concentrate on her marriage and her family. *A year ago, I thought those two things would never be mine.*

Audrey played with Peter's nose before laying an openmouthed, wet kiss on his eye.

"So gross." Peter cringed through his amusement. "I'll go so you can get to your date."

"I'll walk you out." Susan opened the door. "Be right back."

"Sounds good." Reynolds stuffed his hands in his pockets and winked.

She stepped onto the front porch with Peter and Audrey, laying a couple of quick kisses on the baby's cheeks. "Glad you two found some common ground."

"Who, Reynolds? I didn't give him the benefit of the doubt and I should have. He's not like all those assholes you dated."

Susan shook her head in confusion as the happy sounds

of kids playing a game of touch football in the park filled the afternoon. "I had no idea you thought they were assholes."

Peter rocked back and forth as Audrey played with the collar of his shirt, promptly trying to stuff it in her mouth. "I've always been worried *for* you."

"Why?"

"Sis, you did so much for the rest of us. Time after time, you gave up everything to keep us going. You kept us from being homeless, and I didn't appreciate you enough for it." He shook his head as the sun cast its long shadows across the lawns. "I was too wrapped up in my trauma to notice. I left way too much for you to handle. Then I worried that you'd give up everything for whoever you dated or ended up with like Mom did. I wanted more for you, but I didn't know how to tell you."

His acknowledgment had never been the goal, but to hear it sure sounded sweet. "It's what had to be done, Peter."

"True, but you sure as hell didn't need to be doing ninety percent of it for years at a time." He patted Audrey's back. "It's your time to find your joy. You deserve someone who loves you for everything you are. Is she drooling on me?"

Pulling a burp cloth out of the side pocket of the diaper bag, Susan placed it across Peter's shoulder. "There. I thought … I had no idea you even cared about any of that."

"Of course I do. I want you happy. Loved. Protected. We all do."

Emotions ran down her cheeks. "We'll see how it plays out with him and me."

"Plays out? He loves you. I mean, the guy *really* loves

you, and you obviously love him. What he did to make your dreams come true? Susan, he's a good guy."

"I do love him, but I'm scared." Audrey grabbed Susan's finger and gummed the tip with abandon. "She's hungry."

"Love is scary, but when it's the right person, it's worth it." Peter waved to his two kids, Polly and Diggory, running up the sidewalk. Diggory pushed a stroller.

"Don't let fear tell you what to do. I lost the first ten years of my kids' lives because Simone worried I'd reject her and them." He swallowed hard as the memory of their late mother must still be hard for him to process. "Don't let it rob you of any more time because that drunk bastard's stolen enough from us."

She couldn't begin to add up the minutes, the days, the years that fear dictated her decisions because of one selfish person's choice to drive drunk that spring morning so long ago.

To force its release from her would be nothing short of liberating. "We've let him steal so much from us, haven't we?"

"We're all here now. All of us get a new start and a new outlook on life. A place to talk about it out of the public eye." A tight line replaced his mouth. "I don't think any of us have dealt with what happened that day."

"After all this, it's apparent I haven't," she joked despite the seriousness of the moment. "Amazing Reynolds wants to be with me after all my baggage."

"You need to stop short-changing yourself. I wish you could see how amazing you are, the way the rest of us do."

Peter thumbed over his shoulder. "The way he does."

"Thank you, Peter. That means the world."

"Hi, Aunt Susan." Polly stomped up the stairs as Diggory waited on the sidewalk.

"Hi, kids. Ready to take care of Audrey tonight?" Susan inhaled all the goodness along with the crisp autumn air. A few houses already had Halloween decorations out, and she gleefully wondered how much candy she'd need to buy.

"I've the games picked out and we have a high chair ready." Polly gently took the diaper bag from Peter. "Let's go, Dad. *Jeopardy!* is about to start."

"Be right there." Peter turned to Susan and nudged her with his elbow. "If you don't marry that guy, I might. Except Shelly might get upset."

"But I already married that guy." *And now I don't doubt as to why.*

"Then why are you outside right now when you've got a sitter?" He raised an eyebrow before descending the stairs and placing Audrey in the stroller. "See you tomorrow."

The baby kicked her feet in excitement as they buckled her in and headed toward their house down the street.

"Bye, Aunt Susan!" Diggory waved as he sang along to the classic Queen tune, "Somebody to Love."

She waited for them to pass several houses before she faced the door.

For years, she waited, hoped, and begged for a chance to have someone who simply wanted her. Not who she could be or what they perceived her to be, but her right now. Today.

Susan found Reynolds sitting in the secret library, pulling a book off the shelf. "Have a nice talk with Peter?"

"I love you." For once in her entire life, Susan let the words flow without pause.

Without guessing or questioning.

"What?" His eyebrows arched in surprise.

"You are the most logical, practical, responsible man." She wiggled out of her jeans and tossed them.

"You know, you're sexy when you quote seventies hit songs."

He gets me. Crooking her finger, she inhaled the spicy scent that always followed him, allowing it to drift across her skin.

And now he gets all of me. "I love you."

He tossed the book on the chair, obviously not interested in reading anymore. "You do?"

"I do." Slowly, she unfastened each button of her shirt. "And I like this library."

"I just bet you do."

Before unbuttoning the last one, she cupped his face, leaning in until their foreheads touched. "I love you for everything you are and everything you've believed in. And for helping me believe in good things again."

"And I love you because you're you." His hands drifted down her arms, but before he pulled her closer, he asked, "Did you want to go out to dinner?"

"No."

"No?" He raised an eyebrow as his eyes scanned her from top to toes.

She shrugged off her top, revealing the gold Princess

Leia–inspired lingerie. "No. I want to stay home and make memories."

"I love you even more."

The End

To my readers

Thank you for reading Susan and Reynolds's finding their happily ever after and being patient with me as it took far longer than I anticipated to write their story.

I hope I gave this adoption story its proper dues, as expanding a family through adoption can be tricky and heartbreaking. It was for us, and although each journey to give a child a forever home is unique, the pain and angst are constant companions even in the smoothest of cases.

Whether you choose foster/adoption, private, or international adoption, I strongly encourage you to talk with others who've gone down that same path. Find what will work for you and your family.

Understand that even though this story focuses on infant adoption, please know (as of 2021 statistics) there are over 300,000 children in the US waiting in foster care for their forever families. The average amount of time a child spends in the foster care system is three years, and many times, siblings aren't adopted together.

Even if adoption isn't possible for you, please consider volunteering or donating to local groups and organizations that help kids with everything from clothes to education to mental health and wellness advocacy.

For more information on foster care and/or adoption, check out these resources:

5 Books You Should Read About Adoption
adoption.org/5-books-about-adoption

Recommended Adoption books by GoodReads
goodreads.com/shelf/show/adoption

Adopt US Kids
adoptuskids.org/adoption-and-foster-care/parenting-support/for-adoptive-parents

Child Welfare Information Gateway
childwelfare.gov/topics/permanency/adoption

Foster Love
fosterlove.com

If you've adopted, I'd love to hear your stories.

Find me on social media and on my website.

Website
patriciawfischer.com

Facebook
facebook.com/PatriciaWFwriter

TikTok
tiktok.com/@PatriciaWFischerauthor

LinkedIn
linkedin.com/in/patriciawfischer

Tule Author Page
tulepublishing.com/authors/patricia-w-fischer

Instagram
instagram.com/PatriciaWFischerauthor

YouTube
youtube.com/channel/UClvsb9RRvsG_XqqTeMMficg

Authory
authory.com/PatriciaWFischer

LuvCentral
luvcentral.com/signup/2BwtGD

Spoutible
spoutible.com/PatriciaWFwrites

Amazon author page
amazon.com/stores/author/B00A7DWSH8

Thank you for reading.

Acknowledgments

To everyone who patiently wondered if the fourth Davidson sibling would get her story, it's finally here.

Susan comes to Marietta, and we quickly discover she's had a secret connection to that mountain town for quite a bit now, but that's not the only thing Susan's kept from her siblings. She brings untapped emotions and a lot of hope for a new beginning, and I promise she gets one.

One of the BIG reasons Susan gets her happily ever after is due to the amazing encouragement and extreme persistence of the Tule team.

There aren't enough words to voice my appreciation to Jane Porter, Meghan Farrell, Kelly Hunter, and Monti Shalosky for believing that I could not only finish this book, but edit it down from 95,000 words into the 75,000-ish range.

My first few drafts were really wordy.

A huge thank-you to my bestie writer peeps Sasha Summers and Teri Wilson, both of whom brainstormed with me numerous times and kept asking, "Have you finished your book yet?"

Big hugs to my parents, Valera and Chuck, who always had books in their hands and encouraged me to think outside the box.

Finally, I would not understand the foster/adoption process without going through it with my sweet husband, Steve, and our girls Emma and Katelyn, as we increased our family of four to six by adopting Alex and Sophie.

If you haven't read about the other Davidson siblings, you can grab their books here and happy reading.
tulepublishing.com/authors/patricia-w-fischer

If you enjoyed *Adopting With The Doctor*,
you'll love the other books in…

Marietta Medical series

Book 1: *Resisting the Doctor*

Book 2: *Challenging the Doctor*

Book 3: *Doctor for Christmas*

Book 4: *Adopting With The Doctor*

Available now at your favorite online retailer!

More Books by Patricia W. Fischer

Men of Marietta series

Book 5: *Burning with Desire*

Available now at your favorite online retailer!

About the Author

Native Texan Patricia W. Fischer is a natural born storyteller. Ever since she listened to her great-grandmother tell stories about her upbringing the early 1900's, Patricia has been hooked on hearing of great adventures and love winning in the end.

On her way to becoming an award-winning writer, she became a percussionist, actress, singer, waitress, bartender, pre-cook, and finally a trauma nurse before she realized she needed to get her butt to a journalism class.

After earning her journalism degree from Washington University, Patricia has been writing for multiple publications on numerous subjects including women's health, foster/adoption advocacy, ovarian cancer education, and entertainment features.

These days she spends her days with her family, two dogs, and a few fish while she creates a good story with a touch of reality, a dash of laughter, and a whole lot of love.

Thank you for reading

Adopting With The Doctor

If you enjoyed this book, you can find more from all our great authors at TulePublishing.com, or from your favorite online retailer.

TULE
PUBLISHING